FOUR TIMES A VIRGIN

IRRESISTIBLE ARISTOCRATS
BOOK 2

SUZI LOVE

FOUR TIMES A VIRGIN

A Regency Noir, a darker historical romance set in London.

When confronted by the self-assured Countess of Dorchester, the Duke of Stirkton is stunned to discover that this breathtakingly beautiful widow is the naïve girl he met years before at a country inn and has searched for ever since.

The countess will do anything to prevent her younger sisters being forced into marriages as sordid as hers was, even if it means joining forces with the tormented duke and revealing the horrors of their intertwined pasts. Though Max is desperate to make amends to Carina for his late grandfather's wrongs, they realize that a fresh torrent of evil might be unleashed.

Can they expose their enemies, yet keep their loved ones safe? Because only then will they feel free to be together.

 Formatted with Vellum

PROLOGUE

1820, *December 1st; Monthly Report to Maximus Meacham, Duke of Stirkton, from Mister William Gibbons:*

....deep guilt drives your search for these women but please remember, your grandfather died barely three years ago. Until then, your hands were tied. Our current tally is five established in trade, ten compensated, five deceased, and nine relocated onto your various estates. If the girl selected for you in Dorchester was, in truth, a titled lady, she most likely married and left the district. Our chances of finding her are slim...

1821, February 1st; Missive to Bill from Max:

.... apologize for using our slight blood relationship to pressure you into starting this search. Our quest to locate these women has revealed the extent of my grandfather's degradation, and I wouldn't blame you if you wished you'd been born into any family but this one. I'd like you to live with me in London, once these debts are repaid and honor has been restored to our family. You're more than my closest relative. You've become a friend, perhaps my only friend. In six months, on my thirtieth birthday, I will marry ...

1

1821, April 1st; Duke of Stirkton's residence, Mayfair, London

"You want me to be your mistress?" The Countess of Dorchester's sculpted brow rose in an exaggerated show of disbelief.

Being the object of someone's ridicule might be a novel experience for Maximus Meacham, Duke of Stirkton, but it wasn't one he cared to repeat, even if the woman laughing at his proposal spoke like a queen and looked like a goddess. Max brushed an imaginary speck from the sleeve of his evening jacket and pretended he couldn't see her half-hearted attempts at smothering her chuckles with her gloved hand.

"And I'm to be at your beck and cal for precisely one month?"

He looked up and caught her inspecting him from head to toe. When her gaze lingered around the area of his groin, his muscles contracted, his body heated and his bollocks tightened. He turned away. If the Countess knew that her one lingering appraisal of his manly assets could turn a cold and controlled duke into a lustful male, he'd lose control of their situation and his years of planning would amount to nothing.

The Countess would take what she'd come for: his grandfather's lists, and his fantasy of having her as his lover—even for four weeks —would evaporate faster than his dreams of a happier new day had, when his grandfather had thrown open his bedroom door each morning and berated him for failing to arise and greet the dawn. He glanced sideways. His breath seized and he mentally revised his description of her beauty. With porcelain skin, auburn curls, and emerald eyes that hinted at a Scottish lineage, the Countess had grown into one of the most stunning women he'd ever laid eyes on. Max's comparison was based on intimate knowledge of some of the most exquisite women in England. Not even his imagination had done her justice, and he'd spent many long nights picturing how she'd look when, or if, they ever found her again. Wondering if she'd aged gracefully, or more importantly, if she'd lived disgracefully after he and his grandfather had turned her young girl's life on its head? Though his fantasy woman had carried a girlish countenance and had worn significantly less clothing than this girl who captured his attention in an ill-lit room at a country inn.

He risked another look at his unexpected visitor. This lady wore a gown that wrapped her body as closely as a lover's arms, and he knew from the pile of bills he paid to whichever modiste that month's mistress preferred that the Countess's outfit would have cost a pretty penny.

While he snatched quick and gentlemanly looks at the Countess's face and dress style, she continued her own perusal. Her study of him and his entire body was so slow and intense that he felt his skin heat and prickle. As the Duke of Stirkton, he was well accustomed to being watched. Young pups copied his dress style. Toad-eaters mimicked his behavior in futile attempts to ingratiate themselves into his life. Conservative groups applauded his somber public behavior, while cartoonists ridiculed his straight-laced demeanor and suggested he take a mistress. Or two.

Whichever way people viewed him, no one had dared ridicule him to his face. Until this evening. The Countess had side-stepped his butler and marched into his drawing room as if an unannounced call upon an unmarried duke was something she did regularly. Max had informed her, in great detail, of the extensive search he and his cousin had undertaken to locate her and the other women. She'd huffed and rolled her eyes. Normally, his month-about- mistresses gleefully accepted his proposal because sharing a duke's bed for a month would set them up for the rest of their lives. Apart from the financial benefits, he was a generous lover. One benefit of his abnormal upbringing had been an early and full education into what women wanted in a bed partner. Until the Countess had laughed at him, he'd never had reason to doubt his sexual prowess. In the brief time she'd been in his house, she'd challenged several of his beliefs.

"It's the ideal solution." And something he needed. "I will help you search my grandfather's boxes by day and, in exchange, you'll make yourself available to me in the evenings." Max waited, unsure what to expect. An odd situation for a man who prided himself on reading adversaries as easily as he tallied the accounts.

"Ah, I understand." She nodded, and the crimson curls artlessly dangling from the knot

on her crown bounced around her shoulders and settled on the bare flesh exposed above the fashionable square-cut of her evening gown. "You're jesting."

His body's acute, and for recent times, abnormal physical response, distracted him. He

envied those curls and their freedom to touch her lightly-tanned skin. "I never jest."

"You're seriously asking me to play your courtesan for this month?" She walked around

him, tiny circling steps meant to disconcert him. "Me?" She threw her arms wide in a

theatrical gesture. "Act like a common cyprian? A demimondaine squeezed in between

business meetings. Or, in our case, between boxes of files." She waited for his nod. "But

why?"

"Why not?" Max's compulsion to provoke this woman, the girl selected for him in

Dorchester and whose name had eluded him for eight long years, was childish. Ridiculous

behavior for a man taught from birth that Meachams exhibited the same haughty arrogance as

the Royal Family, no matter the circumstances. Yet he'd tried to discompose the Countess

from the moment she'd arrived and faced him, toe to toe. He glanced at the ornate clock on

his mantle. Twenty minutes had passed in a flash. He feared blinking in case the erstwhile

Lady Carina Woods vanished as swiftly as she had from the Dorchester inn, swept away in an

elegant but discreetly blackened carriage.

Now, the widowed Countess looked cool, calm and more magnificent than any of his

dream manifestations. Even while looking at him as though he was an escapee from Bedlam.

"What you're proposing is ludicrous."

6

"TO THE CONTRARY, my proposal is serious, sane, and expedient." Though he knew his idea

sounded insane when voiced aloud. "Before I agree to your searching through my

grandfather's documents, I need your agreement to my terms."

He was a fool, an obsessed idiot who'd been thrown into confusion at her unannounced

arrival and hadn't taken his usual time to prepare his argument. The moment she'd set foot in

his house, a life-time of training had been forgotten as he'd scrambled for ways to secure her

attention and her promise. By habit, he glanced towards the portrait holding pride of place on the long wal. He shivered when his grandfather's eyes, blue and as cold as arctic ice chips,

stared back at him. The late Duke had controlled every step of Max's growing years and had

taught him, with the aid of his riding crop, rules that must be followed so the family name

and reputation would continue, unsullied by weakness or doubt.

Max's first sexual experience had been on his fourteenth birthday, another lesson, with

the woman selected, instructed and paid for by his grandfather. Max's tutelage in ducal

dominance in the bedroom had been scheduled on his calendar alongside accounting lessons,

because Augustus had believed that regular sex was a messy yet necessary part of a duke's

life in the same way food ensured a man's physical wellbeing. Max was trained to control his

sexual responses, harden his heart and view a woman's body as a means to an end, while his

companions were employed on a rotating monthly basis. If their month passed with no

complications, each courtesan was well compensated. Women were to be scrutinized for

cleanliness and sensuality with the same objectivity a duke was expected to give to the side of

mutton or slab of beef served by his chef each night. But after years of searching for this

particular woman, Max feared that adhering to those rigid Meacham rules would be as

impossible as disobeying Augustus had been when he was a child.

"A proposal? You issued a ducal command." The disappointment in the Countess's

statement drew his gaze, and his thoughts, back to her. "And you believed I'd accept as if I was a well-trained whore. You may be accustomed to women rushing to do your bidding, but

I'l never again be ordered about by a man."

Her hands-on-hips stance demonstrated her rejection of him better than any words, yet he

couldn't stop imagining how her hips would feel under his hands instead and if his fingers

would stretch to touch the edges of her femininely-rounded stomach. She'd spread her feet

wide beneath a dazzling sea-green gown, and he wondered if her legs were long enough to

wrap his waist if he held her up against the wall beneath and pounded into her softness. With

her height, her legs would drape nicely over his shoulders, he decided, while he took her in

every way he'd dreamed of for so long.

7

"YOU'RE A WIDOW. AN EXPERIENCED WOMAN." He raised an eyebrow, daring her to

contradict him. "Surely I'm not the first man to ask you to be his mistress?"

The rational part of his mind argued that contracting her as this month's pleasure was a

sound business decision. His irrational side wished she'd protest and declare herself as

innocent as the night they'd met. "I'm reputed to be a decent lover. I can give you what you

need." He ran his gaze suggestively over her curvaceous lower body and up to her plump

breasts, barely confined in a tight-fitting satin bodice. Lady Dorchester made an unladylike

sound, somewhere between a grunt and a growl. Good! Only fair that the Countess feel out of sorts, considering the turmoil her unexpected appearance had caused him.

"Real y?" She matched his deliberate appraisal of her offerings with one of her own and,

predictably, his body reacted with surge of lust.

"The attributes of the women I choose each month matter little to me," he said,

addressing the wall again. "Though I have a preference for hair like yours--red and vibrant."

"I prefer to think of my hair as auburn."

He turned to study her hair and smirked at her sensitivity over its color. If he was a poet,

he'd say it reminded him of a fiery summer sky. But he was a hot blooded male, who'd rather

tell her to spread her locks across his pillows and her naked body across his silk sheets. Or

even better, insist she trail her hair across his naked chest each time she rose and lowered on

his erection.

Naturally, he couldn't say any of those things so he rebuked her sarcasm with some of

his own. "Auburn?" He shrugged. "Going back to my proposal, a month together should suit

nicely, because it wil take you a few weeks to ful y search my grandfather's files and this

way I'l have you close by for whenever the mood strikes."

"Oh, how romantic." She clutched her hands at her chest. "I fear that being too often in

your company wil overwhelm my delicate female senses." She made another ineffectual

attempt at smothering her laughter. "Although as you've pointed out, your terms would mean

that I'd perform as a courtesan and I'd be *on hand*, or *under hand*, and I'd have you, *in

hand*."

"How droll, my lady," Max said evenly, despite feeling a little wounded. "And excel ent

use of the double entendre."

"I beg your pardon for my flippancy," she said, without showing the least bit of remorse.

"But your assumption that I'd topple into bed with a man I've only met twice is arrogant,

galing and insulting."

His training hadn't prepared him to deal with an independent and contrary woman, as he

8

WAS ACCUSTOMED TO DEFERENCE, not defiance from women.

"As you're against marrying again and my wedding is some time away, becoming lovers

is an expedient solution. I was selected as your first lover, so it seems fitting that I shall be

your last."

"You misunderstand." She shook her head and several loose curls lifted and flew.

"Though I'll never marry again, I'm young and wealthy and able to please myself when it

comes to sexual liaisons."

Carina's plans to have sex with other men disturbed Max, because he'd clung to an

image of her as an innocent girl who needed his protection in the same way she had in the

Dorchester inn. Imagining her spreading her hair across the pillows of some unknown man,

or men, made his jaw clench until his teeth ached.

For three years he'd waited to make amends, and yet, in half an hour, Carina had tossed

every one of his long-held beliefs and pent-up yearnings back in his face. Not that he blamed her, because demanding sexual favors from a young countess wasn't something he normally

did. But she'd marched back into his life and he had no intention of letting her walk out again

until a few things were resolved.

"Neither a husband nor a man is necessary to relieve a woman's bodily cravings,"

he said casually, while he watched for signs of betraying emotion.

A whip's sting on his grandson's bared buttocks had been the old Duke's favored way of

teaching Max about women's needs and wants, and though he didn't consider himself an

expert, he did understand the tricks women used to manipulate men and appease one of their

cravings: an unrelenting desire for wealth. He knew, to the penny, the cost of extricating

himself from one of his monthly companions if she refused to leave his cottage.

Though much of Augustus's sex education had been strange and useless, Max had

learned how to detect human flaws, especially in women, and to use this knowledge to his

advantage. However, he couldn't fathom Carina's wants and needs.

The Countess wasn't cowered by his status as women of the lower classes usual y were,

and nor did she bend over backwards to ingratiate herself as females from the higher echelons

did. To the contrary, her emotionless responses to him and his suggested arrangement both

frustrated and maddened him. He felt out of his depth already and had no idea how to save

himself.

"Nevertheless," she said, waving a casual hand between them, "a generous lover can provide a woman with more intense pleasure than she can give herself, alone in her

bedchamber. I imagine that some men could provide the same thrill that you presumably

9

DERIVED from deflowering virgins at Madame Laverne's on each of your birthdays."

He stiffened. How did she know where he'd been initiated into fornication? She'd

arrived tonight seeking access to his grandfather's journals, so he'd assumed she knew little

about his life with his grandfather, or about the girls purchased for him twice a year, as

regular as clockwork. Underestimating the Countess could prove a costly mistake. She might

have come here for reasons other than needing some information from his grandfather's

papers and he, as a wealthy duke, had good cause to suspect everyone's motives.

Surreptitiously, he began his ritualistic exercises. Tightening and releasing the fingers on

both hands was a relaxation technique he'd learned years earlier to hide distress and never

allow thoughts or emotions to be seen.

Adopting his ducal voice, he repeated the dictum taught to him with the aid of a whip-

thin birch rod on his fingertips. "Ridding those girls of their virginity wasn't meant to be a

pleasure, for them or for me. If Meacham money wasn't used, then another man would have

paid to be their first. My grandfather believed that regular sexual relief allows men to

concentrate on their estates and finances, rather than be governed

by the whims of an aroused
   prick."

Lady Dorchester muttered an idiom he couldn't quite identify and he wasn't certain if

   she scorned the way he'd been educated or if she approved. She wandered around his room,

   then meandered close-by and passed almost under his chin. He made the mistake of sucking

   in a deep lungful of air and, instead of it steadying him and his wayward thoughts, he inhaled

   her scent. Desire struck him squarely in the chest and the rush of arousal was so sharp and

   strong that, although it was out of character and dangerous, it felt right.

If the old Duke had stil lived, Max's backside would have been whipped raw, because

   this sort of normal male reaction was forbidden for a duke as it robbed the thinking brain of

   blood.

Carina's head tipped back as she stopped and looked up at him and, in that moment, he

   knew that years of instruction were useless when he faced the one woman he'd never been

   able to dismiss from his mind. Her jewel-colored eyes sparkled like the priceless gems in

   jewelry he vaguely remembered his mother wearing. She was silently asking something of

   him, though a man whose main claim to fame was an ancient title and a hard heart was

   unlikely to be able to give her whatever she needed.

Amazing that in such a short space of time she'd managed to confound and befuddle him

   when others had tried for years to bamboozle him and couldn't. Lust could always be

   explained as physiological, but his compulsion to hold this

woman in his arms and assure her

10

THAT ALL WOULD BE WELL WAS incomprehensible. Only once before had a woman affected him

this way, but when he'd been asked about that evening in Dorchester he'd lied and told his

grandfather that the girl had been nothing special. The Duke had been vindictive when

thwarted, and Max had feared for Carina's safety if the old man had suspected him of

harboring feelings for the girl, even if they had been only pity. Contrarily, he'd prayed that

Carina had left England and was an ocean away, and yet he'd also longed to be with her

again and finish what they'd agreed to never start on that il -fated night.

"...You believe that twaddle?"

He pulled himself out of what his grandparent had termed his useless day dreaming and

searched for a suitable response, despite having no idea what she meant.

"It's always served me wel."

"So not one of the girls or women you've paid over the years has ever excited you or

pleased you?"

"That's exactly what I'm saying."

"You felt no emotion at al?"

He swalowed. "None." He'd played the part of a cold-hearted aris-tocrat most of his life,

yet now the role made his skin itch and his stomach churn. His inability to toss out one of his

usual sarcastic retorts angered him, though it wasn't Carina's inva-sive questions that galed him, but rather his curt responses.

"Rubbish!" She stabbed a finger into his chest. "You, Your Grace, are lying through your

teeth."

He raised an eyebrow and fixed her with his most intimidating stare. "As I have

explained, *madame*, I am the twelfth Duke of Stirkton. I do not lie."

If they had been present, his business associates would have advised Carina to not toy

with him, but they were alone in his drawing room and she was carelessly baiting him, with

no thought to how he would react. The innocent girl from Dorchester that he remembered had

matured into a forceful and resourceful countess who'd tracked him down and confronted

him, while he and his cousin hadn't discovered any hint of her location.

"And I'm the Countess of Dorchester." She flicked a dismissive hand through the air and

glared at him. "Who gives a damn? What matters to me is truth." Her voice dropped to a

whisper. "And justice."

For the first time, she wouldn't look him in the eye. Her fingers knotted over the folds of

her skirt and when she finally raised her face, sadness clouded her eyes. Now they appeared

as deep and murky as stagnant pond water.

II

"I'D BEEN DOSED with laudanum that night at the inn. Besides which, I was only ten and

eight years. I was grateful for your understanding. You saw every-thing. My age, my terror and that I'd spat out most of the dose the Earl had poured down my throat. Though I cannot

recal exactly what you said."

"I didn't say anything." Max shook his head. "Such intimacy was forbidden when I was

with the girls my grandfather arranged."

"Did you know that the old Duke wrote reports on everything?"

Max flinched. His grandfather's appaling behavior stil burned his gut like a stab from a

hot poker. "By the time I met you, I knew."

"So you also know he secretly watched you."

"When he paid for girls at brothels, he demanded reports on my technique because

discussing my performance was supposedly a necessary part of my education."

"Huh! Watching was also a way for him to keep control when not in the room with

you." Carina raised a brow. "Though standing in dark corridors and peering through bored

holes also fed his more perverted obsessions."

Max couldn't answer while he fought the surge of bile clogging his throat. He'd been

physically sick after discovering that his grandfather had watched him through peepholes, the

old man taking his own pleasure while his grandson performed as his proxy. The girls

working those rooms had been accustomed to twisted sexual desires and would have ignored

Augustus standing with his eye glued to a peephole and living vicariously through his

grandson. The old voyeur had probably watched Max's every thrust and retreat in and out of

a girl's body and imagined they were his own.

But for Max, that deep betrayal had begun his quest to uncover every one of the old man's secrets and to make amends. That night had also prompted Max's desire to control

when, where, and with whom he had sex. The cottage where he conducted his liaisons was

owned by him and only he, and his workman, knew how many times the locks on doors and

windows were changed, and only his handyman knew that walls were also checked.

"My grandfather didn't alow any form of compulsion in his life, or mine," Max

muttered, using his best Meacham voice—cold and without inflection.

"Despite outward appearances, he was ruled by at least one evil compulsion and he

indulged himself for at least two decades."

"You're mistaken. My father and uncle were the Meachams who suffered cravings and

weaknesses. Drink, gambling, and unsuitable women. Because of them, I was taught to avoid

those temptations and to protect my future son from any inherited weaknesses."

12

ANOTHER OFTEN REPEATED lesson had been that men couldn't bear heirs nor suckle babies.

Women were created for men's use and to bear children, nothing more. After reaching the

age of twenty-nine, Max had followed in the footsteps of generations of Meachams and

negotiated for a bride. In six months' time, on his thirtieth birthday, he'd marry the chit

selected for him years ago. He'd perform his duty, producing the required heir and a spare as

quickly as possible, and then establish his duchess at his main estate where she would raise

his children, leaving him to continue living mostly in town, his existence barely disrupted.

"Do you deny that he frequently pandered to his evil side and without any thought to

those he hurt?"

"You've no proof to support those accusations."

"I do, but that discussion must wait, because I can't stay long and we've other things to

decide. But your declaration that you never gained, or gave pleasure to your virgins is clearly

untrue."

Max shook his head, despite guessing what was coming next. Memories he'd fought long

and hard to repress flooded his mind. His grandfather's worst-ever fury had erupted the night

Max had challenged him over his Peeping-Tom actions, but Augustus had underestimated

Max's own anger and his growing size and strength.

"...because," she said, "I remember the first time I was sold very clearly."

"The first time!" Shock was quickly displaced by savage rage at her implication.

"Oh, yes. A man as depraved as the Earl wasn't about to stop at one attempt. His greedy

nature was encouraged by your grandfather's fat walet. He needed me carrying a child and

he didn't care who fathered it. Not long after seling my first virginity to you, the Earl—"

"—did it again." He shuddered at the thought of Carina being led like a slave to an

auction block.

"Twice more after you."

Merciful heaven, he'd been wrong. English aristocracy oozed with far more evil than even his distorted upbringing had led him to believe. He leaned head-down on the mantle and

tried to swalow past the constriction in his throat. Her late husband's treachery outstripped

Max's imagination, even though during the years he'd searched for Carina and the other

women he'd imagined plenty of horrors. Though Augustus had equaled the Earl in treachery

as his schemes had grown from callous to malevolent as he aged.

"Did the Earl have more plans?"

"The next victim to be offered my so-called virginity had been selected, but the Earl died

prematurely."

13

CARINA'S chilling revelations were more disturbing than an emotional outburst, and he

couldn't help but wonder if she'd seen murdering her husband as the only way to avoid her

virginity being sold to even more men. He'd lied to Carina about not recalling their

rendezvous, because that night was etched in his mind and she was one of the women he'd

failed to locate. When he'd entered the Highway Inn in Dorchester on the night of his

majority, he'd sensed that bedding his assigned virgin would change his life, but he'd never

imagined just how much impact that one night or one girl would have.

Max and his cousin had searched high and low for Carina, despite knowing that women

forced to prostitute themselves often died at a young age through circumstance or disease.

The breath caught in his chest as a new thought occurred to him. "Who was it? Who was

the Earl seling you to next?"

"Ah, we've come to the crux of the matter at last. I risked coming here because I need

you to tel me his name."

Max frowned. "How would I know?"

She hesitated. "To answer your other question—"

"I didn't ask another question."

She gave a smal brittle laugh. "Like everyone else, you want to know if I kiled my

husband."

"Did you?"

She smirked. "That, Your Grace, is for me to know and you to never find out."

He stared, open-mouthed. "You're a cool one."

"Not as cool as you taking a virgin each year with less emotion than asking a lady to

dance with you at a bal."

Max bristled. Each year on his birthday, he'd been taken to an experienced prostitute,

and after he'd turned eighteen his companions had been virgins. According to Augustus,

bedding virgins prepared a duke for dealing with his untouched wife, and as those girls were

destined to lose their virginity to the man paying the best price to the brothel nun who owned

them, Meacham money might as well win.

"Women were for enjoyment and al were wel compensated."

"Incorrect on both counts. The Earl may have been paid, but I received no compensation

for surrendering something that a lady is taught to save for her marriage night. Secondly, you

were shown how to gain physical release but never enjoyment because, like the Earl, the old

Duke couldn't perform the act himself. You were a substitute, and someone they despised,

because you were capable of finding pleasure with women while they couldn't.

14

"How do you know these things?"

"I've spent three years collecting information and preparing for my next step."

"I've no interest in whatever you think you know about me."

"But the things I know wil surely shock your betrothed."

"At last, the real reason you're here. Blackmail. I alow you access to my family papers,

and in return you'l not speak to the girl I'm to marry and not reveal my sordid past."

"Not al your past wil be of interest to your future family members. Merely the

procession of courtesans who live in your cottage on Brent Street."

Max kept his breathing even. He wouldn't alow any interference with his marriage plans

or his vow to wed on his thirtieth birthday. Neither his grandfather's passing nor the

Countess's arrival would disrupt his plans, one of which was to follow Meacham tradition

and sire his heir soon after his thirtieth birthday and while he was in his prime.

Young brides like Lady Alice Johnston expected that a mistress would be part of her

husband's life once they'd gone to bed together enough times to produce a son and heir.

Unfortunately, gossip about a duke spread faster than normal and Alice would be

embarrassed about the news that her husband had kept a string of mistresses, even if they

hadn't al occurred at the same time.

"I can destroy your reputation."

Carina threw back her head and laughed. "Your good name wil suffer far more than

mine, if I reveal your family's depraved secrets." She shrugged "My reputation was shredded

long ago."

She shook her head and her curls flew around her head. They looked like fire yet they

swung as softly as cool silk, and again he saw her lying on a bed with her hair fanned out like

an open clam-shell.

He dragged his gaze back to her face. "Our past is entwined so exposing me wil also

expose you. Therefore, you shal present yourself here tomorrow morning at ten, when I'l

present you with the first box of papers and you'll agree to my terms."

"There'll be no terms except mine."

He paced the length of his room with his hands clasped behind his back and didn't look

at her. Negotiating tactics; he sensed he'd need every one he could employ to stay a step

ahead of Carina. "In exchange for the names of those two men and for my help uncovering

the third," he said in a cool voice, "you'll entertain me for a month."

"Your wealth can buy you a companion in any brothel in London and your title would

ensure you were invited into beds al over the city."

15

"NONE of those women interest me at present."

"By some ridiculous whim, you've fixed your attention on me, despite the fact that I've

only been here for twenty minutes."

"My mind has been fixated on you for a lot longer than twenty minutes."

She frowned. "I'm unsure whether I should be flattered or insulted. Is this supposed to

ease your guilt?"

Damn the woman for she was far too astute. He studied the portrait of Augustus and

reminded himself that a Meacham never relaxed their guard, because someone might

discover the chink in his armor and get under his skin—someone like the Countess.

"I don't agonize over past events."

"No regrets? No guilty conscience?"

"None."

"Why then, ye of little conscience, has your mistress's house stood empty for so long? Is

it a year? Or even more?"

Max stiled. "I've no intention of explaining myself."

"I realize you're past due for your month of physical release but, sadly for you, my body

is no longer for sale. I'l not play whore for you, or any man, ever again."

With her head held high and without a backward glance, the Countess of Dorchester

walked to the door and through it, leaving Max alone in his drawing room with the blood

running hot through his body and no willing woman available. Nobody had stirred him this

way, not his body nor his mind, since going to a country inn to bed a virgin.

He'd tried to treat a sweet girl with care, as gently as he dared, knowing that they may be observed. Risking a beating hadn't mattered as he'd tried to aleviate her fear by whispering

words of instruction and comfort and despite it being forbidden, kissing her. Over and over.

Tonight, that girl had appeared before him as a beautiful woman. And she was still unlike any

of the others he'd bedded, before or since.

Alone, his body tight with arousal, Max addressed the spot where the Countess had

defied him. "I wil have you again, Lady Dorchester. One way or another, your body wil be

mine once more."

16

2

———

oods House, Lawnton Place

"What if he doesn't come?" Carina spoke over her shoulder to Gertie, her loyal friend and companion for many years. "When I threatened to expose al the Duke's past secrets, I was shamming. I can't reveal anything from that time in case it's traced back to my husband and his immoral deeds."

The older woman raised her head from her mending. She was seated straight-backed, regal as always, her elegant skirts spread above the green and gold pleats of the fashionable settee. The trappings in Woods House were new, purchased with an eye to enhancing Carina's status as a countess and a widow recently arrived in town for the ritual of a social season.

"Carina, there is nothing to be gained by fretting yourself into a state. As you said, the only way to deal with the Duke of Stirkton is to present him with a façade even more remote and cold than his is reputed to be."

Carina had deliberately donned her finest carriage gown and leather walking boots so the Duke would view her as a well-occupied lady who could spare only a few scant minutes to receive a caller, even if it was he who was calling upon her. On her sixth turn past the bow window overlooking the street, she glanced at her heavily shod feet and sighed. Gertie was correct: her ceaseless pacing in boots was wearing unwanted patterns in her lovely new Persian carpet.

The overly-ornate ormolu clock, also bought to flaunt her wealth and status before the ton, informed her it was twenty minutes before the hour. The non-fashionable time at which she'd instructed the Duke to arrive was a deliberate ploy, another trick to keep him off balance and give her an advantage. It was also a half-hearted attempt at keeping this, their second meeting, as secret as their first last evening. Nothing remained secret in London for long, especially in these exclusive gardened squares where servants shared gossip from house to house before their masters had arisen for breakfast.

"I stayed cool and calm last night even when he asked—" Carina half-turned back to the window so she wasn't facing Gertie. "No! *Demanded* that I agreed to his terms of becoming his latest courtesan. To service his needs, was how he expressed it."

Gertie gasped. Despite the depravity her friend had viewed during her life, such vulgarity from the Duke upset her. "You didn't mention that His Grace propositioned you, and in such a crude manner. Perhaps this is a mistake after all and we can find another way to verify the whereabouts of those dreadful men who paid your husband."

"I'm not scared of the Duke of Stirkton, nor his demands. I'm confident I can coerce him into giving me what I need. Then we never have to see him again. Ever."

"My dear, I suspect that you mightn't *need* to see His Grace, but you're drawn to him nevertheless. And though his standing doesn't intimidate you, the old emotions he dredges up for you scare you to death."

"No, Gertie, the past needs to be resolved once and for all. Then we can concentrate on sorting out Georgie's problems."

"Now that we're in London, we can ensure that your sisters are introduced to some gentlemen; *decent* gentlemen."

"We must move faster on that account too, because our disgusting stepbrother is already making plans to sell them off to the highest bidder in the same way he did with me."

"Oh, no, not already. Poor, poor Georgie. She hasn't recovered enough to be in the same room as men, and certainly not enough to be put in the hands of another husband."

Carina walked to the settee, dropped down next to her friend and took Gertie's free hand. "I'l fight Peter if he tries to sell Georgie for a second time, and I'll do whatever it takes to stop him." She clutched Gertie's fingers. "The worst part is knowing that al Peter's plans and the horrors he's brought into our lives are simply to fill his ever-diminishing coffers."

Gertie's brow creased with worry lines and reminded Carina again of how lucky she was to have found such a stalwart friend after the Earl's death, at a time when most of the county had labelled her as a murderess. Gertie had convinced their village that Carina was a giver rather than a taker and too kind a person to have taken the Earl's life, no matter how much that evil old man had deserved to have it snuffed out.

"We need to reintroduce Georgie into society in a slow and careful manner," Gertie said.

"Without having to deal with your brother."

"Stepbrother!"

"I apologize, and I can well understand why you hate any hint of a blood relationship between you."

"I despise Peter and I always have, and so do Georgie and Lucy. Oooh! As for that scheming wife of his—" Carina shuddered. "There's something cold and calculating about Clara and I've never trusted her."

Gertie nodded. "There was something sinister and unsavory about the way she watched the girls yesterday when we visited. As if—"

"Go ahead and say it. As if she wished someone would abduct the girls, or even murder them in their sleep."

"No, it was more like she was totting up in her head how much money the two of them might fetch if she sold them to a bawdy house."

"Good grief!"

Carina jumped up and resumed her pacing as she thought about Gertie's observations.

Her friend was an excellent judge of people and their motives. "Either way," she said at last,

"Peter wants more gambling money and Clara...Well, I can't even guess at her motives, but it's obvious the girls can't stay in that sinister household."

"If we put our heads together, we'l come up with a plausible excuse to remove them.

After that, we can work out how to keep the girls away from Peter."

"We're running out of time and I dread to think of Georgie's future, and then Lucy's when she reaches a marriageable age."

Carina glanced out at the square for the twentieth time and clutched the window casing for support when she saw that striding along the pavement towards her house was an exceedingly tall man, dressed in up-to-the minute fashion and wreathed in an aura of power and control. The Duke of Stirkton cut such a superior figure that men stepped aside and women turned to stare as he passed them on the footpath. The fact that he was oblivious to their attention and admiration made him more interesting, and for the first time in many years Carina felt a glimmer of hope.

"Oh, Gertie, yes, yes," she said, clapping her hands and spinning in a giddy circle before the window. "I think Georgie's way out is about to present itself, and sooner than we thought."

Gertie joined her at the window but groaned aloud. "Oh, no, no, no, Carina! Not him. The Duke of Stirkton is not the best person to help us introduce the girls to gentlemen."

"Why not? He may not be a perfect solution but, with his influence in society, he may provide our best way forward."

"You were only going to ask to see his grandfather's papers. Look at whatever the Duke may have already found, whether it's letters, directions, or anything else to help us work out the names and locations of those two men."

"And to reveal the identity of that fourth man who paid so much money to spend a night with me." Carina gave an exaggerated shudder. "To take my fourth virginity."

"Thank the good Lord that man hasn't come looking for you in the last three years."

"My original plan was to ask the Duke if I could see his grandfather's old papers. But he may be more help than we expected, a veritable Good Samaritan. And the best thing is that the Duke need never know. With a little subtle coercion, he can be made to believe that helping the girls is entirely his idea."

"Good heavens! His Grace was correct to label what you're doing as blackmail. The man is no fool, Carina, and the more involved he is in your plots and deceptions, the more of a threat he is to us."

"It's his fault, not mine. He raised the stakes by stipulating that I must go to bed with him in exchange for helping me, so it's only fair that I increase my own demands. The Duke was raised to protect the Meacham name at all costs and he can't afford to let me expose him."

"I think you're underestimating the man. He'l not be manipulated by anyone and especially not a woman. After all, he was raised to think of women as objects to keep his house and warm his bed, and nothing more. The Duke refuses to dance more than twice in an evening and barely acknowledges women, apart from the wives of business associates."

Despite knowing Gertie meant her insights as a warning, Carina was more intrigued than ever with the man and used the safety of her curtain to hide behind and study him. The perfection of his clothing indicated the pretty penny he spent on his appearance, although his wealthy estates ensured he'd never need to agonize over any merchant's accounts.

Maximus Meacham held his head at a haughty angle, his long legs striding up her steps, his large frame stretched as tautly a hunting tiger's. Though it wasn't his outer trappings but his innate hauteur that commanded attention on the street.

"If Max has such a low opinion of women, it'l be even more satisfying when I bring him to his knees."

Gertie put her hands to her head and moaned. "You've that look on your face again and it never bodes well."

"Nonsense. I'd never upset someone of His Grace's standing." She gave Gertie her best falsely innocent smile, and reinforced her lie by fluttering her eyelids, pursing her lips, and clasping her hands to her bosom. "I always, always, play fair. At least, with anyone who plays fair with me."

Her theatrical performance made her long-suffering friend drop her head in a fit of despair and when Gertie finally looked up again, she scowled at Carina.

"But do you consider that the present Duke played you fair, or did you wrong? Please, please, do the right thing and lay the blame where it belongs: with your step-brother, your husband, and the late Duke. Max was controlled by an evil old man and his tortured childhood would have destroyed a weaker man, the way it did his father and uncle."

"How can you defend him after what he did to me?"

"Small villages keep no secrets. Everyone knew the Duke abused his sons and then later his grandson. Birch branches were readily available and easily replaced."

The door knocker clanged three times in a row and their butler shuffled as fast as he could to answer. By the time Tompkins announced their caller, Carina and Gertie sat with their sewing basket between them and were working on their mending. They rose and curtsied in unison, and Carina hid her smile when Max was forced to sketch an impatient bow.

"Your Grace, how nice of you to cal." The only indication of his irritation was one raised eyebrow as she took her time introducing her companion.

"Lady Dorchester," he said as soon as she'd finished, "I am here as commanded."

Carina made a show of looking at the clock. "And early, so you must have been eager to see me again, Your Grace."

"Do you have any more tests for me, my lady? Because it wasted the time of two footman to follow your carriage last night and locate your residence."

Carina experienced a small pang of guilt at Gertie's hissed breath. But her friend merely said, "I'll ask Thompkins to bring refreshments," before she rushed away, leaving Carina face to face with a man whose heated looks could ignite a fire.

"I'm a busy man," he snapped, once Gertie was out of earshot. "May we now discuss our arrangements for the next month?"

"Fine, let us discuss terms. I possess several letters that involve you." Max paced her drawing room the same way she'd been doing, creating the same whorls in the same carpet.

He made a quick assessment of her room, noting the clock, the settee and every other indication of her wealth. She clasped her hands and hoped he wouldn't guess why she was flaunting her new social status. Finally, he stopped beside the fireplace and fixed her with his dark stare, while reaching up to caress every curve of her gilded time piece. She shivered when she imagined those same sensual strokes drifting across her body, and when he recognized her helpless reaction, a flare of pure male interest lit his eyes with heat.

"Letters," he repeated in a low voice.

She willed herself to not lower her gaze and reveal any hint of weakness. This man would squash a weak woman like a bug under his boot.

He said again, "You've letters." A tiny quaver in his voice showed his displeasure. "From whom?"

Good, she wanted him to be flustered, or at least as aware of her as a woman as she was of his masculinity. "Letters from several of the women you've kept at your Brent Street cottage over the last two years."

He stiffened. "What possible interest would I have in letters, or any other worthless pieces of information you've acquired in order to blackmail me?"

"Blackmail is such a harsh term for our partnership. I've my own set of rules for our time

together and if you don't agree to them, I'l be forced to make these letters public."

"My poor deluded Countess, half the men in England keep mistresses and no one cares."

He shrugged. "Try blackmailing some of the married men instead of bachelors like me." His casual dismissal of the evidence she'd painstakingly collected over three long year stirred Carina's irritation and she itched to burst his arrogant bubble. The old general who resided near her at Dorchester swore that the best defense was offense. Along with sage advice, she'd sweeten her offense with a little honey. Before she left London, she'd put an end to the Duke's treatment of women and show the arrogant man that women, or at least the one woman he was presently dealing with, were as capable of deciding their own fate as men.

"Your Grace. No, no, that's far too formal, and I prefer your given name."

He stiffened. "I'm addressed by my title, Stirkton. My given name is Maximus."

She'd need a large jug of syrup in addition to that honey. "Maximus is too formal for two people who've shared such intimate times." At his shocked look, she pretended to cough to cover her laughter. "As we're to be such good friends, I'l cal you Max."

His hands clenched at his sides and he sucked in a long breath. If she rattled his composure often enough he might be desperate to get rid of her by handing over the notebooks, and then she could go back to where she belonged.

He dipped a sketchy nod of agreement. "Address me that way if it'l make our agreement run smoother, but in return, I will cal you ... Carina."

Her name rolled off his tongue in a slow and seductive wave that sent ripples of awareness up her spine. Despite his blanked expression, her suspicions were aroused. His sensual voice was most likely another expert weapon that he'd developed after he'd spent so much time with practiced courtesans. The Duke's arsenal of sexual tricks was obviously larger than hers, as she'd had limited experience dealing with the male gender.

"Please do. Friends don't need formality. I've been introduced to your betrothed, Lady Alice Johnston, who I understand is barely eighteen years old."

A muscle jumped in his cheek and he flexed and relaxed his fingers several times. She'd found his Achilles heel and she was more than capable of applying pressure until he acquiesced to her demands.

"Yes, Lady Johnston is a young girl."

Interesting that he wouldn't meet her eyes. "And a very sheltered young girl."

Having only a moment before resumed his pacing, Max halted in his tracks but kept his back to her. "I'm sure I don't have to warn you, Countess," he said, without turning around, "that I'd take it amiss if anyone upset Lady Alice."

"She's so innocent and so..." She waited until he turned to face her before waving a nonchalant hand. "...So virginal."

Max made a noise that was almost a gasp, before resuming his slow pacing around the fringe of the carpet.

"Lady Johnston and her family would be dismayed, shocked even, to hear the details about Brent Street and your past." She waited until she held his complete attention. "Such a shame to expose someone so sweet and pure to the sordid realities of gentlemen's lives. To be the object of gossip." She gave a sigh worthy of a Drury Lane drama and watched his teeth clench.

"Lady Dorchester—"

"Carina."

He dipped his head in acknowledgement of her small victory. "Carina, do you remember the concept I explained last night about women being interchangeable? One bride is the same as another."

"Not when this particular girl was selected by your grandfather years ago for her perfect lineage."

"Do your worst. London swarms with fresh chits whose blood

lines are as impeccable." His voice had an edge to it when he said, "I'll not submit to coercion."

She strolled to an elegant corner table and retrieved the sheaf of papers weighted down by a paperweight. "Then perhaps these may be of more interest."

"What? More irrelevant missives about my unbecoming behavior."

"These are testimonies dictated to me in the presence of witnesses by the girls your grandfather purchased as your birthday gifts in the years before me. And, in one case, by the husband of one of the girls. Your grandfather paid him a handsome sum to remove her from the area, so there'd be no chance of you meeting her again."

Goading Max was dangerous. He wasn't known in the city for his largesse, but rather for aggressive business tactics. Bribes to his household staff had revealed that his servants were treated fairly, though Max's aloofness discouraged familiarity. Chambermaids weren't subjected to unwanted advances and wages were paid on time. His houses and estates ran like well-oiled machines, rather like the Meacham men.

However, she'd wager that Max would be hard pressed to name more than a handful out of the hundreds of servants who worked in Mayfair, or on his estates in Stirkton. It had taken her three long years after the death of her husband to piece together enough information to feel prepared enough to confront Max. Even then, she'd prayed she didn't regret her decision.

"It seems you have something I want after all. How much do you want for them?"

"I explained that it's not money I want. The one good thing about my marriage is that I'm now extremely wealthy. Oh, and that he was incapable of pestering me in bed. Such a relief to not have another man paw at my body like an animal."

He swiveled so fast that one leg knocked hard into the side of a chair, though his eyes were so wide with shock at her words that he felt no pain. "Did I do that? Paw you like an animal?" A jumble of emotions raced across his face, regret followed by horror and, for such a rigidly self-contained man, his outburst made him more human and, somehow, more manly.

No, no; too much was at stake to let down her guard, no matter how much she longed to appease his fears. Eight years had passed, and she no longer believed in fairy tale endings because life was hard and harsh.

But the air sizzled with awareness, and the bond that had tied them years earlier tugged again, and tugged hard. Releasing the breath she didn't realize she'd been holding, she shook her head. "No, you spoke to me and took time to comfort me, even though it cost you dearly."

A deep shudder racked his tall frame. He dipped his head for a moment before re-meeting her gaze, but his light gray eyes had clouded to a stormier, angrier hue.

"What it cost me doesn't matter."

"You earned another beating for daring to speak to me."

His shoulders slumped before he straightened again, but his momentary lapse confirmed the truth of Gertie's story that his kindness to a frightened virgin had been rewarded with a beating. She pulled a handkerchief from her skirt pocket and surreptitiously dabbed her eyes.

"Grandfather disciplined me often, but it was no harsher than I deserved."

"Utter rot! If you believe you deserved his punishments, then I pity you because no boy—"

"Man! I was a man. I'd reached my majority when taken to you, and I knew how to follow rules."

"No, you weren't allowed to develop into a man at a normal pace, because that evil old man robbed you of your youth."

Three men had paid the Earl for a night with her and yet she didn't hate any of them. One of them she'd remembered fondly because, considering what Max had tried to do for her when he was only a youth himself, she couldn't help but be grateful that he'd been the first. By the second, and third, she'd been more confident and had handled the situation better.

"You know nothing of my upbringing," Max said, turning his back once more, though she didn't need to see his face to perceive his tension. His shoulders were stiff, his spine rigid and his hands pushed back his coat tails.

"Oh, but I do know. I lived close by the inn where we met. My husband was so tight-fisted that he refused to travel far that first time because it would have cost more."

He turned and stared at her, focusing his unnerving stare on her face, her hair and then her figure. "I don't recall seeing you in the area."

"We led a reclusive life because my husband detested being around people who were either happier or wealthier than him. He allowed me to visit our local village once or twice a week to purchase essentials, and nothing more."

"And yet you claim to know of my upbringing."

"Higher ranking families govern rural areas, so their comings and goings are discussed in great detail and, from there, news travels."

"Did you know who I was that night?"

"No. I'd glimpsed you from a distance when you rode your great black stallion along the lanes, but I'd never been close to you, so I pictured you as either a hero who'd save me from the Earl, or a villain wanting to rob me of my virginity."

"I did not rob you of anything," he enunciated each word. "Meachams aren't thieves. My grandfather paid for that night."

"Yes, well, I'm afraid I can't agree with you about that. However, we were discussing your betrothed. Blonde, blue eyed, perfect lineage, and I imagine sweet and demure."

"Lady Johnston possesses every quality a man of my standing requires in a bride."

"Marrying a duke is a feather in her cap and a bonus for her parents."

"I never concern myself with such details but, yes, marrying a duke will certainly raise their social standing. My family is one of the most revered in England."

"Still, I fail to see what you gain, besides a womb in which to nourish your heirs." She couldn't seem to stop poking her finger into his haughty demeanor, hoping it would deflate a little and lower him from his elevated status to a more normal level.

"After I met your Lady Johnston, I confess that I was puzzled as to why you were marrying an unworldly girl when you're widely acclaimed as a man of extraordinary

brilliance. And a girl of eighteen years..." She shrugged. "To be perfectly truthful, she didn't appear to be the sharpest young lady in London."

"This is an outrage." He strode towards the door, while yelling over his shoulder, "I didn't come here to be insulted."

Gertie walked through the drawing room door at that moment, followed by Thompkins, two maids, and the tea trays. Max hadn't been paying attention and as he rushed towards the door, he collided with Gertie, knocking her to the floor. Carina sank on one knee beside her, while Thompkins struggled to balance the wobbling tea trays before the maids dropped them.

"Gertie, speak to me. Are you hurt?" When Gertie shook her head and tried to rise, Carina eased her back down. "No, no, lie still. Until I'm sure that you're uninjured."

Max hovered over them without moving or speaking and, in fact, Carina decided he looked terrified, frozen in place. However, Gertie's wellbeing was her foremost concern, not the extreme reaction the Duke was having to the accident, even if he'd been the cause of the mishap.

"I'm sorry. So sorry." Max's pallor was whiter than the victim's as he repeated his apologies over and over. "I didn't see you."

As he repeated it, his tone became more frantic, which seemed at odds with his public image of self-control. He was acting as if he'd killed Gertie. Then he stopped talking and peered down at Gertie's face, before dropping to his knees and grasping her hand. This show of emotion seemed so alien to his nature that Carina rocked back on her heels to gape.

Ignoring her, Max spoke to Gertie. "I recognize you. Your home was near our estate in Stirkton."

"Yes, Your Grace." From her position on the floor, Gertie managed a weak smile. "I grew up in the same area as you. My mother was a great friend to your mother when they were girls. Clarissa married your father and went to live on your estate, and that was when she... changed."

"Perhaps...Would it be possible...Would you mind...?"

Carina's gaze swung between them, amazed at the instant connection her friend had made with the Duke. Her own interaction with him was prickly and disturbing, while Gertie related to him as if they'd conversed a hundred times before and liked each other.

"...If I called," the Duke continued, sounded abnormally emotional. "When you feel improved, of course, and have recovered from my clumsiness."

Both had forgotten Carina's close presence and spoke to each other as if sharing tea and a gossip. Max was gentle and kind and Gertie, distrustful of most men and for good reason, turned pink-cheeked and gazed at Max as if he'd hung the moon.

"I'd like to hear about my ... my mother. I recall very little, and the staff at the Hall changes so often that nobody there remembers her."

Max dipped his head and touched his forehead to Gertie's who, in turn, reached up and touched a finger to his cheek. Stunned yet fascinated by the unfolding scene, Carina shuffled her knees closer to Gertie. Her old friend clasped her arm and raised her brow in question.

Upon Carina's nod of confirmation, Gertie smiled. "I'd be delighted, your grace. There are things you should be told now that your grandfather has passed on."

When Max frowned, Carina forestalled anymore questions by helping Gertie to her feet and summoning the two maids to assist her friend upstairs.

Speaking over her shoulder she said, "I must settle Gertie in her chamber and then I'll return. Thompkins will serve tea, or if you prefer something to settle your nerves, there's brandy."

"Thank you." Max bent in a polite bow. "I await your return with great anticipation." He glanced at the other's retreating backs before bending closer. "You'll not put me off, Carina. Talk of the past and our night together has stirred my interest in you even more, and I find myself eagerly anticipating our liaison over the next few weeks."

His warm breath whispered across her earlobe and blew over her neck, setting her pearl earbobs swinging in what she was certain was a deliberate move. "I looked forward to being beside you, day and night."

Her body shivered involuntarily at each raspy murmur. Drat the man! She hadn't considered the Duke would, or could, unbend and tease her in return, and she was helpless to deal with it, or with him. She'd prepared herself for a beastly Max and had been confident she could repel any advances he made. But this smooth-tongued Max left her weak-kneed, tongue-tied and unable to summon her normal defenses.

"I think of it," she said, striving for a cool and steady tone of voice, "not so much as a relationship, but as two friends—good friends—prepared to assist each other with a mutual and delicate situation."

"Real y my dear lady, why not lay al our cards on the table and tel the truth? You're already known as a possible murderess."

When he raised one haughty eyebrow and waited, Carina wondered why she'd allowed this condescending man a moment of pity, or why she'd weakly wavered at his few short words of seduction. The Duke and, yes, she admitted it, his masculine and muscular physique, had drawn her physically, despite her mind putting up considerable resistance. Max presented more danger to her now than when she'd been a bewildered girl served up to him.

"So please, my not-so-innocent temptress, let's cal our association by more correct terminology."

His looked at her with determination, distrust and distaste, before spitting out his accusation. "Blackmail!"

Carina gasped. She strode to the door without a word and she pushed all thought of perhaps forming an amicable partnership with Max from her mind. The Duke of Stirkton had played her for a fool. Tugged at her feminine softer side in a deliberate ploy to disconcert her and allow him to claim victory in this round.

This, however, was merely another preliminary skirmish in their month-long war, after which time she'd wilingly retreat, or perhaps flee before her virtue was claimed once more.

3

Maximus waited until Lady Dorchester's butler closed the doors to the drawing room behind him, before lifting his shaking hand to his mouth and taking gulping down a large

dose of brandy. A few minutes earlier, by pure accident, he'd almost harmed a woman, which

was the very thing he'd sworn would never happen again.

When he'd seen Gertie lying on the floor, he'd been sharply reminded of the beast he

might be now had Augustus lived further into his growing years. Max's greatest fear was

turning out like Augustus in adulthood and flying into rages and, even perhaps, harming a

woman. Brought up to follow family dictates or expect fierce retribution, his younger self

had learned to hold himself together. But he'd laid in his lonely bed night after night and

wondered why other lads his age, even those of the lower classes, appeared to be happy when

he was so miserable.

On the other hand, he'd not end up like his father and uncle, both of whom had been

undisciplined and disorganized and had suffered dearly for those weaknesses. His own life

was mapped out, and his forthcoming marriage and the begetting of his heir was his duty—to

preserve the integrity of the Meacham name. Until reconnecting with the Countess of

28

DORCHESTER LAST EVENING, he'd believed himself one of only two people who knew the family's

sordid secrets, and who knew of Max's tireless work to make amends for the barbarities

Augustus had caused.

Max strode to the window and stared out at the street, but all he could think of was the

Countess speaking to the women with whom he'd had liaisons and wondering what they'd

disclosed. And, more importantly, how the Countess's disclosures would affect his carefully

laid plans. He'd brazened it out and lied that losing Alice's cooperation mattered not a whit,

but, in truth, failing to carry out part of his life's work would weigh heavily on his

conscience. Augustus was dead and buried, yet completely rejecting his rigid ideas and plans

was akin to Max abandoning England and going off to climb a Tibetan mountain.

Nevertheless, looking at Carina as she'd defied him this morning, he'd been sorely tempted

for the first time in many years—eight to be exact—to claim the woman he wanted, drag her to his lair and plough her until they both collapsed from an excess of pleasure.

Carina glided back into the room, skirts swirling and gave life to his dream. How she'd

retained her strong spirit despite the torments she'd been subjected to was a mystery, one he

was determined to solve. She was vibrant, womanly, intelligent, and he craved her in his bed

with a compulsion so opposite to his nature that it disconcerted him.

"Max, thank you for your patience."

Carina's auburn hair had been twisted high on her head when he'd arrived, but as she'd

become more animated, wisps had escaped until tendrils had teased her neck and a rosy color

had tinted her cheeks. Her eyes glowed as green as a cat's, and Max barely stopped himself

reaching out and touching her face, tucking a wayward curl behind her ears, or nipping at her

earlobe. Most of all, he wanted to bend his head and taste her essence, to touch his lips to her

skin and absorb some of the zest and energy she radiated. Her character was as far removed

from the reserve of his betrothed as ice was from fire, and for once in his miserable existence

he longed to warm himself before a blazing fire instead of staring at an empty hearth.

Regretfully, he cleared his head and said, "I'm so sorry I caused such a mishap to your

companion. How is she faring?"

"She insists she's recovered. Nevertheless, I suggested she rest a while longer."

"A wise decision. Please convey my deepest regret for what happened. I'm not usual y

so bumble-footed."

"You were upset and rushing to escape."

"Leaving," Max snarled. "Not escaping."

"But I upset you by speaking of your grandfather watching you pleasure a woman."

29

"AND I REITERATE that pleasuring a woman takes more time than I can alow away from my

duties." He caled on his practiced iron-will and forced himself to visibly relax. "Anyway,

why would it upset me to speak of something so normal and something that provides physical

relief for a man?"

"And what of women? Is being bedded normal for them, too?"

"I cannot speak for al women," he said in his most formal voice, "but delaying the

inevitable in the bedroom is waste of time for women who are being paid to lie down and

alow a man to spend himself inside them. I've far better things to do than participate in idle

chit-chat when both parties are eager for a rapid conclusion."

"After you're married, how many hours— Oh, no, how silly of me. With your busy

schedule, how many minutes or seconds will you allocate each night in the dark to visit the

bedchamber of your young bride? Five minutes?"

Max sucked in another sharp breath. "Alice and I will spend no more than the usual few

hours together each month, not that it's any of your concern. In fact, I mention it only to

make you aware before you spend your required month with me, that the maximum time I

ever allocate to an intimate rendezvous is an hour."

She raised a haughty brow and glared at him. "Contrary to your assumptions, I've not

agreed to spend a month with you."

He gave her a smal smile. "Ah, Carina, that's not in any doubt. You'l do whatever I say

in order to obtain those names you want so desperately."

"I'm not desperate for anything. 'Tis simply more expedient for me to obtain them from

you so I can move on to the next step in my plans."

"And what are your next steps?"

She shrugged, as if it mattered little. Yet, the fingers she traced around the swirls carved

in her marble mantle, appeared to tremble. "To locate the two men to whom I surrendered my

second and third imaginary virginities, and appease my curiosity."

"And the man your fourth purported virginity was sold to? What do you intend for him?"

"As I've informed you," she stated in a cool tone, dropping her hands to her waist to grip

them in a tight knot, "that's my concern and mine alone." Her bright curls bounced again as

she added, "And certainly not yours."

Max felt his pulse quicken and his face grow hot, so he brought into play well-practiced

techniques learned from an Oriental master years earlier. Slowing his breathing, he expanded

his ribcage from his diaphragm upwards, knowing this form of physical relaxation quickly

took the edge off his fury. Techniques like this, practiced in secret, had enabled him to

30

. . .

FUNCTION and to avoid lunacy many times during his growing years with Augustus.

He refused to be fobbed off this time, and he'd make Carina aware of his influence and

standing, and that without his help she'd never succeed.

"Tel me this at least: why are you so obsessed with destroying that fourth man when

you've had no connection with him."

"I need to face my demons, al of them, if I'm to put the past behind me."

"But he didn't even touch you?" He narrowed his gaze at her. "Did he?"

"No, he didn't get the chance. The Earl died, and I retained what you caled my fourth

virginity."

Carina shivered, and Max was angry on her behalf since two men had got the chance to

be with her. As he must also count himself, the tally was three men. She too began to pace the

room, her hands twisting the fabric of her skirt into knots as she walked.

Yet something drove him to prod her to reveal more. "Then I repeat, why?"

She halted and stared straight ahead, eyes wide, and said with utter disgust, "Because, he

paid an enormous sum of money and because he's possibly—"

"Possibly what?" He wanted a believable answer. "What could be so hideous about this

man that he causes even you, an otherwise calculating schemer, to shake?"

"I can't and won't say anything more until I verify my suspicions. But if you refuse my

request and stop me locating that man, I'l thwart every attempt you make to marry by sending copies of my letters to every prospective bride you approach."

"There's an endless supply of women in England who'd marry me today."

"Sooner or later, the mud I've slung about wil stick and your titles won't stop the

gossiping or the speculations and the staring. You'l be reduced to buying a lower class of

bride and sullying your esteemed lineage, and your grandfather will rise up from his grave

and haunt you and your new bride."

"I've already searched some of Augustus's papers but I've found nothing about the

virgins he bought for my birthdays. You've gathered more than me and I need you to tel me

how you acquired such private information."

"Only after you fulfil my terms, al my terms. But, for now, my middle sister is a widow

who needs to be brought out in society again, and my younger sister is ready for a season."

He glanced back at her and frowned. "What does any of that have to do with me?"

"You're going to use your influence to help me launch my sisters."

Max spluttered. "Me? You can't be serious. I avoid society when-ever possible and I've

no intention of attending any events simply to convenience your sisters." He shook his head.

31

"Don't you have male family members to escort you around town?"

"The girls have a guardian but, unfortunately, he is the difficulty."

"And why is that?"

"Peter sold me to my husband and married Georgie off far too early to a despicable man.

Our younger sister, Lucille, approaches marriageable age but I'l
not let our step-brother ruin

her life in the same despicable fashion."

"If the man is your guardian, he has lawful rights."

"The law may say that a male relation has the right to control a
woman's inheritances,

her dowry and, to a certain extent, whom she must marry. But
nobody should be allowed to

sel women to depraved men where they'll suffer unspeakable
atrocities."

"I'm not sure what you want of me."

"Merely to pretend to have a friendly relationship with us so my
sisters are protected."

Carina was making demands he'd normally refuse, if anyone
dared ask him such a thing;

but he looked forward to the time when she became his, and with
more enthusiasm than with

his month-about-mistresses. He reminded himself that Carina
was a warm receptacle for his

release, nothing more, and pushed aside thoughts that she was
also the woman for whom he'd

searched for eight years.

"Fine. I'l play the part and gain *entrée* for you, and your sisters, to
events around the

city for one month."

"Good, then I—"

"I'm not finished!" Not looking at her, he snapped out his orders.
"At the end of that

month, you'l remove yourself from my life, completely, regardless
of whether or not your

sisters have met marriage- minded gentlemen."

Carina glared at him, but his focus was on her hips where her
hands pulled tight her skirt

and coincidentally displayed her lush curves, while her chest rose
and fell rapidly and her

breasts tested the strength of her bodice fabric. He'd been with countless women whose

bodies were both more alluring and beautiful, having prided himself on bedding the most

exquisite courtesans in London. However, Carina drew him for reasons other than beauty,

lineage or family titles. This was lust, desire and arousal; a purely physical response that he'd

assuage quickly and then put behind him. As soon as he'd bedded Carina, he'd focus on

softening his bride and ensuring that she came to their joining without fear. If necessary, he'd

allocate time each week to display his eagerness to become a groom.

"For three years," Carina said, "I've not been beholden to any man, so I loathe having to

stay in London one hour longer than necessary. But I'l put up with any discomfort in

32

EXCHANGE FOR GIVING my sisters a few outings where they'll see that decent men do exist, even

if our family hasn't encountered very many to date."

Max ignored his sharp pang of regret at Carina's desire to quit the city so quickly at the

end of their association. Change disturbed him, so he should be pleased that any interruption

to his routine would be short-lived.

"I look forward to that day as much as you," he lied. "To recap, for one month I'l

arrange entertainments for your sisters, and we'l do a combined search of the boxes stored in

my attics. We'l exchange reports, and you'l give me al letters in you possession that concern me."

Her smile held a hint of triumph as she quickly ushered him from the room, but if she

imagined that she'd be gaining everything she wanted without paying the piper, she was

sorely mistaken. She'd attempted blackmail and threatened his smooth transition into married

life, so she'd not flee from him until he was satisfied they'd both accomplished their goals.

He crossed to the small desk where her letters rested and reached for writing paper. Carina

gasped.

"Never fear, my dear lady," he said over his shoulder. "I'm leaving your instructions and

not stealing your secrets."

"My instructions?" She read the paper he passed over, and he watched and waited for her

predictable reaction. Her eyes widened and her pretty mouth dropped open. "You're ordering

me to appear at Brent Street at two o'clock." She glanced down again at the note shaking

between her two clenched fists. "In two days' time." She scowled at him. "How dare you?

You've yet to prove yourself trustworthy, especial y when your arrogant, condescending and

insufferable attitude to women has been proven time and time again." Max raised an eyebrow

and waited for her tirade to finish. "Only a fool would commit to you, especial y physically,

until you've given me something that I want."

"I'm the Duke of Stirkton and I do not lie. So, yes, two days hence, our liaison will

commence. The sooner we start, my dear, the sooner we can be rid of one another."

"You're an abominable beast and a—"

"Monster?"

"Monster of a man. And if I refuse your despicable terms?"

"Then you'l learn nothing about the men you seek. Can you surrender your quest so

easily after three years plotting against them, and me? No, you'l be there. Meantime, I'l be

here at four this afternoon and we shal drive through the park. Make sure you're ready, as I

dislike standing my horses for long."

33

MAX TURNED and walked to the door, tensed and ready for her predictable reaction. He

already knew she had a temper. A vase hit the wall beside him but he kept walking, hiding his

smile. Then, as he strode down her steps, Carina's voice could be clearly heard as she vented

her fury on a now empty room.

LAWNTON PLACE; a quarter past four that afternoon.

CARINA PACED with customary military precision around her drawing room, stopping on

each rotation to peer out window in the same way she had earlier that morning, only this

time, on every second rotation, she glanced at her clock. Carriages came and went along her

street, and she fumed over the upcoming arrival of one particular gentleman's carriage.

Gertie, Georgie, and Lucille sat in a subdued row on the settee and listened to her rant.

"Fifteen minutes late."

"But," Gertie murmured, "this morning you taunted His Grace for arriving early."

"Ooooh! The Duke of Stirkton is insufferable and inconsistent." Gertie laughed, then

covered her mouth with her 'kerchief in a futile attempt to smother the sound when Carina

directed a black expression her way. "He expects us to meekly await his arrival as if we've

nothing better to do this afternoon." She gestured to her two sisters who wore their best day-

gowns. "Look at us. We're like lambs to the slaughter."

"My dear, wasn't it your idea that the Duke should take Georgiana and Lucille out and

about?"

"It may have been my idea," Carina huffed, giving Gertie another glare, "but I'd no

intention of being trapped into accompanying that man, because having to share the same air

as him irritates me beyond belief."

"Yes, you definitely seem out of sorts. Yet, you're not as angry at the Duke as you

were."

"What do you mean?" Carina snapped. "Of course I'm angry. Maximus Meacham thinks

he can bend me to his wil as if I were a green girl."

"Methinks thou doth protest too much, my dear."

"Spare me your theatrical nonsense."

"I simply meant that having spoken to the Duke in person after eight years of trying to

hate him, you're seeing him as a man, with al the strengths and frailties of every man and

woman, even you."

"I left frailties behind me many years ago and now concentrate on my strengths." She glanced at Georgie, who looked ready to bolt from the room. "Gertie is correct, darling, and

34

THE DUKE OF STIRKTON is merely a man, so you've nothing to fear."

"But he sounds to be such a fierce man," Georgie whispered, her sapphire blue eyes

luminous with unshed tears. "I can't be near another large and fearsome man."

"Not al big men are as coarse as your late husband."

Georgie nodded but looked unconvinced, and Lucille's posture was ramrod straight, her

fingers pleating the green satin ribbon hanging from her waist. Carina met Gertie's eyes in

shared understanding. When Georgie's husband had died, nothing had been left of the vibrant

and robust girl who'd been married at seventeen and she frequently suffered nightmares. If

offering her sisters a new life included spending time in the presence of Maximus Meacham,

then it was a small price to pay, though she needed to find a way to avoid going to Brent

Street in two days' time.

Nature provided her with a simple excuse and she'd bet that the Duke was too upright

and uptight to question her over her monthly courses. On Wednesday morning she'd send a

missive explaining her indisposition, and before Max could summon too many arguments

she'd be gone. She'd been proclaimed a virgin three times, and if there was to be a fourth

man in her bed she'd selecting him, and not for money or titles or desperation.

She longed to spend one night of passion, the sort of shared desire that penny dreadful

novels made seem possible. But her next night with a man wouldn't be with the one selected

by the late Earl because, if what she suspected proved true, the very idea was unconscionable

and illegal. Even after living with depraved Meachams, Max would be shocked if she shared

her suspicions with him; this level of evil would repulse even the most hardened of men.

At last, a large and elegant carriage displaying the Duke's coat of arms pul ed up before

their house, and Carina braced herself for the arrival of Maximus Meacham in all his

pompous glory. His long legs appeared out of the coach door before the footman could lower

the step and he leapt, fit and lean, onto the footpath. God help her, the man was glorious.

Thompkins announced their visitor, "His Grace, the Duke of Stirkton," after which

Carina took her time introducing her sisters and enjoyed Max's obvious impatience.

"May we proceed, ladies, as I'm engaged for this evening and I dislike tardiness."

Carina pointedly looked at the clock, before smoothing her skirts and making a show of

checking the girls' outfits.

"Yes, it would be unseemly to keep sweet Lady Johnston waiting," she said, as she

breezed past him towards the door. She waited until the footman was seating her sisters in

the Duke's luxurious coach before she spoke in a low voice that only Max could hear.

"Because Alice's parents are known to be sticklers for the strictest of propriety and we

35

WOULDN'T WANT THEM, or Alice, to be upset."

She dipped her head to hide her grin when he snapped, "I do know how to behave."

"And did I tel you our exciting news? When I explained to Lady Johnston that we were

dear, dear friends of yours, recently returned to town, she graciously extended an invitation

us to dine with them, and you, this evening."

Max's eyes darkened from deep brown to angry black. "You're dining at the same place

as I am tonight?"

"Yes, isn't that wonderful?" She patted his arm and gave him a guileless smile. "And

Alice suggested that you cal here and to take us up in your carriage."

Max's open mouth resembled a gaping fish, until the waiting coachman cleared his

throat to signal they should move along. Carina picked up her skirts and placed one booted

foot upon the first step before adding, "One morc thing." She let him see, and comprehend,

her gloating expression. "Do not be late, as I so dislike tardiness."

Max gritted his teeth, while Carina settled herself into the seat with several small wiggles

and leant forward to rearrange her skirts far enough that her breasts pressed into the deep V

slash of the bodice of her burgundy carriage dress. Every twitch, every quiver of exposed

pink flesh, captured Max's spelbound gaze, as she doubtlessly intended.

To add to his torment, Carina shifted her shoulders and thrust her bosom further into his view, daring him to forget his manners in front of her sisters and Gertie. He hunched into his

corner and ignored the complacent look on her face. The Countess would learn that nobody

outwitted a Duke of Stirkton, ever. To his irritation, they encountered a line of acquaintances

at the park, and he was forced to show a polite face and introduce the ladies to the procession

of gentlemen eager to make the acquaintance of well-bred, pretty young women previously

unknown to them.

Carina leaned out of the carriage to converse to Lady Secombe, while her son engaged a

reluctant Georgiana in a discussion of the weather. The young man was immaculately attired,

as befitted the first son of a viscount, and judging by the way he gazed at Georgiana he

regarded her as a diamond of the first order. Max studied the young ladies in his carriage for

the first time, having been distracted by Carina previously, and noted the new flush on the

cheeks of shy and retiring Lady Georgiana due to the rapt attention of young Lord Secombe.

A scheme unfurled in his mind, much like the smile unfurling on Lady Georgiana's face

at some jest from her new admirer. The sooner Carina's sisters were launched, the sooner

their elder sister would be free to concentrate on their liaison, and him.

Lady Georgiana's quiet beauty, and her vulnerability, would ensnare a young cub like

36

.   .   .

SECOMBE and his devotion would see her protected at all cost. And despite Lady Lucille

appearing for the first time in public, she wasn't a gauche chit for, like her sisters; she

radiated warmth and sincerity, and though self-contained, energy and passion lurked below

the surface. Judging by their crowd of gentlemen admirers, the girls' success was guaranteed,

which should relieve Carina's worries, not to mention the added bonus for him of having

more time alone with her, and also more time to discover the truth about that fourth man.

He was close to uncovering the identities of the two men who'd bedded her after her

night with him and when that happened, he'd claim vengeance and save her having blood on

her hands again, if she had indeed hurried along the Earl's demise. The least he could do was

ensure her time with her sisters was incident and murder-free.

Several gentlemen had persuaded Carina to stroll along the paths with them and others

implored her to dance with them at this week's bals. "Gentlemen, step back," he said loudly.

"Alow Lady Dorchester room to breathe." His growling astonished them al, especial y him,

considering that he sounded like a jealous lover. Though he intended becoming her lover,

he'd never been a jealous one and he wouldn't be starting now.

The animalistic desire to rut with a mate had been held in check because of who he was,

where he was, or who he was with. But at twenty-nine, those raw and lusty urges were

screaming for release. His unbridled lust would terrify sheltered Alice. But when Carina had spoken of taking a man to her bed, he'd longed to be the one to unleash her suppressed

passions. He longed to see her quake with release and to find pleasure alongside her.

Every few minutes, Carina glanced between the shoulders of her admirers and studied

him with pursed lips and a small frown. He closed his eyes and anticipated the excitement of

Carina warming his bed. Despite the Countess's cool, calm façade, if he applied the right

pressure she'd agree to his terms and be his for the taking. Though he'd much rather she

came willingly to Brent Street, and into his arms.

4

The Countess of Dorchester slipped the strings of her beaded reticule over her gloved wrist with slow precision, before sliding from her snug corner towards an outstretched hand.

Accepting the Duke of Stirkton's assistance, she stepped down from his ducal carriage.

An hour earlier, Max had collected Carina, her sisters and Gertie from Woods House

WITH MUCH POMP AND CEREMONY. During their slow journey through crowded streets to the

outskirts of London, and the sprawling residence of Lord and Lady Johnston, Max addressed

Georgie, Lucy and Gertie with unfailing politeness, but to Carina he said nothing. Despite

being personaly dispatched to a coach's equivalent of Coventry—the squashiest corner—

Carina smiled.

As Gertie remarked several times, the well-sprung carriage was the height of luxury and

the livery of the Duke's servants immaculate. Georgie, Lucy and Gertie sat forward on the

edge of their seats, peering past the lace curtains and lapping up every knowledgeable word

the Duke spouted as he described the passing sights.

Despite herself, Max's behavior had impressed Carina as well, even though none of them

were impressionable girls. Footmen had helped her sisters descend from the carriage, and

they now climbed the steps to the imposing front door, skirts lifted to prevent soiled hems.

Noticing Max's scowl, Carina couldn't resist a little more goading. "You seem a trifle

disconcerted. But don't concern yourself on our account, because your carriage is wel sprung

and we've arrived safely and in good time. Dreadfully impolite to arrive tardily at the house

of your betrothed."

Max's face muscles barely moved, yet undercurrents of emotion swirled beneath his

rigid features. His left eyelid twitched and his heavy breathing stretched his evening jacket

until she feared the buttons would pop.

"I'd never cause the slightest unrest for the girl I'm to marry, nor her family, and I shal

be displeased, most displeased," his eyes narrowed in a fierce scowl, "if anyone upsets their

evening."

"My goodness." Carina made a show of clutching her chest. "Is that a threat?"

"More of a warning to behave wel or suffer the consequences."

"Once again, you've underestimated the influence of rumor and innuendo. I hold the upper hand in our battle because you've more to lose from rumor mongers. Every shred of

dignity I possessed was stripped from me long ago." She turned to where the butler awaited

them and murmured, "In a Dorchester inn."

At his sharp hiss of inhaled air, she wondered if he was capable of human emotions after

al. An intriguing possibility, although she'd no intention of exposing her feelings. She'd

schemed and plotted various ways to make this shadowy man from her past suffer a fraction

of the torments she'd endured, and now she enjoyed watching him squirm the way women

did when under the control of bombastic men. Holding the whip hand over Max, for even this

one evening, would be worth it.

38

His fingers clenched over hers until, with exaggerated care, he loosened his grip and

placed her hand on the sleeve of his black evening coat. "Let us proceed. The sooner we dine,

the sooner Alice's family can be rid of our tiresome presence."

"Ah! A sentiment similar to the ever-so-romantic one you expressed regarding your

cottage? The sooner our liaison commences, the sooner we'l be bored with each other."

With great difficulty, she restrained herself from looking him in the face. His labored

breath delighted her, because dealing with a man of his ilk meant using any means to gain the

advantage. Influencing Alice might prove advantageous, as her parents were anxious for the betrothal to proceed smoothly. So if she insinuated that the Duke should be kept under tight

control, lest he stray and embarrass them, they'd apply pressure to bring him to heel.

While Max placated his future duchess, he'd have little time to meet at Brent Street and

she'd be free from liaising with a man she didn't yet trust.

"I've always believed," he murmured close to her ear, while the maid relieved them of

their cloaks, "that unpleasant tasks are better undertaken quickly rather than drawing out the

agony."

"Like pul ing a tooth?"

"Exactly."

She smiled at him while sauntering towards the drawing door where a patient butler

waited. "I disagree. Some episodes, though considered unpleasant at first, are better enjoyed

if time is taken. It's a lesson I learned one night eight years ago. Do you remember?"

Lady Johnston peeked around the doorway and saved him from answering. "Your

Grace," Alice whispered, staring with wide blue eyes before dropping into a deep curtsy. "Is

something amiss? My parents are waiting to welcome you, and the Countess of course."

Alice's feeble smile failed to touch her cheeks, or her eyes. The corners of her smal

mouth turned up just enough that a meagre glimpse of perfect teeth was allowed, and not one

wrinkle lined her face. Carina repressed a desire to roll her eyes, because Alice's mother had

assuredly lectured since birth to her hapless offspring about the correct way to smile. Young ladies were taught that moderation in all things were of uttermost importance and that smiling

freely might cause premature wrinkling on a lady's forehead. Besides that, excess emotion

was supposedly reserved for the lower classes who knew no better.

Max matched Alice's polite reserve by blanking his own expression. "Lady Johnston—"

Displaying an overly-sweet smile, Carina said, "Max dearest, do not stand on ceremony

on my account." She tapped his rigid arm with her folded fan. "I'm confident that you're on

more intimate terms with your entrancing young friend. Come, come, don't be shy." She

39

RAPPED MAX'S FOREARM AGAIN, before leaning towards Lady Johnston and saying in her loudest

whisper, "In private, I'm sure you cal each other adorable little names."

Alice's bowed mouth dropped open and showed that her front teeth were not perfectly

even, or perfectly white. She couldn't speak and her hands, gloved in white satin with lace

and bows, fluttered between them as if touching her future husband was as unthinkable as

calling him a pet name.

"Oh, no. One cannot address His Grace without his ful title. He is, after all—" Alice's

pale blue eyes widened and she said with awe, "the Duke of Stirkton."

Max looked out of his depth, an unusual state for him. Goading him might stop her worrying about dinner and the catastrophes that could occur during formal and drawn out

dining. She'd attended few formal occasions, partly because of her fear of being recognized,

but more because she'd been sickened by her husband fawning and toadying over people with

titles. Local squires had caled to gawk at the Earl's much younger wife and to then spread

malicious gossip about the couple.

Max turned back to his young bride-to-be. "Lady Johnston, I would be honored if you

would address me with less formality as, in a short time, we wil be married."

Alice's blush spread up her fair skinned neck up and reddened her scalp under her pale

blonde hair. "My mother would never forgive me, were I to forget for even one minute who

you are. Your titles are some of the oldest in England and your estates the largest."

Carina watched with blatant amusement while Max's scowls, shot in her direction during

each of Alice's downward glances, only increased her enjoyment. As they entered the foyer,

she placed her hand on his tautly muscled forearm and surreptitiously walked her fingertips

up and down. "I agree, Alice, that merely being in the Duke's presence might cause a lady to

swoon."

Alice, poor chit, appeared ready to faint at Max's feet and land on his black evening

shoes. A predator like Max was going to eat this timid girl for breakfast in the first month of

their marriage. Forced to extricate himself from Carina's clutch to support his betrothed's withering form, Max glared at Carina and, for an instant, guilt rose up like bile. His anger

was justifiable because this blameless girl didn't deserve shabby treatment from her guest.

"Lady Johnston," Max said in the sweetest voice she'd ever heard him use. His face

showed genuine compassion so perhaps he did comprehend the terror Alice felt in his

presence, especial y if she'd been taught by her mother that catching a duke was the dream of

every debutante, and that she must obey him without argument because of his social standing.

"My dear, do not overset yourself. Lady Dorchester is teasing. If you and your family

40

FEEL MORE comfortable addressing me by my title until after we marry, I shall accede to your

wishes."

Lady Johnston bobbed yet another curtsy, but was in such a rush to escape Max's

presence that she almost tripped over her skirts. Max muttered something under his breath,

and Carina took pity on Alice and led her away.

"Shal we follow my sisters, *Alice*?" Hopefully, her emphasis on the name would shoot

another arrow into Max's thick hide. "There's no need to stand on ceremony with any of us,

and I'd be honored if you would cal me Carina, as my sisters do."

Alice nodded. "Certainly. It's only the Duke of Stirkton that I cannot address casual y."

In an overloud whisper, Carina said, "In public you can continue to use his title." She giggled. "But in private, I'm sure Max would enjoy you being more playful."

Alice glanced over her shoulder at Max who was straining to hear their conversation. His

brooding expression would intimidate the most daring school-room miss, yet his resemblance

to the devil incarnate exhilarated rather than intimidated Carina.

She'd witnessed first-hand the evil that men could commit and for a time had viewed

death as the only way to extricate herself from the devil's clutches, but her accursed strong

mindedness had prevailed and she learned to confront life rather than death.

If she'd died, their stepbrother would have shown no mercy towards her sisters so, for

their sake, she'd fight long and hard. Anything to keep Georgie and Lucy out of their

stepbrother's clutches.

"Max," Carina said, "please reassure Lady Johnston that you're not about to pounce and

gobble her up."

Alice gasped in pure terror. Her reaction to Max seemed extreme, yet Alice had been

sheltered by her parents, and Carina had been tossed to the wolves at an early age. Carina had

more reason to fear Max's wrath and to expect some retaliation to her blackmail threats, yet

Max appeared more frozen than frightening and more tormented than wicked.

Max smiled at Alice. "I hope we become friends during our marriage and then you wil

become more comfortable using my Christian name." He glared at Carina. "And

disappointing your parent is unthinkable. Rules serve a purpose and without them there would be anarchy in the world."

Carina clapped. "Bravo, Max. An astute yet subtle way of reminding us of our faults, and

of our obligations to proper society."

Neither Alice nor Max spoke until Lord Johnston stepped forward to greet them with his

hand outstretched. "Your Grace, we are delighted to have you dine with us. My daughter has

41

BEEN SO LOOKING FORWARD to it, have you not, Alice?"

"Yes, Papa. Mama and I spent the day deciding the menu and selecting gowns."

Alice drew breath and her developing breasts rose up and ballooned over her décolletage.

Max went goggle-eyed for a second and Carina smothered a gurgle behind her gloved hand.

Alice rushed on with an obviously well-rehearsed question which she directed towards the

man peering down at her face. Or rather, from that height, he was most likely able to see

down her dress al the way to her toes. "Do you not think," she said as she twirled a little to

show off her flowing satin skirt, "that this is the most exquisite blue you've ever seen?"

Carina rolled her eyes until Max glared at her over Alice's shoulder. "A beautiful color

and it matches your eyes perfectly."

Alice looked down at her gown and frowned. "But my eyes are pale blue, not dark like

the gown, nor medium blue like the lace."

Carina chuckled. "You sil y man," she said with a shake of her head. "Alice wil imagine

you pay no heed to her coloring or to her beauty. Her eyes are the palest shade of blue

imaginable."

Max blushed, or as close to that human condition as his disposi-
tion alowed. "A careless

mistake. Your eyes are pale blue and your hair is ..."

"Golden like sunshine?" Carina beamed at their stunned faces.
"Max might conceal his

poetic bent but he gives women the most breathtaking compliments." Max and his poetic bent

looked ready to throttle her in the drawing room of his future
father-in- law's house, because

she couldn't picture him spending enough time with any mistress
to offer her flowery

compliments. "And Max extolls your virtues endlessly, Alice."

"He has?" Alice looked stunned.

"He's delighted that he can hold long discussions with you about
his estates, and he

eagerly anticipates the day you will seize the reins and organize
his households." She put a

hand to her brow. "Is it four or five, Max, which Alice wil be
responsible for?"

"Seven."

"Oh dear, oh dear." Alice sank into a chair and fanned her face.
"Mama!" She grasped

her mother's wrist and tugged her closer. "However wil I
manage?"

Lady Johnston perched beside her daughter and stroked her
hand. "You'll be the

Duchess of Stirkton, so of course you'l manage. Dukes and
duchesses are the highest ranks,

if you discount the Prince."

"Because," Carina muttered, "one always discounts royalty when
the Duke of Stirkton is

present." The three Johnstons had identical blank expressions,
but Max looked unamused.

42

LADY JOHNSTON TRIED to placate her pale daughter. "I shal remain with you, darling,

because His Grace knows understands that you're too young to cope without your mother's

guidance. We shal al reside with you for part of the year."

Max growled with disbelief, horror, or both. Thankfully, the butler announced dinner and

the gentlemen escorted the ladies to the table. Carina was partnered by Alice's brother, her

sisters were allocated escorts, and Max escorted his betrothed, though not before scowling at

Carina. The message in his eyes warned of retribution, but nothing he did compared to the

danger her sisters were in if she they didn't meet, and marry eligible gentlemen.

Carina turned her charms on the young man beside her. "Lord Johnston—"

"Please, Lady Dorchester, cal me Brendon."

She knew the old biddies wouldn't approve of such informality, but the Colonel had

taught her that in for a penny, in for a pound. "Certainly, Brendon."

She flashed him an enchanting smile and clutched his arm. Ahead of them in the

procession, Max forgot to shorten his strides to accommodate the constraints of Alice's blue

satin skirt, and she stumbled and would have falen if Max hadn't put both hands on her waist

and pulled her upright.

Carina held her breath. Brendon shrugged.

"My sister and the Duke are an unlikely match, don't you think?" Brendon guessed why

Carina kept her mouth firmly closed. "We both realize that my downtrodden sister is out of

her depth with the infamous Duke of Stirkton."

Although his honesty surprised Carina, she held her tongue.

"My sister is beautiful and charming when you know her as I do, but my mother

smothers her good qualities. From the time Alice toddled, she was told her only purpose in

life was to snare a lofty title. The man behind that title was unimportant."

"But without a husband and a title, a woman is less than dirt under men's feet and can be

passed from pilar to post with no care for her welbeing."

Brendon studied Carina with his intense blue gaze and more intelligence than he'd

displayed before his parents. "Ah, this happened to you. Your eyes show your pain quite

clearly."

Waiting in line for a footman to seat her, Carina considered her companion. For a young

titled gentleman, Brendon seemed level-headed and deserving of a sensible answer.

She dipped her head in agreement. "I cannot stand by while others suffer the same fate."

She glanced at her two sisters who were paying rapt attention to their partners' conversations.

Brendon followed her gaze. "You're worried that your sisters will also be shuffled from

43

PILAR TO POST."

She assessed Brendon from his stylish haircut to his well-shod feet, the way an

unmarried lady evaluated a bachelor's worth.

He threw back his head and laughed, the enjoyable sound of a man easily pleased. "Are

you deciding if I'm a delicious pudding and you want to eat me, or a prospective groom and

you want to marry me?" She smiled and shook her head. "Ah! Perhaps for one of your

sisters?"

Carina matched his laughter, enjoying being with a man who expressed his emotions so

freely. "I apologize. Was I that obvious?"

"I feel like a side of beef hung at the market."

She chuckled. "Worrying about my sisters is making me crazy."

"I forgive you." Brendon glanced to where his own sister was being seated at the head of

the table next to the Duke. "I also worry for my sister. She's too immature to cope with

Stirkton. My parents were foolish to push for this marriage before Alice enjoyed her first

season, or gained some experience dealing with men."

Carina pitied Alice who was a sacrificial lamb being offered up to a god. Surviving

marriage to a man as potent as Max would take a lady of indomitable strength, or he'd

dominate her and squeeze the life out of her as easily as he'd squash a cockroach under one

highly-polished boot.

As the Countess of Dorchester, Carina was seated down the table from Max, the highest

titled gentleman. She sighed with relief that both her sisters were now seated and engaged in

conversation with their dinner partners. For the first time in years, Georgie paid attention to

the topics discussed around her and Lucille, with her friendly demeanor, was happily

conversing with both ladies and gentlemen. Georgie's recent withdrawal had become so

severe that Carina and Gertie had feared for her sanity.

Carina studied Max's severe profile and marveled anew at how
unfair life was that he'd

gained titles and wealth by accident of birth, yet had devoted
himself to maintaining that

inheritance and passing it on to future generations, in contrast to
her step-brother whose only

interest was his immediate situation and which gambling hells he
could afford to visit. Apart

from his titles, wealth, and aura of power, Max's features were
ruggedly masculine, which

together made him breathtakingly handsome and infinitely
desirable.

Was that enough to agree to become his mistress? Not if there was
a way to avoid it.

Being close to Max and giving herself to him was a dangerous
temptation because, once

again, it would mean surrendering her soul to a stranger.

44

5

D inner progressed without mishap and Carina's fears about her sisters' ability to cope
dissipated, alowing her the first glimmer of hope she'd felt in many months. Georgie was

displaying her best side and seemed her old self, sensible and capable, and not a quaking

mess who was terrified of large men, especially their step-brother.

For her own part, Carina enjoyed not only Brendon's company, but this brief respite

from her own worries and a chance to talk and laugh instead of being on guard every

moment. Lady Mitchell sat opposite them, and each time she regaled her audience with titbits

of gossip her purple turban bobbed so violently that its spiraled feather dipped towards her

food. Diners all along the table watched with open-mouthed fascination and counted down

the seconds until the tip of the feather acquired an additional hue.

Cream *lobster bisque* was narrowly avoided, and thankfully she missed the salmon

mousse because the color would have clashed dreadfully with the purple of her gown. The

third course, served by an also-amused footman, was *Crème d'Asparagus* and an exact match

for the grass-green ruffles bouncing gaily around the lady's enormous bosom. Carina was

able to hide her growing amusement behind her napkin, until the poor unassuming asparagus

proved her undoing. Brendon whispered in her ear and her small bubble of mirth quickly

escalated into full-blown laughter, when their nonsense and amusement triggered laughter all

along the table too.

Carina's hand stil covered her mouth when she lifted her head and encountered Max's

dark stare. On one side, his bride-to-be prattled to his profile, while on the other, her mother

gushed and waved her hands but was also unable to capture her future son-in-law's attention.

Max's facial expressions during the first courses had fluctuated between boredom and

frustration, but he now appeared furious.

She understood his boredom and the frustration, considering his dinner companions. But

his fury was directed down the table at her, though what she'd done to earn it was a mystery.

"My lady," Brendon whispered, "for some obscure reason Stirkton is hurling

metaphorical daggers in your direction. The two of you have been close friends for many

years?"

"Quite correct." She gave Brendon an agreeable smile and lied through her teeth.

Nothing was going to upset her sisters tonight. "His Grace and I met several years ago, but

45

I've no idea why he seems out of sorts." Another blatant lie.

After that, dinner became uncomfortable. Each and every time Carina glanced down the

table, Max's attention was fixed on her and waves of fury emanated from his tense body.

When the final course was consumed and the ladies left the men to enjoy port and cigars,

Carina was the first to rise from the table and walk to the door.

"Where are you rushing to, Lady Dorchester?" Lady Dorothea Johnston placed a light

hand on Carina's arm and pointed down the halway to where two footman waited. "Tea is

being served in the drawing room and when the gentlemen join us, we shal have music."

Lady Johnston's voice rose an octave, "Dearest Alice plays the pianoforte brilliantly. His

Gracc wil be captivated when he hears her repertoire for the first time."

Forced to follow Lady Johnston to the drawing room, Carina said, "I'm certain His

Grace wil be enthralled." She envisioned a bored-to-tears Max falling asleep every night,

while his young wife valiantly tried to snare his attention with her music. Max didn't appear

the type to content himself with unvaried evenings of mild enter-tainment. Attempting to cage

a prowling beast like Max in a quiet drawing room each evening would be akin to trying to

hold a tiger by the tail.

Georgie and Lucy came to her on the elegant green and gold settee and sat, one either

side, as the ladies' tea ritual commenced. Slipping her hand into Georgie's, she asked quietly,

"Are you enjoying yourself?"

As usual, Lucy spoke first, her voice bubbling with happiness, and didn't give Georgie a

chance to do anything but nod. "I'm having such a wonderful evening." Lucy gripped

Carina's other hand. "Mr. Templeton was a most entertaining dinner companion. And,

Alice...I mean Lady Johnston, although she implored us, Georgie and I, to address her as

Alice, as you are such great friends with the Duke and she wants us to become bosom

confidants...She told us, Georgie and I," she leaned around Carina and smiled at her sister,

"that she hasn't many good friends, or at least ones her own age in town in whom she can

confide, you know, share one's secrets wishes with, and she realy, realy wants us to—"

"Lucy, sweetheart," Carina chuckled as she patted her sister's hand, "take a breath. It's

good you're enjoying yourself because I was worried you might be overwhelmed." Slanting

her glance towards Georgie, she added, "Both of you."

Her fear that Georgie wouldn't emerge from her cocoon of silence long enough to

engage in conversation had almost made Carina send a note of regret to their hosts. She'd

worried that Georgie would feel overwhelmed being with this large group of men but,

although she'd watched her sister as closely as a hawk al night, Georgie had showed no sign

46

.   .   .

OF PANIC.

"Are you enjoying it, too?" Her sister lifted her head and Carina saw happiness on her
face, a long forgotten emotion that gladdened Carina's heart.
"The dinner was easier than I expected and everyone has been most kind." The corners
of Georgie's mouth turned up and she came closer to a genuine smile than Carina had seen
for a long time.
Carina swallowed down the lump in her throat and offered up a prayer of gratitude.
Georgie's late husband had repeatedly abused her until her confidence was destroyed. Time
and patience were needed before she could rediscover her courage. Carina brushed aside her
tears before Georgie noticed and lifted her head, but shivered when her eyes met the direct
gaze of her adversary.
Max stood a small distance away and stared at her with unblinking black eyes. She
needed to be outwardly strong, even if she quaked like a jelly inside. Max read her far too
easily, when she needed the reverse to stay a step ahead of him. She needed his grandfather's
journals and she had no time to lose, because the longer she stayed around Max, the more
susceptible she'd become to his sexual advances.
The Duke was a constant reminder of her past life and a time which she wanted to stay
buried. The only way to banish her pain once and for all was to deal with the men involved
and then disappear. Ideally, her sisters would have found decent husbands before her own

plans came to fruition, and then she'd be free to travel to the exotic places she'd read about.

Max stepped closer and she braced herself. "Now you've joined us, Alice can play for

you. She's eager to demonstrate the musical expertise she's acquired during her seventeen

years." Despite her polite smile, Max understood her message. Alice was young, innocent,

and immature and he was trapped into going ahead with a marriage he'd loathe, because a

gentlemen couldn't cry off from a long term arrangement like his. His attendance was

mandatory at Alice's planned musical performance, and at the altar on his wedding day.

He spoke to his hovering fiancée, despite not taking his eyes off Carina. "I'm eager to

see and hear you play since your mother has extolled your musical talents for several weeks. I

look forward to not just this performance, but to the many we will enjoy during our

marriage."

Lady Johnston senior had hovering near them, waiting for a chance to take charge of the

conversation once more. She popped up like a bird eager to catch the early worm at Max's

elbow and chirped in a bird like voice, "Your Grace, you'll not be disappointed. Our

delightful girl looks like an angel, plays and sings like one, and embroiders with as fine a

47

STITCH AS AN ITALIAN NUN. Your furniture will be enhanced by her needle-worked linens." She clasped her hands and heaved a heartfelt sigh. "Alice shal make you a wonderful wife, and

my husband and I are delighted that we'l be able to visit you often."

Carina started to laugh but smothered her blunder with a cough. The Duke's jaw

tightened and his fists clenched while his future mother-in-law gushed about how much they

looked forward to spending time with the married couple, insensitive to Max's loathing of her

plans. Carina put her hand on his arm, intending it to be another careless irritant, but she

surprised herself when she rubbed his taut arm with her thumb in a placating gesture. She was

being sily. He didn't need comforting, especial y not from her, and she needed to direct her

pity towards Alice, not Max.

"Oh, Max," she gushed in an overdone voice, "how lucky you are. At last, you'l have

close family, after being alone for—"

"Not alone!" The clustered women al jumped at this sharp rebuttal. "My grandfather

was with me."

"However," Carina said, "the late Duke's ideas were somewhat old fashioned and often

not in keeping with society's normal rules. As a young gentleman, deciding which of his

rules to accept must have been a constant trial for you. Though I believe you're now sorting

out for yourself which rules to apply to your present life and which to disregard."

Alice's eyes widened and Lady Johnston gasped. "Lady Dorchester," the older lady said,

drawing several short breaths before she could continue. "No one in this room can say what may, or may not, have influenced either the late Duke or the present one. In any case, the past

is of no consequence." She fluttered her gloved hand in the air like a fairy-godmother waving

her wand and wiping the entire subject from everyone's minds. "Thankfully, His Grace now

has us, the entire Johnston family, to assist him and his bride in adjusting to married life."

The aforementioned bride had plonked herself without ceremony into a nearby chair and

sat as if carved from stone. Her fingers twisted the folds of her skirt into haphazard pleats and

her bottom lip trembled. For once, Max noticed her distress and, stepping closer to Alice,

bent to speak in a soothing tone.

"Lady Alice, please don't upset yourself. Lady Dorchester aludes to the time after my

grandfather's passing when I was old enough to form my own opinions. Until then, I'd

followed my grandfather's teachings to the letter. Nevertheless, everyone grows and matures

eventually, and so it was time for me to move ahead with my life and put the past behind

me."

Max dipped a brief nod in the older Lady Johnston's direction. "I'l be celebrating my

48

THIRTIETH BIRTHDAY VERY SOON. So you, my dear lady, may leave all decisions regarding Alice

and our marriage in my hands and rest assured that your daughter's happiness will be

foremost in my mind at al times."

Carina clapped her hands, attracting the attention of al standing nearby. "Oh, wel said.

A striking speech. And knowing you as intimately as I do," she said, pretending not to see

Max's glower and unspoken warning, "I'm positive that in al your future undertakings with

this delightful family, you shall be the consummate gentleman. Caring, selfless and

considerate of al their wishes."

Lady Johnston frowned, swiveling her head from Carina to Max as if sensing wrong but

unable to pinpoint the problem. She looked to her daughter and fluttered a limp hand in her

direction. "Alice, please play for us, now. Your Grace, would you be so kind as to turn the

sheets of music at the pianoforte?"

Max bowed deeply to all the ladies. "My pleasure, my lady."

He took Alice's arm and escorted her to a wel -polished instrument standing proudly on

spindle legs on the raised stage in the corner of the room. Lady Johnston clapped her hands to

attract attention and watched while her guests found seats. Alice began to play and a hush fell

over the gathered onlookers as her talent shone.

Several songs later, Carina's gaze drifted around the room to survey the attending

gentlemen. The cream of society was gathered here tonight, probably due to the attendance of

an influential duke. Several gentlemen claimed close acquaintance with Stirkton, so he hadn't

kept himself aloof from all society. And his investment and trading ventures would throw

him into constant contact with his peers and other investors, plus her investigations had uncovered the names of several elite clubs to which he subscribed.

Despite having to mix with men and women often, the upright and uptight Duke of

Stirkton held himself at a distance, which was more mental than physical. Perhaps, Carina

mused as Alice's fingers ran over the ivory keys to produce a passionate sonata, Max's

solitary upbringing prevented him from disclosing more of his private side.

She blinked several times and straightened in her chair to look over at where Max stood

engrossed as he turned the pages of sheet music, and realization dawned. Whenever she'd

teased him, Max had been disconcerted and unsure how to respond because he'd had no

siblings to roughhouse with and to tease, as she'd done with her sisters. From beside her,

Carina heard Lucy's long sigh.

"Look," Lucy said, pointing at the dais to where Max gazed down at Alice with an

expression of stunned awe. "See at the Duke's expression and how he looks at Alice. Perhaps

49

HE'S TRULY GOING to fal in love with her."

Carina's stomach clenched and, without thought, she rubbed a hand over her middle to

ease the ache, hating herself for being upset at the idea of Max in love with someone. It

would suit her plans a lot better, so why did it disturb her?

Georgie chuckled and both sisters looked at her in surprise. "Having Max fal in love

with his wife would make their marriage so much easier.

However, His Grace appears more

in love with the sonata than the musician."

The three women swung their eyes back to scrutinize Max's features, normally

shadowed and dark, but which were now lit up as if from an inner fire. Georgie's

observations were correct, as they always were, because she had an instinctive awareness of

the emotions of others, even ones they were at pains to hide. Carina tried to fit this newly

revealed aspect of his character with what she already knew.

By his transfixed look, the music held him in thral, and when Alice's hands moved to

pound out the final cords his eyes drifted closed, as if in ecstasy. With his face relaxed, its

harsher crease lines were eased and the curves and hollows of his sculpted face stood out

more in relief, increasing his already large masculine appeal.

When he later walked to join them, Georgie spoke first as if she was the best of friends

with the Duke. "Oh, my heavens, Max, was not Alice's playing simply breathtaking?"

With one of his brief bows of acknowledgement, a slight bending from his lean waist, he

said, "It was indeed breathtaking, Lady Georgiana. I recal my mother playing the very same

sonata when I was much younger and I would sit and listen, entranced by the music."

Once more, Carina felt that tug of guilt. Her treatment of him had been abominable all

evening and her only excuse was that some imp in her nature prodded her to stir the rigid man

out of his customary unbending stance. She longed to ruffle him until he snapped, broke his

self-inflicted chains and allowed himself to act more like a normal person and less like a

duke.

After hours wavering between tormenting Max until he exploded in front of his future

family and was compelled to fulfill her request and get rid of her as fast as possible, and

pitying him for being unable to extricate himself from a situation his grandfather had locked

him into, the long evening finally drew to a close. Even Max groaned his relief when they'd

at last escaped the suffocating atmosphere at the Johnstons' house. Lord and Lady Johnston

gushed over Max's status, his elegance and his titled acquaintances, until Carina feared she'd

disgrace herself and be physically ill on their front steps.

Carina meanly pictured a future for the detached Duke of Stirkton, in which the Johnston

50

FAMILY DESCENDED upon him and his wife, *en masse*, several times a year. Max sat at the

pinnacle of London's social ladder and the Johnston family, the elder lady in particular,

dreamed of seating themselves alongside him in the rarified air of the city's *haute ton*. If she

was a gambler, she'd lay odds that Max would send the Johnstons running, with their tails

between their legs, before he and Alice celebrated their first year of wedded bliss, or perhaps

wedded disharmony.

Carina's only disquieting moment happened as they were seated in the ducal coach and

rolling through the heavy road traffic to Woods House. Georgie shared a bench with Max, squeezing herself into the corner to avoid any accidental contact with his broad-shouldered

frame and stretched out legs. Her cloak slipped off her shoulder and she shivered. To

Carina's great surprise, Max was the first to notice. He moved to pull the cloak over

Georgie's shoulder but when his arm stretched out, Georgie flinched and threw up her hands.

"No!"

Max's hand hovered midair before he dropped it back into his lap. "I regret having

frightened you, Lady Georgiana. I was going to adjust your cloak, as you appear to be

suffering from cold. I apologize that my coach isn't warmer." He gave Georgie a smile that

was full of understanding, yet she huddled in the corner and her shoulders shook.

Carina jumped into the breach. "I apologize, Max, but Georgie doesn't care to be

touched, especial y by men."

At the same moment, Georgie leaned a few inches towards Max. "Your Grace, I'd be

most grateful if you'd assist me with my cloak. I suffer with the cold more than most people."

For the next ten minutes, no one spoke. Lucy's face showed her astonishment and Carina

was stunned that their sister accepted a man's touch, and had even invited Max to touch her

clothing.

Sensing the change in Georgie's attitude to this particular man, Lucy said, "Your Grace,

you must come to Woods House and hear Georgie play. She also plays like an angel."

"Oh, Lucy," Georgie said, her hands rising to cover the hot flush rising on her cheeks.

"His Grace wouldn't wish to waste his valuable time listening to my efforts at an instrument."

"On the contrary, Lady Georgiana, it would bring me great pleasure to hear you play."

"And," Lucy said with a mischievous glint in her eyes, "Carina sings beautifully. In fact,

al three of us adore music."

"I also adore music, "Max admitted. "It is one of my weaknesses."

Carina, having recovered her equilibrium, couldn't resist one last jab at Max. "One of

your weaknesses?"

51

"ONE OF SEVERAL, I'M AFRAID."

"Surely, Your Grace, you're not admitting to succumbing to common frailties like

ordinary men? I assumed that the revered Meacham name guaranteed you'd live without the

common impulses and customary sins of mere mortals."

Max grunted, half laugh and half rebuff. "I think, Lady Dorchester, that if you continue

pushing and prodding this particular Meacham, you'l discover that I'm as human as the next

man, and that I'm capable of committing a wide range of sins. But you've already compiled a

list of my sins with the help of your sleuths, haven't you?"

Tension emanated from her sisters and pervaded the carriage's enclosed space as they

awaited Carina's reply and, most likely, dreaded her next cutting response. But she, of al

people, knew how stressful this long evening had been for them and how difficult it was for

Georgie to ride in this small space with a man. If she created any more unpleasantness for her sisters, she'd deserve to be horse-whipped.

She laughed. "*Touché*, Max, *touché*. You've bested me this evening."

"No." Scant inches below the red-leather padded roof, he shook his head in a slow

motion of denial. Carina watched, fascinated, as the lamp light reflected the gleam from

several blue-black streaks that lifted and swung and shone above the rest of his dark hair.

Their sinuous slide as they settled back into place made her yearn to stroke and soothe them,

or to trail their silky softness between her fingers.

"...Al evening, as earlier it seemed you wished to cause me embarrassment. Why was

that, Countess?"

Carina's attention snapped back to his face and away from her fanciful wanderings.

She'd missed what he said and stared at him with her mouth open, looking and feeling like a

complete ninny. "Umm..."

"Could it be that my presence makes you nervous? Anxious?"

Silence reined after that enigmatic comment. Georgie and Lucy were no doubt replaying

in their minds the evening's events and trying to analyze Carina's interactions with Max

during the evening. They'd subject her to rigorous questioning when they were safely above

stairs and away from eavesdroppers, demanding confirmation that her relationship with Max

involved more than a week or two of sifting through old papers. In the way that only close

siblings can do, they'd doggedly poke and prod at her, until her thoughts were muddled and

she let slip something to give away her turmoil where Max was concerned.

Her tired mind couldn't formulate an answer to soothe her sisters and appease Max's

curiosity. However, she gained an amnesty when the carriage pulled to a stop before Woods

52

HOUSE. "Oh, look, we've arrived home."

Leaning forward, she grasped the door handle and jerked the lever upwards before the

footmen found their places outside. Her shove on the door almost knocked the wig from one

footman's head as the well-oiled door swung outwards. Without waiting for assistance, she

clambered from the carriage in an ungainly manner, stretching one foot to the footstep and

then the other down to the road. Her slipper hit the shiny Macadam surface and she slithered

sideways, only the quick thinking of the stunned footman saving her from sprawling face-

first. His white gloved hand shot sideways and grasped her hard around the elbow until, by

sheer brute strength, he steadied her.

"Oooh," she shrieked as she tottered on her toes, before finding her balance and being

able to settle back on her heels. "Oh, my goodness," she gasped, dreadfully relieved that

she'd not ended as a legs-in-the-air spectacle in front of all these men.

From behind her, Georgie and Lucy gave twin gasps of horror as they descended with

the assistance of another servant. Worst of all, her butler rushed down their front steps, or as

close to rushing as an old man with rickety legs could manage while using the wooden railing as a hand-over-hand crutch.

"Oh, my lady, good gracious," he said, one hand clutching the rail and one at his chest.

He was unable to move out to aid her, and the color of his face resembled a newly scrubbed

sheet and his wilowy frame rocked back and forth on spindly legs. "Are you harmed, my

lady?"

Carina murmured her thanks to the footman who'd saved her, before wrapping both

hands around her butler's arm. The poor man wore only a night-shirt half-covered by a

loosely-tied dressing gown, and the bones of his forearm had shrunk so much that the woolen

sleeve drooped, two sizes too big.

"I'm quite intact, but let's get you inside and out of this damp air. Your joints wil pain

tomorrow if we don't warm them."

He nodded his balding head once before turning back to the railing and gripping it two-

handed, obviously more exhausted than his stiff pride would allow him to admit. It was past

time he retired to her country estate to live out his days in comfort, away from the London

damp, but he wouldn't be convinced. Straightening, she righted her clothing and moved

closer to her butler so she could assist him up the steps, which from down here and with a

shaking old man on her arm, seemed further than the peak of the highest mountain in

England. Before she could force her own shaking legs to step up, Max moved around her and

firmly grasped her butler's arm.

53

. . .

"TAKE HIS OTHER SIDE, FREDDIE," he said, and then waited until his footman slipped into

position. With barely any exertion on their part, they encouraged the older man up each step

and to the door Georgie held open, while Lucy dodged past and yelled orders to other staff

members arriving on the scene.

"Betsy, take him to the kitchen fire. Get Cook to fix him one of her hot toddies and then

make certain he goes straight to bed. And be sure to put a heated brick at his feet."

Carina stood, one hand gripping the rail beside the top step, and chuckled at Lucy's sharp

orders. Thank goodness her younger sister was no shrinking violet and coped with dramatic

situations with the flare of a sergeant major in charge of a platoon. Despite Lucy's excess of

energy, she remained a firm favourite with the servants because she was prepared to roll up

her sleeves and work beside them if necessary. Georgie peered out the front door at Carina

with her brows raised in silent question and her teeth worrying her bottom lip.

"Do you need help, Carrot, because you look done in?"

Carina groaned aloud. "Do not cal me that name."

Georgie covered her mouth but couldn't control the giggle that escaped. "Oops! Sorry. I

forgot that you think it's childish."

"It's not that, it's..."

"Yes, I remember. Papa cal ed you that. Carrot-top was his special name for you."

Georgie's sigh held so much longing and regret that Carina felt guilty for chastising her

sister, especially after hearing that girlish giggle, a noise she'd waited weeks to hear. She let the footman pass her and then wrapped her arm around her sister's waist. They walked side

by side through the door and directly into Max's path, and into the solid wal of his chest.

"Ouch!" The sisters made identical noises of hurt and rubbed their noses.

"So sorry, ladies." Max stretched out a hand to each sister to steady them. "Ah, Carina,

you do seem to be creating chaos wherever you go this evening."

The Duke looked at her solemnly before giving them a wide grin, a remarkable contrast

to his normal stern and forbidding expression.

Georgie and Carina stared in amazed awe until Georgie managed to recover.

"Oh, no, Your Grace," she said with a shake of her head, "it was my fault entirely."

"Then I shal bid you goodnight, Georgie, if I may be so bold as to address you so

informally."

Georgie went weak-kneed with admiration when Max took her hand and grinned again,

and Carina had no inkling as to why Max had been able to create such a miraculous change in

her sister's attitude towards men. A short time ago, Carina had irritated the Duke either into,

54

OR OUT OF, a sulk but now, for God-alone knew what reason, he presented them with smiles,

dazzling smiles that could make a woman fall at his feet. Radiant, sultry, sexy and seducing

grins, the type that practiced rakes used to seduce women into throwing away long-held

values and sliding naked between silk sheets.

Georgie giggled again and Carina groaned, hoping the other two would guess her

feelings and her opinion of such unusual behavior. The idea of Max unbending to seduce

women was ludicrous, because he'd always seduced by waving a wad of banknotes under

women's noses. Max dropped a kiss onto the back of Georgie's gloved hand, and her level-

headed and man-shy sister treated her seducer—damn! Treated her hand kisser to a long,

languishing sigh of delight before slowly drawing back her fingers in an exaggerated

movement that made Carina want to snatch Georgie's hand away herself.

"Georgie," she snapped, "take this." She thrust her handkerchief into Georgie's hand,

"Wipe your chin and then go and check on Lucy." At Georgie's stunned look, Carina added a

lack-luster, "Please."

Max's smile deepened and, showing hel ish injustice considering Carina's expanding

vexation with him, two dimples appeared. The left dipped into a crease a smidgen deeper

than the right. Cherub-like, and ones she'd never seen before, they softened his face and

made him appear more relaxed than any duke had a right to be, considering she was as far

from relaxed as a hungry baby was content. She wanted to sigh aloud like Georgie and even

drool like her sister was doing. She closed her eyes so she wouldn't stare at the enraptured

pair any longer but, from beside her, she heard her smitten sister give another long and loud

moan.

"Lady Georgiana, or rather, Georgie, I think your sister is offering you her 'kerchief in

an act of subtle irony. I assume the handkerchief indicates her belief that you might swoon,

simply because I showed good manners."

"For goodness sake," Carina said, glaring at him. "I wanted Georgie to realize that she

was in danger of drooling down your evening clothes, but only because you're the first man

in a long time to kiss her hand. Twinkling those gorgeous dimples doesn't mean that I, or my

sisters, wil fal at your feet any time soon."

Georgie made a snuffling noise that could have been laughter before she covered her

mouth, muttered goodnight, and scuttled inside. When she pulled the door closed behind her,

Carina was shocked and then annoyed. Her sisters had effectively abandoned her with a

bachelor on her doorstep—this unknown Max, the side of him she'd sensed that he kept

locked away, having long ago tossed aside the key. This playful, amorous and mind-

55

BOGGLINGLY ATTRACTIVE SIDE that was far, far more dangerous to her well-being, and three years

of planning, than the ton's bitter and jaded duke that her men had reported.

His lips twitched over some inner humor and he placed a cupped hand to his ear.

"Pardon, my lady, but did I hear you mention dimples? I think gorgeous was the word used to

describe the aforesaid dimples."

"Ooh!"

She had a childish desire to grind her heel onto the top of his perfectly-shined evening

shoes and it took all her willpower to not surrender to that whim. When she opened her

tightly clenched eyes, she discovered that his twitching lips had widened into another of those

incredible smiles.

"Unfair," she muttered with a groan. "Dimples on a grown man." When she threw her

hands up, he chuckled. "Unfair. And excessive."

Using the index finger of each hand, he pointed towards his cheeks. "Even gorgeous dimples?"

Max's teasing manner was so out of character, so disconcerting, that her mind whirled,

incapable of adapting to the abrupt change in the individual standing before her. Legs astride,

hands on his hips, he bent from the waist to almost touch her nose to nose. When his eyes,

forever shielded, dark and predatory, began to shine and twinkle with open good humor, all

rational judgment and good sense deserted her. This time impulse proved stronger than

willpower.

"Damn you, Max, don't you dare be nice to me now."

Her left foot shot out from under her skirt and stomped down hard. Fortunately for Max,

lightening fast reflexes plus a stride's distance from her foot saved him from injury.

Unfortunately for Carina, jarring her already sore foot on the parquetry flooring didn't save

her from hurt.

"Oooh," she groaned, hopping on one foot. Max reached for her and supported her

weight as she reached down and rubbed at her painful ankle, but continued to mutter, "Damn,

damn, damn." When the twinges subsided, she eased her foot to the floor and balanced

without his aid. Darting a wry glance up at Max, she shrugged her shoulders. "I apologize for

my childishness. I suppose you may cal it retribution."

He shrugged, a careless imitation of Carina's gesture, however he offered no more

smiles. No more dimples. Already, she missed those dips and creases that shifted his features

from austere to striking. Sil y to crave them when she'd been shown so few.

"Retribution, indeed. Although, why my being nice to you would scare you so much, I

56

CANNOT COMPREHEND."

When she barked out a laugh, he glanced away for a moment and then back, but in that

instant she could swear she'd glimpsed hurt and pain flash in his expression.

He swalowed once, and again, before saying, "I'm not a complete monster, you know."

She nodded. "I do know, because I've witnessed your kindness. But that was many years

ago, Max, and you and I aren't the same people anymore. It's impossible to go back."

He sighed, a sound of regret that softened Carina's resolve. "You're no doubt correct.

But on our way forward, we can at least forge a truce, a temporary peace. Would that be

acceptable even if my attempts at levity have failed?"

Again she felt a stab of displeasure, though for the main part she was disappointed with herself. She'd handled her short interludes with this unusual man very badly and she

regretted her contrariness. However larger goals were her current focus and she couldn't

allow herself to be distracted by a few moments of stolen pleasure on a doorstep.

"A truce would be more than acceptable, Max. Thank you for a delightful evening. You

made my sisters exceedingly happy."

"Only your sisters? Perhaps tomorrow I'l succeed in making you happy also, my lady."

She gave a smal laugh and shook her head. "You're doing it again: being nice to me and

making me laugh."

"Ah, yes," he grinned and held her gloved hand. "Because in the morning, I'l be

wearing my stern face again and no one will ever know that you referred to the hollows in my

cheeks as...gorgeous dimples."

As he turned and strode down the steps, taking them two at a time with his long stride,

she muttered, "Incorrigible as wel ."

"I heard that and be warned: I don't lie abed al morning, so I shal arrive at precisely

nine o'clock. We should decide how to search my grandfather's boxes and share what we

each expect to find, otherwise we'l be spend months in the attics and get nowhere. Until

then, goodnight Carrot-top."

"Carrot-top," she spluttered. "You heard! Hels bels, I shal throttle my sister."

As she pushed the heavy door closed, she heard off-tune whistling on the street. Peering

out, the only person she sighted was the Duke of Stirkton, a non-whistling type of man if ever she'd seen one.

She trudged up to her bedchamber and tried to squash the image of a playful, dimpled

duke, one who whistled, and instead picture Max as she knew him best: a man who scowled

more than he smiled, a man who was stern and bitter, and unfortunately for her, a man who

57

HAD THE MOST GORGEOUS DIMPLES.

6

At precisely nine in the morning, the Duke of Stirkton dodged through the steady stream of horses and carriages to traverse Lawnton Place and mount the scrubbed steps to Woods House once more. The difference between today's arrival here and the one last night was that now a keen sense of anticipation put a spring in his step and stripped the scowl from his face.

Al night long, he'd alternately puzzled over the inconsistencies in the sisters' stories and construed a dozen ways he might push and prod at Lady Dorchester the way she did him, in the hope that she might inadvertently disclose the names of those mystery men. After jogging up the last steps, he raised his hand to knock at the same moment that Lucy pulled open the door.

He turned to the bustling street and sucked in a deep breath of smog-ridden London air.

"Isn't it a beautiful day, Lucy?"

"Good grief, Max. When Carina told us at breakfast that you were acting strangely when

you departed last evening, I didn't believe her. But she was teling the truth."

Max threw both hands in the air as he stepped inside the house. "Isn't a man entitled to

smile occasionally without the world assuming he should be locked away in Bedlam?"

Lucy's laughter sounded child-like, free and quite delightful. Max was struck with

another of those abnormal urges to abandon his ingrained reserve and chortle with her. She

leant both hands on her knees and continued laughing in great loud gulps, until he worried

that she was now laughing at his silliness rather than with him.

"Of course you may smile," Lucy said as she straightened. "It's only that..." She went

into another peal of laughter. "The thought of you, the Duke of Stirkton, cal ing Carina

Carrot-top is ..."

"Lucy, please stop." Gertie walked into view with her hands demurely clasped at the

waist of her yellow sprigged muslin gown and simple pearls swinging at her ears. Max wasn't

fooled. Gertie looked ready to burst into giggles as wel. "I apologize for Lucy's merriment at

your expense. She meant no harm. She cannot reconcile her image of a duke relaxing his

guard enough to tease and to cal her sister by a pet name."

Max studied Gertie. "And you can conceive of such a thing? For this high-born duke in

58

PARTICULAR?"

Gertie didn't meet his gaze but he was certain she was smiling. "Most definitely. You

can display both sides of a high ranking peer. The haughty, hard-working, supreme ruler of

his lands."

"Humph! Most of my acquaintances believe that sums up my entire character."

"Yes, but we know better. There is that other side to you, the one few are alowed to see.

Your mother was forced to hide a lot of her softer side as well, so you have that in common

and something else to remember her by."

"Why do you imagine that I want to remember her for anything?"

Gertie placed a hand on his arm and drew him to a halt in the hallway. The elderly butler

was making his way towards them, his gait uneven, as if he suffered pain in his joints as

Carina had said.

"Your Grace—"

"Please cal me Max as the others are doing. Strangely, I've quickly become accustomed

to it and I might even come to enjoy it. Most people avoid such familiarit y with me, for fear

that the taint left by my upbringing might touch them and corrupt their morals."

"That's blatantly untrue. The shield you've erected around your-self in order to survive

and succeed makes people wary of you, though I suspect your defenses would crumble easily

if the right pressure was applied. Then others would see you as you really are, accomplished

yet modest, strong yet compliant."

Max was so stunned by Gertie's assessment that it took him several seconds to realize she had walked away, leaving him standing alone and bemused in the center of the

fashionable entryway. At their first meeting, he'd formed the opinion that Carina was a strong

and resourceful lady who'd turned cold and uncaring, due to the pain and indignities life had

subjected her to. An innocent pushed into becoming a knowing adventuress through no fault

of her own, but through the evil experiences thrust upon her.

Nevertheless, the distinct possibility remained that she was also a murderess. The late

Earl had deserved to die and few would mourn him, yet the doubt lingered that Carina, in

desperation, might have hastened his death. As the highest title in the county of Stirkton and

surrounds, Max performed the duties of magistrate and he now wondered why he'd not been

informed, nor cal ed upon to write the report, at the Earl's demise.

God knew, Carina had suffered more than she should have in her short life and the bleak

misery she'd endured should have hardened her beyond repair, and yet, when her sister had

recoiled from his touch in fright, Carina hadn't been frightened. She'd been filled with

59

COMPASSION AND LOVE, with no sign of terror.

Despite suffering anguish guaranteed to turn most women's minds, Carina showed

fortitude, courage, deep caring, and the sort of strength Max most admired, despite him being

in no position to admire her. They were two people who'd been wronged seeking a resolution

to their problems, and nothing more.

For him, the resolution was connecting with her and having her in his bed once more.

For him, the resolution was also finding out, at long last, if his actions had ruined her life.

Until then, he'd find no peace in his marriage.

No, that wasn't a direction he'd alow his mind to wander in, nor his body. There'd be

time enough for his body to respond when they were secluded at his cottage, because in

public, he'd keep a tight leash on al his reactions to Lady Dorchester, physical and mental.

His pledge lasted three minutes, or the time it took for the butler to announce him in

Carina's study. Other tonnish women seated themselves before pretty writing tables where

invitations were inscribed and answered and correspondence was attended to, but not Carina.

As in everything he'd observed about her, the Countess was different.

She was seated before a desk that took up most of the room, and her green damask skirts

were spread over the edge of an equally large chair. On the other side of the desk, and facing

her, lounged a gentleman.

Max erected his external barricades and prepared for battle, though he couldn't explain,

even to himself, what stirred this out-of-character reaction. Apart, of course, from the

presence of a man in the close and intimate confines of Carina's study, and the sight of that

man leaning forward in earnest conversation with the woman he'd decided would share his

bed. It took all his self-imposed control to appear calm as he strode towards her desk, as if he

had every right to invade this woman's private domain.

He boldly and uncharacteristically snatched up Carina's hand and kissed the backs of her

fingers, noting the tell-tale signs of shock. Ah, ha! Finally, he'd disconcerted her. With

leisurely movements he faced the gentleman, who watched his display with unconcealed

amusement.

Max assumed his haughtiest manner. "I'm the Duke of Stirkton. To whom am I

speaking?"

Snatching back her hand, Carina jumped to her feet and placed herself in direct contact

with his looming body. Max felt the jolt of it to his toes. Her unique aroma tickled his nose

and, like a hunter scenting prey, his nostrils flared. Hearing a loud chuckle from the as yet

unidentified man, he held himself as rigid as a pole and commanded his body and its

60

REFLEXIVE YET animalistic reactions to subside.

Unlike him, Carina didn't give a fig about controlling her emotions. She almost snarled

when, with a flick of her hand, she indicated the gentleman who had risen and who now stood

watching them with a look of bemusement and amusement. Max's fingers twitched as he

suppressed the urge to unleash his inner demon and plant his fist on the supercilious

expression on the man's too-handsome face. As if knowing exactly what Max wanted to do,

the man smirked and Max's annoyance rose a notch, as if the crank had been turned on a

medieval torture rack.

Carina snorted her disgust. "Maximus Meacham, the Duke of Stirkton, may I present to

you my good friend, Mister Jonathon Smythe. Jonathon, apart from being a longtime friend is

also my factotum."

Max forced himself to relax and move around the desk to shake his hand. "Pleased to

make your acquaintance, Smythe." He turned to Carina. "Where did you say you met?"

"I didn't, and nor is it any of your business."

Jonathon chuckled. "Ah, I sense tension in the air. Thankfully, I have the advantage in

our little contest, Stirkton, as I already know where you two met."

Max looked at Carina and frowned. "I see." He didn't understand at al, but he hated

being the odd man out and wanted even more to wipe the complacent smile off Smythe's

face.

Carina interrupted. "Jonathon knows that we met in Stirkton when we were younger.

And that you're helping launch Georgie and Lucy into London society."

"Ah, good." Max nodded and smiled.

"Perhaps you first assumed that I knew something more, Your Grace. Some deeper,

darker secret?" Jonathon questioned with a grin. "Because my paper knife wouldn't dent the

angry atmosphere between you. I'd need sharp swords."

Carina stomped one foot on her thick carpet, which was unfortunately for her made no

satisfactory noise and she was forced to growl. "Jonathon, stop tormenting him. I think we've

concluded our business, for this morning anyway."

Smythe nodded. "I'll be working upstairs for the next two hours." He eyed Max up and down. "Cal out, Carina, if you have need of assistance."

Max bristled. "Lady Dorchester is perfectly safe with me, Smythe. Can you say the

same?"

Carina stepped between them and held up a hand. "Gentlemen, please, I'l not al ow such

ridiculous squabbling in my house. You're like a pair of unruly boys wrangling over who

61

ROLLS THE HOOP FIRST." She waved her hand in a shooing motion to Jonathon. "Now go, go

upstairs. I'l ring if I need you."

As Jonathon walked to the door, he shot Max a warning. As soon as he'd departed, Max

said, "Upstairs? Smythe lives in your house?"

Carina groaned. "No. Jonathon does my bookkeeping here. I keep irregular hours and, as

the Earl left me several properties, we often work long into the night together. When

necessary, Jonathon stays the night and we begin again early in the morning."

Max ran a finger around his neck, under his intricately folded neckcloth.

"And you don't consider it a threat to your virtue to have a single man—I assume

Smythe is unmarried." Carina nodded. "An unmarried and unre-lated male living in your

house wil surely cause gossip."

Carina stared at him, wide-eyed, before throwing back her head and laughing so hard that

groped for the arm of her chair and dropped into it. "Do you realize how bizarre that

statement sounds? You, being concerned over my virtue? Do you mean the virtue that you

yourself robbed me of many years ago?"

Max felt his neck and face heat. "I meant..." He ran his hands through his hair. "Damn it

al, I've no idea what I mean. Yes, I do know. I'm stunned and horrified that you'd alow

Smythe to remain overnight, tarnish the reputation of your household and further hamper

your sisters' chances of holding their heads high in society."

Carina sighed. "Georgie's life was destroyed and her name sul ied years ago when she

was sold into marriage by her guardian. I hoped that being seen in your company might erase

some of that nastiness from people's memories and alow her to create at a new life."

"I'm confused. I understood that your sister was a widow."

"I suppose it's better you hear the story from me, rather than someone else's version of

the truth. Georgie's husband died of consumption nine months ago, after which her husband's

family returned her to our stepbrother."

"Returned her? She sounds like a trading commodity they purchased and returned

because they were dissatisfied with the merchandise."

"That's exactly what happened. They purchased her to bear a child for their sickly son,

the second son of a viscount. Unfortunately, he couldn't give them their heir."

"He was incapable of performing his marital duties?"

"Yes. He tried at first, but he wasn't strong. Rather than apportion blame where it

belonged, they condemned his wife. They forced Georgie to visit his sick bed, to try to

encourage him..."

62

. . .

"To arouse him?"

"Yes. However, she failed."

"So they returned her?"

"It was better that they sent her back, because I can now try to protect her."

"What does she need protection from?"

"Not what, but whom. Her husband's relatives were cruel, and if she'd continued living

with them...well, who knows what would have happened? One cousin, also titled, had

decided that as Georgie was available and living close by in his uncle's house, he needn't

exert himself. Choosing a bride could wait because he had a pretty woman readily available

whenever he was forced into seclusion in the country to escape debt collectors. It would be a

simple task later to take over his cousin's wife because, after al , he'd arranged Georgie's

first marriage to his cousin, for a share of her dowry of course, but also because Peter, our

stepbrother, has some hold over him. I don't know what yet."

"Would it be so terrible if Georgiana was married to this cousin, especial y if he's to

inherit a title one day?"

"You don't understand. The family didn't treat Georgie wel."

"You mean her husband mistreated her? Is that why she was afraid of me touching her in

the carriage last night?"

"No, not her husband, because he wasn't strong enough to be violent. Besides which, he

mainly avoided his wife as he didn't like women very much, if you grasp my meaning."

Carina's frankness shocked Max. He'd been involved in plenty of crude male

conversations which discussed sex, including the illegal practices between men, but hearing a

woman speak of them was disconcerting, despite his own upbringing. "I take your meaning,

though it's not something a woman would normally be familiar with."

"Ah, but you forget, Your Grace, that I'm not the usual sort of young woman. You and

your grandfather made certain of that."

He flinched under the weight of the truths she spoke so casualy. "I never forget, not for

one moment." He struggled to regain his composure. For some reason, her poisonous barbs

struck home, each and every time. "So if Georgiana was mistreated, I assume you mean that

she was reprimanded."

"Reprimanded! Her eldest brother-in-law punished her every month that she failed to

become *enceinte*. More than once, she suffered broken ribs. He damaged her hearing by

boxing her ears, and twice he twisted her wrist so badly that until she fainted with pain."

"Good Lord. And nobody stopped him?"

63

"WHO? For much of that time, I was in Dorchester trying to survive myself."

As Carina paced and revealed more of Georgie's history, Max blamed himself more and

more.

"And, as you explained when we first spoke, Max, men view women as interchangeable.

A wife belongs to her husband and has no rights of her own. Isn't that how English law

works?"

He turned away. English law stole women's rights and alowed men absolute power.

Men could inflict pain, destroy lives, and with no interference or repercussions. Dukes were

even less likely to be accused of assault than other peers. He didn't agree with it, but if he

spoke up in parliament and tried to change those laws, his peers would think him insane.

"I'm sorry," he finally managed.

"What did you say, Max? Surely the great Duke of Stirkton isn't apologizing to me, a

mere woman. What are you sorry for? Robbing me of my innocence?"

"I don't wish to discuss that chapter of our lives, because nothing can change what

happened. Though I do regret that because of your husband, and me, and the other two men,

you were unable to go to your sister when she needed you."

Carina dropped her head and buried her face in her hands.

"Oh, no. Please don't cry. It's not too late. With my help, your sister wil once again

hold her head high in society. Assisting her is the very least I can do to try to make amends."

She lifted her head. "I'm not crying. I never cry. Not anymore."

"I'm pleased—"

There was a knock at the door and Carina called out her permission to enter. Her sisters

hurried into the room. Lucy walked straight to Max and curtsied, a courtesy he returned with

a bow. Georgie hovered closer to the door, as if she might still turn and run. Max stepped closer and bowed. "Ladies, a delight to see you this morning. I trust you enjoyed last

evening's entertainment."

Lucy's answered in a rush, "Oh, yes, Your Grace. And this afternoon, we shall drive in

the park with Alice and several of the others from last night. Are you accompanying us?"

Max searched for a polite reply. He'd been betrothed for some months and only once had

he been forced into accompanying the ladies to the park. Now he realized a refusal would

reflect badly on him and, for some reason, he wasn't comfortable with Carina always

thinking the worst of him. In the past, he'd erred far too many times with women thanks to

his grandfather's strict doctrines, though in the last few years he'd worked tirelessly to make

amends. He'd vowed to become a better person than his aloof and tyrannical grandfather.

64

HE SWALOWED. "I'm unsure if Lady Johnston expects me to join her, but it wil afford me

great pleasure to accompany you." He looked directly at Carina. "Al of you."

Georgie made an indistinct sound, leaving Max uncertain whether she was dismayed that

he would be accompanying them, or pleased. Expressing emotions never came easily to him,

but he gave them a smal smile. "That is, if Lady Georgiana has no objections to riding in my

carriage again."

Georgie's mouth tilted up into a soft smile, possibly the sweetest smile anyone had ever directed Max's way. It gave him a nice, warm feeling.

"It wil be wonderful to have a gentleman to protect us, Your Grace."

When Carina and Lucy stared with gaping mouths, Max guessed that this was unusual

for their sister, and a small rush of pleasure filled him that this small and scared woman had

chosen him, of all men, to be her protector. He couldn't recal any occasion when he'd

undertaken the role of protector of women, apart from having a courtesan under his

protection each scheduled month at Brent Street.

Those arrangements were temporary and monetary transactions, whereas he now enjoyed

playing the gallant hero for a group of ladies, and if Carina noticed his smug smile and

recognized it for satisfaction, he didn't care. Hopefully, it might alow her to see him in a

different light, a rescuer rather than a destroyer.

Having committed himself to driving in the park, Max seized this opportunity to

ingratiate himself with Lady Alice Johnston, because if Carina forgot her promise and

revealed their past, he'd need to be seen as committed to his marriage and eager for their

wedding day. Alice was the wife arranged for him and he'd do everything in his power to

ensure that their marriage proceeded without incident.

Until Carina had reappeared, he'd not felt a twinge of unease over the age difference

between himself and Alice, or their future together. His only thoughts had been that Alice's

background and upbringing made her suitable to run his household and raise his children.

Past that, he'd barely given her a thought.

His betrothed's life had been seventeen years of preparation to become the wife of

someone highly titled and wealthy—someone like him. Society and heritage required nothing

more from them, and he'd grown up confident that his life would proceed as planned. Neither

Carina nor her sisters would interfere with his plotted course. Wishing for something he

could never have was what his plain speaking cousin would call, *pissing in the wind.*

65

7

Within moments of reaching the carriageway of the park, the ladies were mobbed. The ducal carriage's emblem attracted attention, something Max regretted when he counted the

number of gentlemen clustered around his coach waiting to speak to one or other of the three

sisters. Even Gertie had her admirers amongst the older paraders who stopped to converse.

Within moments of them pulling to a stop, Carina was asked to give permission for Lucy to

stroll with a group of the younger ladies and gentlemen she'd conversed with at the previous

evening's soiree.

Lucy peered over the open side of the vehicle, talking non-stop with several young

bucks. Seated beside Max, Georgie seemed more comfortable remaining under his protective

wing than venturing out of the carriage and into the rowdy crowd. Again, that unaccustomed rush of protectiveness warmed him through and strengthened his determination to shield

Georgie from further harm.

Georgie wasn't his sister so he'd no legal right to interfere, yet he was going to visit his

solicitor and discuss his options. If these ladies needed lawful protection from their

stepbrother, he wanted to be in a position to provide assistance. Being prepared came

naturally to him as he ran his business ventures and his households in an organized fashion

and without any surprises. Know your opponent and his weaknesses, was his hard and fast

rule.

"Lady Georgiana, feel free to remain in the coach. But if you prefer to take the air, I'l be

happy to stroll with you." Out of the corner of his eye, he noticed Carina's stunned look as

Georgie gave him another endearing and trusting smile.

"Thank you, Your Grace. I'd love to walk, if it isn't too much trouble."

Max assisted the ladies out of the coach and held out an arm to each. Georgie hung on to

him with a tight grip, while Carina hesitated before slipping her arm through his. Yet walking

with these two beautiful women gave him an inexplicable feeling of perfection. Having never

lived within a close family or experienced the worries of a brother who cared for his sisters,

he should be disconcerted but, instead, a weight had lifted from his shoulders and his body

and soul were lighter than they had been in years. He almost laughed out loud at himself and

his fanciful notions.

Two gentlemen Georgie knew from the previous evening approached and she allowed

them to walk her in front, another satisfying accomplishment for his day. Lord Brendon

66

JOHNSTON GREETED Carina with a happy smile that spoke of far too much intimacy.

"Lady Dorchester, how wonderful you look today."

"Why, thank you, Brendon."

"Your dress is a very becoming shade and it matches your eyes exactly."

Max grunted. "I suppose you sprout poetry as wel."

Brendon refused to be insulted. "I do read poetry. At times, I even recite poetry to

beautiful women." He smiled at Carina with an even wider display of perfect teeth. "Do you

enjoy poetry? Because I shal happily recite Byron to you al day long."

Max snorted, despite never making such a crass noise in public before. "We don't need

poetry right now, thank you. Don't you have somewhere else to be?"

"Ah, Stirkton, you cannot be trying to keep Carina all to yourself as you are engaged to

my sister. What is your relationship with Lady Dorchester?"

Before Max uttered a scathing reply, Carina intervened. "His Grace is an old friend,

though on occasion he oversteps the boundaries of our friend-ship. His intentions are

honorable and he's helping us become reacquainted with London."

Brendon's ingratiating smile turned Max's stomach. "Any man would be delighted to assist so lovely a lady. My titles may not be so high as Stirkton's, but our family is welcomed

into the best of circles, and I'm more available than the Duke because I'm not occupied each

day with estate matters."

The younger man's shrewd expression and this absurd verbal sparring annoyed Max.

No time spent with the Countess would be calm and comfortable, of that he was certain. At

the first whiff of her perfume or the tiniest glimpse of bare flesh, he became like the other

greenhorns who clustered around the three beauties. Another bee swarming around the queen

and longing to taste her honey. Max groaned. Images of a honey-pot and the various ways

he'd like to sample hers produced reactions inappropriate for mixed company, especial y

when he was being watched like a hawk by his remarkably obser-vant future brother-in-law.

To add to Max's melancholy, Carina peered up at Johnston and fluttered her lashes like

an experienced coquette. Her performance was most likely a trick to keep him off balance

and make him appear foolish in the presence of a man destined to become his brother-in-law,

but her efforts would be in vain. He'd practiced managing and manipulating people since he

reached his teen years, and was devilishly adept at extracting himself from tricky situations.

"And you, Johnston," he asked with an air of innocence, "don't you have demands on

your time during your day? As your father's heir, I assume you're kept busy from dawn til

dusk. "

67

. . .

JOHNSTON LAUGHED at his attempts to divert Carina's attention. "Not me, Stirkton. My

fastidious father overseas all our business interests and claims that I'm more of a hindrance

than a help."

"Isn't it tedious," Carina asked, "having nothing to fill your days?"

Lord Johnston threw back his head and laughed. "My dear Countess, you've become

immured with country standards and have forgotten the rules for landed gentry in the city. If

my cohorts heard that I soiled my hands by laboring like a country squire, tending stock and

ploughing fields, I'd be a laughing stock amongst my friends. A true gentleman never lowers

his standards and works, and even if forced to involve himself in shipping or commerce to

pump up his coffers, he'd never admit such a mortifying thing in public."

"So titled gentlemen consider any sort of employment lowering," Carina said pleasantly,

though Max noticed her left eyebrow twitch. Having come to London from her rural property,

Carina would be well-acquainted with the work involved in running farms and looking after

tenants. Servants undertook the heavier work but someone of Carina's energetic nature

wouldn't sit in her drawing room and embroider while someone else made all the decisions.

She'd be actively involved.

"You misunderstand me. Some people are put upon this earth to work, for if not, who'd

cook our meals and clean our houses?"

"Perhaps every person who walks this earth and breathes air should be responsible, in

some smal part, for their own welbeing and not leave the burden to others."

"Ah, Lady Dorchester, you're a sympathizer with today's radical movements. Alowing

greater freedom for the working classes is a noble cause, but allow me to offer a word of

caution. If you and your sisters wish to be accepted here, you'd be wise to refrain from

speaking of reforms amongst the higher classes." He shook his head. "Especially not to any

of the older matrons, such as my own mater, as they believe that men will discuss those

things in parliament, in their own time, and that ladies shouldn't admit to understanding

anything about such matters, let alone speak aloud of reform. If you discussed factories or

child labor at a dinner table in my home, my mother would swoon in her turtle soup."

Carina gave a smal smile to acknowledge Brendon's half serious, half flippant advice.

"And you, Your Grace, do you believe the lower classes sole purpose in life is to work and

serve the higher classes? Or are you a supporter of factory reforms and better working

conditions?"

"I take time to ensure that al my workers are fairly treated."

"Impressive, Max. Not many men of your rank open their eyes or ears and notice their

68

EMPLOYEES' work conditions."

Her assumption that all dukes were unfeeling and incapable of change was mildly

insulting to someone who prided himself on using his brain and employing innovative

techniques. "Though my grandfather believed that the distinction between classes must be

upheld to prevent anarchy, I'm in favor of ways that improve the lot of my workers and yet

allow me to remain in command. My titles and holdings bring great responsibility, but above

al, I'm a human being who dislikes seeing other suffer, regardless of their class."

Carina's smile was a genuine expression of understanding and agreement and the cold

parts of his heart were warmed. "I uncover new depths in you every day, Max. New things to

admire."

He shrugged, despite appreciating her compliments; because he'd so rarely been admired

that he felt uncomfortable. His grandfather had doled out praise as parsimoniously as he'd

given food and shelter to his servants, preferring punishment over praise to reinforce his

instructions. "Contented tenants reap better profits for estate cotters, so my manager does

whatever is necessary to ensure they remain productive. In the long run, it benefits all

concerned."

Carina smiled again, and he longed to capture the moment and let the warmth chase

away his nightmares.

Lord Johnston's voice disturbed his reverie. "A touching idea, Stirkton, but maudlin

sentiment has no place in commerce. Even a non-involved son understands productivity is

based on supply and demand. The rich demand and the poor

supply."

"Unfortunately, to pay for the multitude of smal pleasures you enjoy every day,

hundreds of your father's employees work from dawn til dusk in substandard conditions."

The young lord turned and smiled at Carina, once more setting Max's teeth on edge.

"Our pleasant walk wil be spoiled by such dreary talk. Beautiful ladies don't need to hear

about workers' uprisings."

Carina raised an eyebrow. "Not al ladies wilt like winter flowers when the welfare of

workers is discussed, Brendon. On my estate, I play an active role in management, and I did

so even when my husband was alive."

Johnston took hand and placed it on his sleeve. "Perhaps it's time to improve that

situation. Marrying would relieve you of those burdens."

Carina shrugged. "I don't consider it a burden. Quite the opposite."

"Women are wonderful with social obligations, but finances are better handled by men."

He tugged his immaculate cuffs and gave a condescending smile. "One day soon, I'l take a

69

WIFE AND HAVE CHILDREN. My father taught me money management, so my wife's dowry and

his legacy wil be secure."

Carina's breath released on a long hiss. Max felt smug satisfaction that the lady he

wanted scorned this pompous idiot as he did. He folded his arms and waited, but her sisters

called her and denied him the pleasure of hearing her scathing retort. To some extent, Max

also thought of ladies, including his fiancée, as unequipped to manage money. Carina,

however, was different. She was a vibrant and intelligent widow and had no need of a man's

interference with her estates, workers or staff.

Georgiana strode towards him, head bowed, and pressed her small body as close to his

side as respectability allowed. Glancing over her head, he saw three gentlemen on the path

and knew one of them was responsible for her trembling and the gloved hands clutched to her

chest. He took one of Georgie's hands and gently looped it around his elbow and placed her

hand on his coat sleeve, giving it a reassuring pat.

The men slowed when they saw her under his protection, while Georgie squeezed closer

to his side and implored him with adoring puppy eyes to save her. This fragile girl with her

battered heart and frightened spirit tugged at his own ragged soul. Mindful of her fear of

hefty-sized males, Max drew Georgie down a hedged walkway that was wide enough for

Carina to link her arm through her sister's free one, but that excluded Georgie's flock of

followers.

Bending his head, Max listened to Georgie's unsteady wheezing and murmured,

"Breathe, little one. No one wil hurt you ever again." Carina gasped, but he concentrated on

the girl clutching his sleeve. He patted her hand again and said, "Breathe, my dear." Georgie

sucked in a slow lungful of air and he nodded. "Excellent. Now, please believe me when I say

no further harm shal befal you."

Georgie whispered, "I trust you."

Max's footsteps faltered, alongside his heart. Time stopped. He swalowed past the lump

in his throat but couldn't speak, instead turning them to walk back to the fountain. "Ladies,

it's time we departed, so you can prepare for this evening."

Carina leaned around to speak to Georgie, but Max forestaled her. "Not now." He

glanced at the gentlemen trailing a few paces behind. "We can talk later."

By the sharp sideways glances Carina flicked towards him, she was loathe to relinquish

control to any man, most especial y him. He might have earned Georgie's trust but, so far,

Carina had no reason to follow suit. He didn't slow his measured pace but spoke across her

sister's head. "Trust me."

70

FOR LONG PAINFUL seconds he waited, fearing a negative answer. She walked, eyes fixed on

the water foaming from the fountain's ornate sprouts and soaking the paving, and then gave

one quick nod. Two women, with less reason than most to trust men, trusted him and had

accepted decisions made by him on their behalf; he felt ten feet tall.

Though the truce between him and Carina was transient, memories of their past

relationship hadn't blackened his character to the extent that she refused their alliance. Past

the fountain's outer circle of enclaves and stone benches, the path widened and Brendon

seized the opportunity to walk beside them.

"Wel, wel, Stirkton. We're seeing a previously unseen side of your nature. You're
making conquests everywhere, first with Lady Dorchester and now her sister." He looked
across. "Forgive me, Lady Georgiana, but you don't enjoy the company of many gentlemen,
yet you're enamored of the man my sister is to marry. Interesting."

Max opened his mouth to reply, but shut it when a tug on his sleeve and Georgie's
begging gaze reminded him how skittish she was in crowds. He clasped her trembling hand.

"We're friends."

Johnston snickered. "And Lady Dorchester? Also your close friend, Stirkton?"

How dare the bastard speak that way in front of the ladies? Max clung to his famed rigid
control and kept his touch light on Georgie's arm, but the fist closest to Johnston's face
twitched. The man's boyishly-rounded jaw was two feet away from being smashed into
pieces and his handsome features pulverized.

"Johnston, take great care before making nasty and groundless insinuations. Soon, we
shal be related by marriage and your sister would be devastated if her family was at odds."

The other gentlemen looked horrified and edged away from John-ston. "Now gentlemen, I
shal drive the ladies home."

Carina had watched without comment and she now smiled and nodded. "Yes, Your
Grace, how thoughtful. Lucy, we're leaving."

If she'd sided with Johnston, he mightn't have reined in his temper and his fit of
temper—or jealousy—would have been viewed as much more than friendship. The gossiping

ton would ensure that Alice's parents heard about his close friends. Lucy had listened to their

conversation but, thankfully, other than glancing at her sisters with raised brows, she hadn't

questioned why she was being whisked away from her entourage.

Ten minutes later, Max crossed his legs and slouched into his corner of the carriage,

rehearsing his speech in his head, so he didn't sound arrogant and domineering or earn a

reprimand from any of the three sisters. They fidgeted with their reticules and shawls until he

71

COULDN'T CONTAIN his annoyance any further.

He leaned forward. "I forbid you," he said, meeting their eyes in turn, "from forming any

sort of association with Johnston."

Carina stiffened. She leaned forward, nose to nose with him, like a lion preparing to

defend her cubs.

He held up one finger. "I know what you're about to say. The man may be about to

become part of my family, but I don't trust him. Not with your wel -being."

Carina pushed his finger to the side. "I shal decide which gentlemen my sisters and I

mix with."

"You misunderstand. Johnston has his eye on you, Carina, and I mistrust his intentions."

"Rubbish! But even if it were true, it's no concern of yours. You've no right to issue

orders about whom I wil or wil not befriend."

"I can and I wil prevent it."

Her green eyes narrowed as she leaned in until their bodies almost touched, while the

others watched and listened to every word and inference. "Rather than waste your time

issuing orders to me, pay attention to that poor girl who will be your wife. She will have to

cope with your arrogance for the rest of her miserable life."

"What are you implying? There is nothing amiss with my fiancée and me."

"Everything is wrong, you dolt. You terrify that poor timid child."

Lucy and Georgie were open-mouthed with either shock or amusement, though he

couldn't decide which. He pointedly stared out the window at the street vendors and applied

the techniques of meditation, mastered his mind and chose his next words carefully.

"My betrothal period is proceeding according to plan. And Alice is not frightened of me

personally, though perhaps she is a little awed by the attentions of a duke. She's been raised

to show respect and she treats me as a well-bred young lady should."

Carina snorted. "Good Lord! If you believe that rot, you're delusional. Alice's attitude

isn't respect, but abject terror. She's scared of what your nightly demands in bed wil be; that

if she refuses you, you'll punish her. Lock her in the dungeon, torture her as your grandfather

did to you."

Georgie said, "Carina! Apologize to His Grace. At once."

Carina scowled, but motioned that she was buttoning her lips.

Georgie reached along the seat and touched her fingertips to Max's clasped hands. "You

don't frighten me. You're a kind and admirable man, and I envy your bride-to-be."

He relaxed his tense muscles and settled back into the seat's padding, before stretching

72

OUT HIS LEGS. With his hands crossed on his stomach, he raised a brow. "It's comforting to

know that not all women view me as an ogre, or take my well-meaning endeavors to ensure

their safe-being as demands."

"Oh, please, spare me your martyrdom." Carina threw up her hands. "Georgie sees the

good in you, whereas others are only shown your worst side."

Lucy, sitting directly across from him, tilted her head and examined him as if he was a

newly discovered species of the plants she collected. "Georgie's a very astute judge of

character," Lucy said, "and she dislikes many men. She detests big and beligerent males so,

Max," her eyes twinkled and there was an impish twist to her lips, "we must assume that you

have aspects of nobility and kindness, perhaps even gentleness, that you keep well hidden,

and that our sister recognizes and causes her to—"

"Lucy," Carina said. "You're rambling again and you're embarrassing the subject of

your recitation."

Lucy ignored Carina and, to Max's discomfort, finished. "—worship you."

A creeping red blush covered Georgie's neck and lower face, while Max worried that the

heat on his own neck would also turn into a full-blown blush. Georgie didn't look his way as

she said, "Lucy, please stop. I don't worship the Duke, and to voice such an idea is unseemly when His Grace is spoken for and to a girl we have befriended. I merely wanted our obtuse

sister," she shot a glare at Carina, "to see that he has many noble qualities which I'm thankful

for."

Carina rolled her eyes, Lucy groaned and Max smirked. He talied how many points he'd

scored against Carina in their second round of battle. As the carriage rolled towards Lawnton

Place, the sisters chatted amongst themselves of the personages they'd encountered in the

park.

Their list reminded Max of something. "Georgie," he said, "which of those gentlemen

frightened you."

"Oh, no, not one of those walking with us. The man in the trees scared me."

With stunned surprise and a depth of shock etched on their faces that matched his own

expression, Carina and Lucy tackled Georgie.

"In the trees? What was he doing?" Lucy asked, at the same moment Carina began her

string of questions.

"You saw a man? Near you? Did he say anything?"

Their outbursts puzzled Max. Both women strained towards their sister, their faces were

tight with concern and worry that was too extreme to be caused by a lone man standing

73

BENEATH TREES IN A PUBLIC PARK. Lucy curled the cord of her reticule into tight twists that would

not easily be untangled, and Carina nibbled the fingertips of one glove, gnawing on the inanimate object the way she did when troubled.

"Why is that a problem?" Max asked.

After exchanging glances, they dropped their eyes to their laps and Lucy saw the damage

she was doing to her reticule and attempted to unwind it. Glass beads slid down a thread and

pinged as they hit the floor. All three women stretched as one towards the broken strands to

catch the beads before they were lost from sight.

Max stopped their quest with his hands. "I wil replace your reticule, Lucy. Now, explain

what is significant about the man in the trees." He looked at Carina and Lucy, demurely

posed on their seats, but neither spoke. "Any number of men could have reason to stand

under trees in a public park." Stil no response, so he shifted sideways on his seat and reached

out to touch the back of Georgie's hand with a light, two-fingered gesture of reassurance.

"What did the man do to frighten you so much?"

Georgie glanced in rapid succession back and forth between her two silent sisters, her

pale blue eyes widening as she realized that she'd opened Pandora's Box.

"N-nothing. Nothing at al ." She shook her head so fast that her blond curls bounced and

threatened to spil out from her restrictive bonnet. "He...he was j-just a man."

When Lucy spoke, it was in her usual rush of words, coming too fast to make a lot of

sense and over the top of her sister's stuttered explanation. "Georgie... She gets startled, and

if men, as I said before, in particular big men, if they come nearer or perhaps look at her too closely, Georgie doesn't feel comfortable and she....wel..." Lucy appealed to their elder

sister to save her. She spread her hands. "Wel, that's al, realy."

Carina rolled her eyes at Lucy's stumbling attempt to cover up whatever had frightened

their middle sister.

Max looked at Carina and smiled. "Would you like to try and improve on Lucy's pitiable

attempt at hoodwinking me?"

"Not at al." Carina tried for a convincing smile. "Lucy explained what happened.

Georgie feels uncomfortable if confronted by strangers."

"I applaud your attempts at providing reasonable explanations on the spur of the

moment, however, I hope you don't have to play cards with anyone tonight."

Carina rolled her eyes. "I almost dread to ask, but why not?"

"Because your faces give you away. I've never met such hopeless liars." To Georgie he

said, "This time I'd like the truth. Did the man come close to you?"

74

GEORGIE'S EYES were as round as full moons and she was panting more than breathing.

Her hands were wringing each other out harder than his laundress did with the sheets. Despite

enduring a despicable marriage, this brave young lady retained an air of purity. On the other

hand, her sisters gave him identical furious looks that dared him to question them further.

Carina clasped Georgie's hands and stiled their compulsive movements. "Seeing that

man doesn't mean anything. He visited the park, like we did."

Lucy slipped her hand down beside her skirt and laid it alongside Georgie's knee,

probably hoping that she could stop her sister jiggling her leg before Max noticed. "Carina's

correct. That man was nobody. Don't worry about him."

Max scowled at the conniving pair and let them see his disapproval. Their blatant

coercion to stop Georgie from revealing more, implied that some larger crisis loomed. Carina

and Lucy now treated him to identical blank stares, informing him louder than with words

that they weren't going to share their knowledge. Georgie sat in rigid misery after her two

keepers halted her repetitive movements.

Yet her jaw sawed, back and forth, until Max couldn't watch her self-torment any longer.

"Perhaps one day soon you'l confide in me about whatever is bothering you."

"Oh, yes, I wil, Max, yes, I wil." Georgie sighed and to their utter surprise, she kissed

Max on the cheek.

He touched the spot for a long moment. "Thank you. I'm honored that you feel safe in

my presence."

Lucy moaned, clasped her hands in a dramatic pose and said, "Oh, my goodness. That's

the most romantic thing I've ever witnessed." Carina frowned, as if puzzled that her sister

had spontaneously kissed a man. Lucy added, "You're the only man I've seen Georgie kiss of

her own accord since our father died."

The carriage pulled up before Woods House and they went through the ritual of alighting

and entering the house. The younger girls climbed the steps to the upper level, but Max held

Carina's arm and delayed her until they were alone. He dismissed the lingering butler with a

nod and led her down the hall to her sitting room. Without awaiting permission, he closed the

doors and spun to face her.

"Our arrangement shal commence this evening at my cottage, and I'l not be put off this

time."

"I'm sorry to disappoint you but we're engaged for the evening and I must chaperone my

sisters. It's likely we'l not be home until the early hours, after the third or fourth bal."

"Your constant excuses are ridiculous." Max shook her arm.

75

SHE TUGGED out of his hold and rubbed at the spot, and he was filled with guilt. Surely he

hadn't gripped her tightly enough to hurt? His anger deflated fast than a breath of wind could

blow away a child's soap bubbles.

"Need I remind you that your sisters received these invitations due to my sponsorship? I

can easily withdraw my patronage and free up your time."

Carina gave a tinkle of laughter, the sound false and grating. "Oh, but haven't you heard?

I'm now the bosom confidant of your betrothed. Alice asked me to teach her the best way to

deal with a duke who intimidates her. Thwarting me and my plans might force me to warn

Alice of your plans for your marriage. Let me see if I have the correct order."

She held up a finger to indicate the first number.

"One. Purchase a virginal brood mare, following the rules dictated years ago by your bloodline obsessed grandfather. Tel me, have you inspected Alice's teeth or measured the

span of her hips? You'd inspect a new mare that way, wouldn't you?"

By the glint in her eyes, Carina knew her arrow had struck home. The color of her eyes

darkened with her emotions, ranging from ocean green to emerald to deepest jade.

She ticked off the next number, her gloved fingers again waving in front of his face.

"Two. Impregnate said mare through a restricted number of intimate encounters, and as fast

as possible." Another finger lifted. "Three. Put her out to pasture in the country until she

delivers your heir and the spare. Or do Meacham rules allow only one child in each

generation?"

Max screwed his eyes closed, not wanting her to see his agony. She'd no idea how

painful the subject of children was, and no knowledge of the things he'd discovered in his

grandfather's papers. Despite Augustus's rules, he'd clung to the hope that one day he could

break tradition and fill his lonely house with children. Robust, happy children, a mix of male

and female, who'd grow up free and who'd breathe life back into their dying clan.

"Ah, I see by your reaction that I guessed correctly. Does Alice know that after

delivering a son, her days of intimacy with her husband wil be finished?"

He cleared his throat. "There are ways to ensure that no more babies are conceived."

"And, of course, having employed so many bed companions over the years, you'd know all the ways needed to safe-guard the family from diluting the line with more offspring.

You'd have always been wary of some lower class and therefore unworthy woman bearing a

duke's child. Bastard or not, that child would earn her a lot of money. What methods do you

plan on using with me? Withdrawal?" She shook her head. "Far too precarious for someone

who likes to control the odds and eliminate every risk."

76

He moved towards the door, but she strode across the room and blocked his retreat,

placing her bare hand on his chest. Her fingers were so close to his throat that he'd no choice

but to halt and listen.

If he jerked away, he might hurt her again. If she was a cold-blooded killer, he might

become her second victim, though he didn't believe she meant him harm, not physically at

least. Though she did enjoy tearing metaphorical strips off his hide. He imagined her nails

raking trails down his back and over his bare skin, while he stretched like a cat across a bed

mussed from their last vigorous bout of lovemaking.

Now, the warmth of her palm through his clothing disturbed him more than her verbal

blistering of his skin. "...Don't rush off. I'm enjoying this little *tête á tête*." She put a finger to

her lips and the warmth in his upper regions were matched with a rush of heat to his groin.

"Now, where was I?" Her lips pursed and he longed to cover them with his own, to rub against their softness and wallow in their texture and temperature.

When the tip of her tongue touched the end of her finger, every thought fled, except for

how he could encourage her to use that tongue on his finger, lips, and body. He suspected

that in the hard clutch of sexual desire, Lady Dorchester would prove as valiant an adversary

as elsewhere. He'd toss her onto his bed, smother her verbal assaults with his mouth, subdue

her with his questing fingers until she was pliant and malleable and begging him to never

stop.

In his imagination, she grasp for supremacy by rolling him beneath her and then riding

him long and hard, as hard as the stallion needed to cover that virginal brood mare she talked

about. Hell! Did Alice consider herself his brood mare, nothing more; or was Carina about to

disclose that information to Alice?

All the more reason why Carina needed to join him at Brent Street. If their standoff

continued for another fraught week, his desire to have her in his bed would goad him into

doing something unimaginable. The unbending Stirkton that the ton knew would look foolish

when he went down on bended knee and begged a lady to come to him.

"Ah, yes. I was saying that your skeptical nature would make you mistrustful of a

woman's promises. You'd not trust one of your paid companions to prepare themselves by

taking herbal preventatives, and because you trust me even less, I imagine you'll insist on

witnessing first-hand the use of preventatives."

She paced the room and touched furniture, trailing her fingers across a cluster of

exquisite glazed figurines, obvious signs of how wealthy she'd become after the Earl passed.

Trust a lady who possibly murdered her husband? Not likely. He'd not put himself into any

77

SITUATION where she chose life or death, for him or for her.

"The obvious choice for you is French letters."

He dipped his head in acknowledgement and edged away. It was bad enough that the

scent of roses drove him mad, but the heated aroma of arousal emanating from her body

made his senses spin, and it was Carina's temper and heightened emotions that had set them

both off. Her arousal would saturate the air once he brought her to a fevered pitch of longing,

and her scent would fill him while he prolonged her quivering and held off peaking until he

too was ready to climax. The best perfume came with the cream that women excreted from

their secret cavities during sex, and he loved the smell and sight of her flooded thighs when a

woman's muscles and body clenched during prolonged orgasm.

That aroma when a woman reached her sexual heights was what compelled a man to

crawl back between her white thighs, time and time again. Add to that mix the salty tincture

of a man's seed and it was the epitome of—

"Max, did you hear me? Do you intend using French letters for our encounters?"

He gave her an icy glare, first to cool his own ardor, and secondly to dampen the fire in her glowing green gaze. More than one mistress had said his ice-blue stares could freeze the

River Thames and he often used them as a weapon.

"Correct again. French letters control the number of Meachams conceived in a

generation and create less mess, which is a concession to you and one you should

appreciate."

"And I sincerely thank you for taking steps to reduce the messiness involved in our

forthcoming intimacy."

"Sarcasm is not caled for. I'm merely highlighting the benefits to you of having a bed-

partner who is experienced and forward thinking."

"Bloody hel! A bed partner? If this is the only side of you that Alice has experienced, no

wonder she thinks you a cold fish."

"I've certainly never discussed such crude matters with Alice because, unlike you, she

remains an innocent."

Her hand went to her hips and he could almost see steam pouring from her ears. "Exactly

what I've tried to tel you. If you threaten me, or try to interfere in my life as you did by

questioning Georgie earlier, I will disclose the subjects of our little chats to Alice. She may

be so dismayed that she decries your betrothal, perhaps in front of the entire *haute ton.*

Wouldn't that cause embarrassment for a self-righteous, priggish Meacham?"

Max drew back from her before he released his temper. He'd never touched a woman

78

.   .   .

WITH ANGER and he'd not start now, no matter how much she provoked him. Arranged sexual

encounters from his youth had left him with enough mental scars and, from Bil's discoveries,

meeting him may have scarred some of the women. Although, that was debatable, as those

women had sold their bodies in some way or another before he'd met them.

"Why do you taunt me? Do you want to see me lose control?"

She shrugged. "You take yourself too seriously, so I endeavor to ruffle your feathers and

make you forget your dukishness and act like other men."

"I'm not a bird and I'm not other men."

"Or because I'm the only person who dares."

"Madame, are you never serious?"

At his harsh tone, her eyes clouded and her body stiffened. "On the contrary. I've spent

the majority of my life weighed down by somber thoughts and considered deeds and, even

now, I'm under constant duress. Trying to provide for my sisters and to protect them."

"Protect them from what?"

But once again, she wouldn't answer. He wished Carina would soften towards him,

even the smalest bit. She hadn't given an inch in their war and, unlike Georgie, she denied

him her trust. The latter was the most painful. Her eyes closed and he imagined what it would

feel like if, when she reopened them, her thinking would have changed and she'd beg him to

protect her and her family.

After a firm shake of her bouncing locks, she lifted her skirt the requisite half-inch above

the floor and glided towards the door without looking at him. He followed her passage with his eyes as she tripped up towards the stairs and left him standing by himself and feeling

bereft. The aged butler had earlier disappeared and no other servants were in evidence, yet

within seconds the old man appeared around the corner.

"I'm waiting to secure the doors for the afternoon, if you don't mind. Her ladyship likes

everything locked up tight while they take their afternoon rest. Strange thing, I always think,

but Lady Dorchester is very particular about keys and bolts and what-have-you. Her ladyship

is adamant that I then retire to my quarters for an hour before the rush of the evening, with all

their comings and goings."

Max didn't know whether to be amused or outraged at the servant's insolence, but good

manners defeated the urge to issue a strong reprimand. His own staff wouldn't dare address

him in this uncouth fashion, nor would they lock the doors so the household could take an

afternoon rest. Carina not only tolerated the old man's over-familiar ways, but encouraged his

liberties.

79

ANOTHER GLARING DIFFERENCE was that Stirkton House employed dozens of servants, so

doorkeepers were always on hand. Carina was a wealthy widow running a large household in

elitist Lawnton Place and yet she employed a skeleton staff.

With his long stride, he reached the door long before the older man who dragged his feet

behind him. Rather than walking straight out he paused, wanting to make sure the servant was capable of securing the house. These women were too well-grounded to succumb to

flights of fancy over a man watching them; something more sinister was unfolding.

"So Lady Dorchester fears intruders?"

"Yes, Your Grace. My lady worries about intruders. Of course, after the last scare with

the broken library window, one can appreciate that the ladies are frightened."

"You had a break-in? When?"

"The last one was a week ago, but that was the third this month. Probably some

scoundrel trying to sneak inside the house, thinking to steal the silver."

"Has anything been stolen?"

"No, not with our two guarding at night and during the afternoon's rest. The doors are

locked, so no-one can enter and be frightened by the Scottish lads."

He hated the idea of two guards in a house full of women, and he didn't want to ask

himself why thinking of two men watching over her aggravated him so much. Caring so

fiercely about people he barely knew wasn't habitual because he'd grown up more or less

alone, so dealing with his instinctive reactions was difficult. Like wearing another man's coat

and having the breath squeezed out of you each time you moved.

"Who are these Scottish lads?" His vain hope that the butler hadn't noticed his

resentment of the mysterious pair was squashed by the man's low gurgle of laughter.

"Oh, you've no need to show that unseemly shade of green, Your Grace. The Scottish lads are no more than two brutish lumps of dogs, Scottish wolf hounds that've been with

Lady Dorchester for many years. The lads would lay down their lives to protect her

ladyship."

Max heaved a relieved sigh, and ignored the butler when he chortled even harder.

"I've never seen a man look more relieved because the two Scottish lads sharing her

ladyship's house are of the four-legged variety, rather than two-legged males."

Once more, Max was shocked by the butler's levity, yet he couldn't deny his relief that it

wasn't two strapping Scottish men living in Carina's house. Two over-protective dogs was a

blessing, not a cause for jealousy. He shook his head. A servant had given the Duke of

Stirkton orders, hustled him out a door and then laughed at him. His grandfather turn roll over

80

IN HIS GRAVE.

After a word of thanks to the butler, who deserved dismissal rather than gratitude, Max

stepped on to the front porch and paused. The metallic clink and slide of bolts locking into

place behind him reassured him and he walked down to the footpath with a new spring in his

step. His booted foot had barely touched the ground when a movement to the left of the

servant's lower-level entrance caught his eye. Habitually on alert on London streets for thugs

and thieves, Max reached down and slipped a sleek blade from its holster inside his boot.

His footman, standing by his coach, spotted the shadowy figure and gave chase. "Hoi,

you there, what're you about?"

Max ran after the pair, but they were too late to catch the man, who disappeared down an

alleyway that was too dark and too narrow to be safe. The footman bent double, hands to his

knees, and tried to catch his breath.

"Did you get a look at his face?"

"No, Your Grace. He 'ad on a big scarf, so I couldn't get a look at 'is mug."

"Damn! I wonder if he knew me and didn't want to be recognized."

"By 'is clothing I'd say 'e was a gent. Quality trousers under that great coat, fine fabric

like yours. And when 'e ran, 'is boots looked like them ones you ride a 'orse with, Your

Grace. Hessians."

Max looked at him in surprise. This man had been in his employ a long time but, even

so, he'd not known that his staff noticed his clothing and his boots. He then surprised himself

by recaling the footman's name.

"Thomas, thank you for your efforts. Now, I have a job for you. Follow Lady Dorchester

everywhere she goes, and I shall set two more men to watch this house, night and day.

Something is going on here, something sinister. And we need to discover who is threatening

them before one of the ladies is harmed."

He sent Thomas to the far side of the street where his footman could watch without

being seen. For himself, Max was reluctant to climb into his coach and leave. A feeling of

impending doom hung like a black cloud over the house and he, who placed no faith in the

mystical or magical, knew fate had destined him to save these ladies, no matter the cost.

He was Stirkton, a soon-to-be-married duke with no time for fanciful nonsense or

playing knight in shining armor to damsels in distress. No time for pacing like a besotted

suitor outside a house in a bustling thoroughfare, where his emblazoned coach might be seen

and gossiped about by the ton.

Turning to face the bolted door of Woods House, he swore, using a nasty low class oath

81

FAVORED AT SEAMEN'S INNS. The people passing by this exclusive London address stared at him

when he snarled and threw his hands up in the air like a madman.

His acquaintances would laugh at his foolish behavior if they saw his current mad

obsession. Oh, how far the mighty could fall, and in so short a time.

He groaned. The woman who owned that house was driving him insane.

8

The Duke of Stirkton, attired in somber charcoal upon black, stared across wide loops of blond hair and tried to ignore them tickling his chin while he twirled his partner up and down

Lord and Lady Algester's bal room. The past week had tripled Max's frustration and drained

his small store of patience.

Enduring round after round of these tedious *soirées* had driven him to invent far-fetched

excuses so he could legitimately claim a dance with a woman. The dance would be the Waltz

and the woman would be Carina. This present dance was his fifth attempt to complete an

entire set without the debutante in his arms standing upon his feet, or worse, tripping over her

own every time he spoke. He pretended that his wealth and titles overwhelmed these girls,

and not his character. Adding to his discomfort, Carina stood near the wall and laughed, presumable because indomitable Stirkton couldn't converse with, or charm, even one of

Alice's acquaintances.

"Oh, Your Grace, oh, please, do forgive me..."

Yet another white-gowned debutante tramped on his toes and, somewhere below chin

level, stammered the requisite apology. He gritted his teeth to keep from throwing back his

head and screaming, a compulsion that had nothing to do with her insignificant weight

pressed down on his evening shoes.

"...Because, oh dear, I was so clumsy, and I didn't mean..."

Max's eyelids drooped closed for a few blessed seconds of peace as, in his mind and in

silence, he bellowed out his frustration.

When the girl's self-berating rhetoric stopped, he lifted his lids and peered down at her.

Baby-blue eyes formed perfect circles and a perfectly-shaped mouth made a perfect 'O',

while blond ringlets bounced in perfect accord when she swallowed her fright down her

82

PERFECTLY-SHAPED MILK-WHITE THROAT.

"For God's sake, somebody save me."

He knew he'd said it aloud when her perfect skin, no doubt achieved through applying

lemon slices for hours each day, bleached to the color of chalk. And now, the perfect

cherubic chit who'd been forced by an overbearing mama to dance with a duke, would run

home and hide under her bed for a week. Worst of al, she'd inform his future duchess and al her young and impressionable friends that Alice's duke-to-be was a terrifying madman.

"Please forgive me." He gave her what he hoped was a reassuring smile. "My mind was

elsewhere. I know my betrothed's *bon amis* refer to me as Strict Stirkton—"

She gasped, dropped the hand poised in the correct upright dancing position, and took a

tottering step backwards. She covered her perfect mouth with a shaking hand and he barely

stopped himself from groaning, knowing that any sound might cause her to swoon on his

trampled feet. Lifting her fingers from her lips, he held her hand aloft once more and stepped

back into position in the line of dancers.

"One, two, three, turnabout, left glide, right glide ..." He counted off steps and prayed

that she'd slide, by rote, into the sequence of twists and crossed legs and ignore the curious

looks they garnered. This tedious evening, dancing attendance upon the chit he was to marry,

had been another attempt to demonstrate to Carina he was capable of being sociable, but

damnation, his attempts were a catastrophe. For a man who prided himself on correctness,

he'd totted up a long list of errors.

Carina had warned Max, several times, to call his fiancée by her given name to

demonstrate his affection and to encourage her to address him by his Christian name. To

make amends, he'd vowed to entertain Alice's numerous friends, despite each and every one

appearing as terrified of him as Alice was.

Max searched for this one's name. "Mary—"

"Minerva."

"Minerva? You're named for the goddess of wisdom?" For the first time, the girl's lips

twitched up into a natural smile and it transformed her perfect face, her perfect features, into

a far more tantalizing goddess. "With your beauty, they should have named you Cassandra."

She laughed, a sweet tinkling sound, and he smiled back at the tiny enchantress while

they slipped into the dance. "Naming me Minerva is now distressing for Mama, because she

fears I'm living up to the name."

"Your mother doesn't want you to have wisdom and knowledge?"

Another tinkle of laughter. "Oh, no, Your Grace. Young ladies are supposed to be vapid

83

AND USELESS, lest their intelligence exposes their escorts as bumbling idiots."

"Does that include dukes?"

She arched a perfect eyebrow. "Most especial y dukes."

His undignified snort of laughter didn't shock her this time, but amused the girl. He

guided her through the next turn by pressing his hand on her back and grinned. For many

years, he'd avoided balrooms for fear of being trapped by hordes of vapid chits and their

match-minded mothers. Even his long-standing marriage contract didn't deter the more

desperate and determined women.

"Never once have I considered how young ladies with intelligence, such as yourself,

must feel when they encounter so many gentlemen who lack intellect."

"And dim-witted enough to also be condescending, which makes it hard to bite my

tongue."

Amused for the first time, Max ignored the incredulous stares from the dancers around

them and laughed aloud. If he'd been assured of finding others with this girl's combination of

beauty and intellect, he'd have ventured into these staid areas of tonnish entertainment long

ago. Perhaps then he'd comprehend the workings of a young girl's mind and be able to

converse with Alice about more than the day's weather, and perhaps then she might welcome

his obligatory visits to her bedchamber.

After escorting Minerva—the only bright spot amongst the line of insipid

partners—back to her chaperone, he ignored Carina's puzzled scrutiny and made himself

available for Alice and her mother. Fetching glasses of punch was an innocuous activity and

not likely to alarm any young ladies. Though Alice's mother, with her haughty manner and

constant demands on his time, alarmed him.

Girding himself to focus on Alice's friends for another hour at the very least, he bowed

before her and forced a smile, while reminding himself to be gentle, considerate and the

opposite of a monster.

"Lady Alice, the musicians are warming up. Would you do me the great honor of

standing up with me for another set?"

She jumped like a startled fawn, gaped at him, and turned to her mother with a panicked

look. Her reaction was easy to interpret because Carina had described Alice's fears to him that afternoon. But, despite his efforts to help Alice become comfortable in his presence, the

prospect of being in his arms for a second dance scared her half to death.

Visions of their wedding night raced through his head and he shuddered. Unless there

was a dramatic change in their relationship, bedding Alice would be akin to plowing a whore

84

AGAINST A WHARF SIDE wall and then walking away as soon as he'd satisfied a basic need.

Though he'd never imagined emotional attachments or having a clinging wife, he'd never

force himself on a frightened girl in the bedchamber.

What a bloody mess. Money, titles, years of education and training were useless in this

situation and he was floundering, despite having what he immodestly considered as above

average intelligence. The tiniest hint of a revoked marriage contract would disgrace Alice and

shame the name he'd fought so hard to protect.

As he opened his mouth to offer a plausible excuse for Alice and spare her further

embarrassment, Lady Johnston leaned across to her daughter. "Alice! You must never refuse

His Grace. He'l soon be your husband, so you must learn to respect and obey him."

Max flinched. A wife bred to obey a duke's every whim had been his goal for a long

time, but the notion that his duchess would submit to him, despite loathing his touch, turned

his stomach. He clasped his hands behind his back to hide his shudders and heard Alice's meek, "Yes, Mama."

Alice held up her hand and waited for Max to assist her to her feet. He dutifully clasped

her fingers, taking care not to squeeze or encroach on her person. If the girl couldn't endure

his hands on her body during a dance, how the hell would this mousy chit survive being

bedded by a jungle cat? And, yes, he freely acknowledged that he was the hunter in bed and

his companion was prey. Before this, he'd pictured a typical arranged marriage with the usual

sparse couplings in the dark and for only one purpose: to impregnate his duchess.

A duke and duchess slept in separate bedrooms, apart from those few opportune days

each month when Alice would be between courses and fertile. And the onerous task of

teaching Alice about intimacy and calculating fertile days would fall on his shoulders, as he

couldn't imagine Lady Johnston performing her motherly duties and explaining sex to her

daughter. Containing his passion might prove the least of his problems.

Good God! Explaining coupling and reproduction to a girl who cringed at his touch

scared him more than having his teeth pulled, one by one. No matter how he educated her,

vocally or physically, his bride would view him as an animal waiting for his mate to come on

heat, with the end result being submission but no enjoyment. After burying Augustus, he'd

believed himself free to make his own choices about sex; when, where, and with whom.

Memories of those nights during his teens when he'd deflowered virgins or been given

lessons in copulation from whores fueled his nightmares, especially as the next virgin he

deflowered would be his duchess on their wedding night.

He helped Alice to her feet and mentally retreated into his duke-
like shell, executing the

85

STEPS OF COURTSHIP on a ballroom floor by rote. As he turned Alice
towards the music, he

bumped into someone, a soft, warm person who smelled like
roses: Carina—a momentary

reprieve from his anguish.

"Lady Dorchester," he said. "Pardon my clumsiness. Did I hurt
you?"

"Not at al. No one who has watched you dance would cal you
clumsy. Don't you agree,

Alice, that Max is an excelent dancer?"

Alice's gaze was fixed on the floor, but she gave a sketchy nod and
a murmur of

agreement, which made Carina scowl at him as if he was responsible for her reticence.

"Don't let me stop you," Carina said, placing her hand on Alice's
arm and waiting until

the girl looked up at her. "Continue your dance. I do so love
watching happy couples twirl

through a waltz together."

Max watched as his betrothed's eyes widened in appeal, this time
to his nemesis. The

irony made him want to laugh, or howl. A man and woman who
were to be married to each

other, and both preferred the company of another woman, the
same woman.

"Carina," Alice said in an anguished voice. "His Grace and I
would be much happier

talking to you than dancing." She looked up at Max and swalowed, twisting her gloved

hands. "That is, with your approval, Your Grace."

For the first time in his life, Max wished he could cry.

They'd walked towards Lady Johnston's chair, or rather her throne. "Alice." Her

daughter jumped. "His Grace wished to dance the Waltz with you."

Alice bowed her head until Max had to lean in to hear. "Of course, Mama."

He wanted to wring Lady Johnston's bejeweled neck. His hands must have actually

twitched at his sides, because another hand slipped into the one furthest away from Lady

Johnston. He gave Carina's fingers a light squeeze to thank her.

"Perhaps, Lady Alice," he said, ignoring her mother's rudeness, "you'd rather sit with

your friends until supper is announced? Lady Dorchester might stand up with me instead."

Alice sagged with relief. "Oh, yes, yes, please do, Your Grace."

Max walked Alice the few steps to her acquaintances conversed. "I'd be grateful if you

could address me as Maximus, or Max."

If it were possible, Alice appeared more anxious. She gripped the pleats below her

neckline so tightly, he feared her corset-enhanced bosoms would pop over the top.

"It isn't necessary, Your Grace." Alice sent another helpless glance towards her mother,

but the grand lady was engrossed in the tasty morsel of gossip the damsel beside her was

sharing. She turned to Carina. "Do you think I should address His Grace in such an informal

86

. . .

MANNER?"

He scowled at Carina when she used her hand to cover her mouth and her chuckle.

"You've dispensed with formality, Carina, and address me as Max, so surely Lady Alice

should cal me Maximus at the very least." He dared her to contradict him. To his annoyance,

Carina was busy smothering her mirth again.

"Yes, Alice, you should cal him Max, now that you have become closer."

"Closer?" Alice squeaked.

Carina patted her hand and Max squirmed. After the solicitor had read out the terms of

Augustus's wil, Max had rushed to begin his search for the other women but hadn't worried

about his bride. Now he berated himself for not giving more attention to this situation.

"I like to think we've grown closer recently. We'l be more comfortable with each other

when we're wed, because we'l know each other better."

When Alice urged them to waltz by waving her fingers towards the dancing, he steered

Carina towards the floor with a hand to her elbow. But his thoughts lingered on Alice.

"Go slowly with her as she's on the brink of accepting–"

"Accepting the ogre? Strict Stirkton who makes her shake with fear?" Their courtship

was a disaster and their marriage was unlikely to be better.

"You need practice dealing with women."

He spun her in a turn and said, "I deal with women al the time."

Carina turned with him and her lower body shifted into his for support. His thigh

tightened between her legs and, despite the layers of evening clothes separating them, his prick throbbed and grew. Without conscious thought, he bent her back over his outstretched

arm and thrust deeper into her apex.

Her tiny gasp owed nothing to their dancing, and she stilled for a long and wonderful

second before she moved and took up their conversation. "I don't mean the women you pay

at your cottage every month."

"Each second month," he murmured, distracted by the signs of female arousal.

"Truly? I assumed a man with your appetites would require a woman every month."

"I'l not discuss this in a balroom with my fiancée looking on."

He twirled Carina into a complicated series of turns, narrowly avoiding other dancers

and lifting her slippered feet off the polished floorboards. Her grip tightened and he kept her

upright by holding her closer, and at the same time setting his body on fire. Pulling away was

difficult, almost impossible, but he lightened his grasp one finger at a time, though he longed

to fold her into his arms and damn the consequences.

87

IF HE GLANCED across the ballroom, he'd meet the wide eyed stare of his fiancée, or the

accusing glare of his future mother-in- law. These games were over and he needed time alone

with Carina and, by damn, she'd meet him at Brent Street very soon. When the music

finished and he swung her in one last circle before forcing himself to release her.

After bowing to the ladies, he retreated in cowardly haste to the card room. Holding a large brandy, he lounged against the card room wall and was debating joining a game when

Alice's father came to stand beside him. Although his lordship liked the idea of his daughter

becoming a duchess, his mistrust of Max was palpable. Perhaps the man's pre-wedding

investigations had sniffed out some past transgressions and silence was the safest option.

The older man took Max by the elbow and drew him to a secluded area. "I've watched

you with my daughter and I'm disappointed with your behavior. I'd thought that you

understood my precious child better now, and that she was becoming more comfortable with

the idea of marriage and with your character."

"My character?"

"Are you aware that you're referred to as Stern Stirkton, amongst other names?"

"I don't give a damn what others say, and you shouldn't concern yourself with such

nonsense."

"My daughter's welfare is my concern. I want to know that she, and any future children,

wil be cared for."

"Are you implying that I might il -treat your daughter, or my own offspring?"

"I'm implying nothing, but the late Duke's treatment of his son, and your mother, has

been widely spoken about for years. And of course, his dealings with you, his only

grandchild, were appaling."

Augustus had cunningly tried to hide his evil side, so discovering that others had known

was a shock. Naively, he'd imagined the only person who knew the truth was him, though a late night visitor to his house recently had destroyed that illusion. Carina and Gertie had local

knowledge of his estates and childhood, so why hadn't he thought of this man knowing too.

Blind arrogance?

"I'm not my grandfather and I don't conduct myself as he did, especial y when, after his

death...Let's simply say more of his dealings were revealed and I swore to do things better.

The changes I've made are for the better.

"What changes?"

"I can't reveal that, but rest assured I'm working hard to right some of the wrongs." He

broke off and shook his head. "I promise that what you cal my stern nature is under reform

88

AND ALICE WIL be happy with me."

"You're paying too much attention to Lady Dorchester and, for reasons I cannot fathom,

the brood of women related to the Countess. Lady Johnston and I have noticed, and soon

others will remark, that your attentions should be fixed on Alice, and no one else."

"How I pass my time, and my reasons for doing so, are not your concern, sir." He

struggled to keep his breathing regular and his temper steady. Using his height and breadth to

intimidate his father-in-law wasn't a gentlemanly act, but the man's interference must stop.

"I am Stirkton and I answer to nobody but myself." He pointed his finger at the man's

chest. "Do I make myself clear, my lord?"

"Be clear on this: you're reputed to deal with people hardheartedly, but your ruthless

nature doesn't scare me because I can just as hardnosed. I'l not alow my daughter's name to

be besmirched with scandal because, one day, my grandchildren will inherit and they will sit

at the peak of London's society."

Johnston copied Max's defiant gesture and jabbed his finger into Max's chest. "That's

the only reason I agreed to this arrangement all those years ago. I accepted you, in spite of

your family's peculiarities, because your grandfather swore to me that your titles would be

the highest, the most prestigious, that could be available to my family. I've kept my side of

the bargain, given you my girl so you can plant the infamous Meacham seed in her and breed

your heir."

Max's temper spiked again, but this time on behalf of the innocent committed to him

years earlier. His cravat tightened to a noose as blood pumped furiously in his veins and he

clenched his teeth. As with this thug's wife earlier, the duke who was renowned for avoiding

physical contact felt an urge to wrap his hands around somebody's neck.

Johnston was oblivious. "After hearing stories of you partnering low class workers in

trade, I harbor grave doubts about your business acumen."

This disgusting man and his greedy lady purported to value their daughter's welfare yet,

within the same hour, they'd shown that the wants and needs of their daughter were scarcely

contemplated. The grasping pair represented many parents of their class, whose progeny were

ignored until they reached an age when they could be used. Max rubbed a hand over his tight

chest. Acquaintances had long spoken of him as heartless and as having ice in his veins

instead of blood, yet the pains around his heart just now had proved he had a normally

functioning organ.

He'd simply had no opportunity to understand emotion and interpret intense feelings.

Mental supremacy received high praise, and physical excellence was expected of someone

89

OVERSEEING vast agricultural tracts and juggling finances. Emotions had been beaten out of

existence, so little wonder his dealings with Alice were strained. As had been pointed out in

recent weeks, his temperament was bloody appalling and his unsympathetic nature not in the

best interests of a sweet person like Alice. Plus, Alice was trapped between him and Carina

and their ongoing battles; though Alice's grasping parents might prove the biggest problem.

"Believe me, Johnston, our little chat has convinced me that Alice needs my help."

"Good, because I'l be keeping a close on you and you'd better perform to my

expectations."

Johnston made loud smacking sounds as his thick tongue and pudgy lips made short

work of his last drops of burgundy. Max barely concealed his repulsion and wondered again

why he'd been so blind to the failings of this disgusting specimen of humanity. Possibly

because he'd never realy cared.

"I'm not a Russian bear performing on a rope, and I'm trying very hard to remember that

you're my future father-in-law, but I've carried out my duties for the past three years without

interference, and I'l not al ow any now. In order to maintain harmony, I suggest you stop

threatening me, or you'l discover that two can play at that game."

Johnston wavered momentarily before straightening and saying defiantly, "You've

nothing with which to blackmail me." His tongue darted out again, but this time to moisten

his dry lips.

"Did you honestly imagine that we wouldn't scrutinize your deal-ings, in the same way

you investigated us? Very foolish or very naïve. Which are you?"

"This isn't finished, Stirkton. I'm watching you."

"And I you."

Max turned his back on the boor, and strode through the French doors and onto the

terrace that wrapped the receiving rooms. He braced his arms on the outer brick wall and

sucked in blessed fresh air. The conversation had left a sour taste in his mouth and he leant

over and spat into the honeysuckle hedge below, and then wiped his mouth on his coat sleeve.

"Goodness. Not exactly polite behavior for a gentleman at a bal."

He spun around and faced the woman standing next to the open glass doors and twirling

a glass of champagne. Carina made a habit of appearing at his most awkward moments.

She slapped her clutched gloves against her thigh a few times. "You've had a to-do with

Alice's father. Not hard from what I've observed of the man and his rude and lecherous

habits."

His senses jumped to alert and he stepped towards her before rethinking his actions. If

90

GOSSIP HAD STARTED about his acquaintance with Carina, best to keep his distance.

"Has Johnston said something to you? Made advances?" When she didn't speak, but

continued twirling the glass by its fragile stem, he glanced towards the door. "If he's said or

done anything to intimidate you or your sisters, most especial y Georgie, he'l regret it."

"Pfft! It was nothing. He's merely one more buly, and a woman learns to deal with al of

them. What's important is your dealings with him."

He shook his head. "No point asking if you listened. You, Countess, have no scruples, so

of course you eavesdropped. How much did you hear?"

"Enough."

"Enough information to blackmail me with me?"

She laughed. "I'd collected enough delicious titbits previously to start half of London

gossiping about you. What I heard made me revise my thinking about you and Alice, and I

enjoyed hearing you put the oaf in his place. When Alice hears that you're prepared to defend

her against her parents, she'l be eager to marry you."

"Please, don't say anything to Alice. She doesn't need to learn of her father's low

opinion of her."

She shook her head. "Learning that she's a rung on a social ladder and a hatchery for

grandchildren, and nothing more, would humiliate her. Though I suspect she already knows her father's opinion of her worth. I'm glad she's gained a protector."

"Don't pretend I'm some sort of hero, Carina, as I fall far short of being noble and you,

of all people, know that. But I detest powerful men who delight in subduing those closest to

them."

"Augustus hurt you, didn't he?"

He turned away and didn't answer.

"That's why you empathize with Alice," she said to his back, though her voice sounded

closer. "Because Augustus viewed you and your parents as social pawns."

"Oh, please, don't spare my feelings. Say what you real y mean. My grandfather only

saw me as a stud, a breeding stallion for perfect Meachams."

"I'm sorry. He destroyed your chance at a happy marriage before you even met Alice.

All because he was obsessed with selecting the perfect pedigree to complement your

bloodline."

"You're wrong. He did care about me, a little at least. His intentions weren't as

calculated as you've made them sound."

"It's time you accepted the truth. His streak of insanity was a mile wide and if he'd

91

LIVED, he'd have watched you couple with Alice and spied on you through a peephole,

because he needed to oversee every moment of your mating and ensure that the two of you

bred a perfect son and another Meacham for him to torture."

"Torture? A harsh word."

"Perhaps you prefer to remember it as abuse."

"I prefer to not remember it at al, thank you, and now if you will excuse me, I need to

see Lady Alice home safely."

"You mean you need to reassure yourself that her disgusting father doesn't take out his

anger on Alice with his fists."

He sucked in a breath and closed his eyes. Her light touch startled him into opening them

again, but the pity in her eyes made him look away. "How is it, Carina," he said without

meeting her gaze, "that you can read my mind with such ease?" He removed the empty glass

from her fingers before they tightened anymore and she snapped the stem.

"The signs of abuse are easy to spot," she said, "if one knows what to look for. I, like

you, know the tell-tale signs and noticed how Alice flinches when her father raises his hand."

Max placed the glass out of harm's way and nodded. "Tonight when we danced, I saw

bruises on Alice's wrists. Tiny blue marks, as if a man's fingers had pressed down there."

"He uses force to coerce her into—"

"Don't stop now. Tear another layer off my hide and see if I bleed red."

"Johnston used force to coerce Alice into a pretense of happiness in your company. Well,

either him or Lady Johnston."

"Good God! I never considered her mother, although of the pair she's the most

determined to make Alice perform in my presence."

"Al the more reason why you should concentrate on Alice and allow me to investigate by myself. You could send a footman around with Augustus's papers and that'll leave you

free to court Alice in peace, and without my interference."

He clapped slowly. "Oh, bravo, Countess. I was correct, for you have no scruples. Never

let a chance go past to lay hands on those papers. Pity it didn't work, my dear. As a

gentleman, I can't alow you to attempt such an arduous task without assistance."

"You spat in a garden moments ago and now you're worried about appearances?"

"Our arrangement stands as before and I'l send word of a time to meet. You already

know the address. Goodnight, Countess."

He spun on his heel, knowing that in another second they'd both lose their tempers, and

that anger would spur another bout of unbridled arousal. God knew what would happen when

92

DESIRE WAS UNLEASHED, but he did know that a balcony during a ball was neither the time nor

the place to experiment.

He bid an icy farewell to the Johnston family, after Lord Johnston made it clear Max was

not needed to accompany Alice home. However, he employed every seductive skill at his

disposal to draw Alice into an enjoyable conversation before she departed. There might never

be any real love between them, but he'd work hard to ease Alice's fears. It occurred to him

that marriage could become more than anticipated if he contributed more and opened himself up to intimacy. For the first time in his affluent life, greed took hold.

He was greedy for a better relationship with Alice than the fearful one she shared with

her father, and he wanted an unusual ton marriage; one that grew into mutual respect, even

love, instead of loathing.

9

———

Max stood on the pavement outside his Brent Street cottage and drew a deep breath. For two excruciatingly long weeks, he'd anticipated this moment, and he was almost bursting out
of his skin with the need to rush inside and hurry Carina into bed. But he slowed his body and
his thoughts before he stepped over the threshold.

This tumult of feelings, these longings, were strange. Desire for the physical comfort
found with a beautiful mistress was normal; though until the next time they met at his
cottage, he often couldn't recal a lot about the woman's features. This time, he remembered
everything. For two weeks, he'd inhaled Carina's unique scent and absorbed her body heat,
yet tried to ignore both, as he'd stood beside her night after night in drawing rooms and at
dining tables.

He'd couldn't recal what scent fragranced Alice's skin, but he knew Carina that favored lavender during the day, and at night she dabbed sweeter rose behind her ears and between

her breasts. Several times, he'd had to fight the compulsion to dip his head towards her

bosom and inhale. An obsession was an anomaly to him and he had no inkling how to cure

one.

He waited inside until Carina knocked and then opened the door to her himself. No

servants resided, as he preferred to come and go as he pleased. During the day, staff attended

93

TO THE HOUSEHOLD, but at night he preferred the quiet; he never spent an entire night with any

of the women anyway. This evening, he wanted as much privacy as possible. She pushed past

him from the lamp-lit street before her carriage pulled away.

"Countess, I'm glad to have you here at last."

"I almost didn't come."

"We have an agreement. If you want me to continue escorting your sisters, you wil

continue meeting me here."

"I'm wel aware of your terms. Nevertheless, you've not delivered any papers to my

house, nor have you revealed when and where I may begin my search of your grandfather's

boxes."

"I've uncovered more and more of his dealings during my searches over the past year.

But the more I find out about him, the more I realize that, though I was his only family, I

knew little about the man. There are many, many places that he secreted older documents, almost as if dividing the information between a myriad of venues, so that nobody will ever be

able to piece together the entire puzzle."

"Then you'd better have every paper brought to one central place, preferable my house,

so I can access them easier and faster. Because I'l not return here if you're unable to satisfy

your end of our bargain. You might have the luxury of learning things bit by bit, but I only

have a short time before things become ugly, and if something happens to my sisters in the

meantime, I'l hold you responsible."

"I always keep my promises, but threats won't make me rush things."

He led Carina into the parlor, which was a much cozier room than the stark drawing

room at his own house.

"This is nice," she said, after making a leisurely scrutiny of the room. "Not what I

expected."

"You assumed my mistresses were locked in a cold dark cell and fed on bread and

water."

She laughed, an enticing sound that trickled through his awareness like a refreshing

mountain stream and made him want to entice another one from her.

"Something like that. You've a reputation of being cold and distant. Are you going to

prove it wrong?"

"Please, take a seat near the fire. That wil keep you warm in case you're right and I'm

made of ice through and through."

He pulled out her chair at the small table, where a selection of cold food had been laid

94

OUT. That also wasn't usual for his evenings at this cottage, and though the change in routine

was a little disconcerting, he wanted his evening with Carina to be something different:

fresher and better. His hands trembled a little as he poured wine and selected morsels of food

for her to sample, drawing out their time together and savoring the pleasure of having her all

to himself at last.

"Do you normal y serve food to the women you bring here, or am I receiving special

treatment?"

She was teasing him again, but as he'd never tussled with siblings or shared lighthearted

banter with his grandfather, he couldn't toss back a quick-witted reply. The only thing to do

was address her as he would any other woman whom he brought here.

"The women who stay in this cottage know to expect my visits three days a week when

I'm in London. I'l not expect you to live here, but from now on I'd like you to arrive before

me so you are ready and no time is wasted."

Carina choked on her mouthful of wine, spluttered a few times, before wiping her mouth

with her napkin.

She fluttered her eyelashes, as coy as a coquette. "And do you consider spending an

entire evening with me a waste of you valuable time?"

"As I've said before, our evenings wil satisfy us both. Physical satisfaction for me, and

keeping our bargain for you."

She leaned forward so her heavy breasts fell up and over the scooped neck of her

fashionable dress and gave him a glimpse of two rosy nipples. He could barely swallow his

own wine while, without conscious thought, he angled forward for a better view. Flashing

him a knowing look, she dipped a finger under the lace at her neckline and ran it across one

breast and then over the other.

His mouth dried and he ran his tongue over his lips to moisten them, while he gripped

the arms of the chair. Christ, he wanted her.

"We should talk and get to know each other a little better."

A few weeks earlier, he'd have considered any suggestion of connecting with a woman

before sex as a waste of time. Conversation suggested an intimacy he avoided like the plague.

A woman's mind had never interested him before, merely her body. But he craved knowledge

of this woman and yearned for more of the laughter that invariable accompanied her stories.

Entanglements were difficult, and yet he'd formed a bond with Georgie and was comfortable

with the idea of sharing more with Carina.

Perhaps, though, it would be easier to play the cold duke and avoid sentimental

95

SITUATIONS, because he'd learned when young that feelings were easily trampled and hearts

broken. 'No, I haven't enough time for talking." He pointed towards the narrow halway that

dissected the smal house. "The main bedchamber is up the stairs in the front. Go ahead and undress, and then lie on the bed."

A sharp inhalation showed her shock, but his own reactions of guilt and remorse stunned

him even more. Nevertheless, he wanted to clarify their situation so there were no later

misunderstandings. "I've no time for shyness, especial y not from someone I know is

experienced. If I undress you, I'l treat your clothing with less care than you wil."

She made no move to leave the room but stood with her hands on her hips. "So, the great

Duke of Stirkton is prepared to take me by force."

"Of course not. No force is not necessary."

"You mean, your paid whores rush to the bedroom and disrobe, perhaps in the

expectation of receiving more payment for their obedience. Answer me truthfully, Max, have

you ever been with a woman who wasn't paid for, either by you or your grandfather?"

Breath caught in his chest and his hands clenched. Nobody ever questioned him or his

actions. Titles, wealth and his superior air ensured unquestioning obedience, and sometimes

submission, from those he dealt with.

"Perhaps not, however when I bed my bride I'l not be paying."

"Considering Lady Johnston's expectations for your future, you'l be paying dearly for

the rest of your life."

"What do you mean?"

"I mean..." Her sweet smile was so false that it set his teeth on edge.

"...that the lady has calculated your worth to the penny, and I doubt you'l be alowed

any input into either your social commitments or your wife's spending, because her mother wil reside in your home for most of the year."

"How dare you! Hopefully, Alice wil become *enceinte* with our first child within a few

months. She'l raise the child at our country estate, and when she has recovered from the first

birth, I'm breaking with family tradition and scheduling a second child."

Carina laughed. "Your omnipotent powers alow you to control Mother Nature along

with everything else, do they?"

"Meacham males have always been virile, and my experience up til now tels me I'l be

no different."

Her nose screwed up in a puzzled squint. "In al these years of buying women, you've

never slipped up? Not once? Never been overcome with passion and forgotten about

96

PREVENTION? Planted a babe on one of them?"

"Of course not. Taking precautions is a simple matter, and the women who come here

are experienced and take care that there are no illegitimate Meachams. They understand that a

bastard could never be acknowledged."

"And what of me, Max?"

"What of you?"

"I'm different. Inexperienced, and I've no contrivances to prevent pregnancy. To be

truthful, I've never purchased preventatives and I've no idea where to find them. What wil

you do to ensure that I don't catch a child before our month concludes?"

"Very wel. Let's be blunt. With my experience, I can time my

release. Only an untried
   youth cannot withdraw at the correct moment and I left that stage
at fourteen. I've never spilt
   my seed inside a woman."
   "I beg to differ. One woman received your seed." She paused and
watched him as she
   added, "Me."
   He closed his eyes, not wanting to meet her knowing look. Never,
not once, not even to
   himself had he admitted his slip that night. Augustus would have
been furious to learn Max
   had left precious Meacham seed inside a bought woman. Seed
spilled inside a woman was to
   procreate an heir, nothing else.
   "That never happened."
   "Deny the memory if you wish, but you didn't pul out of my body
quickly enough. I
   was a naïve seventeen-year-old who didn't know understand that
a woman could become
   pregnant so easily, but the Earl was more than happy to point out
my stupidity. He was
   ecstatic that I might be carrying your child after that one mistake.
After that, he watched me
   the way a hawk watches a mouse before diving in for the kil
."
   "He was anxious for you to have your menses."
   "Huh! To the contrary. He counted off the days and prayed that I
didn't bleed."
   Max shook his head. "Why would he not want you—oh, good
Lord!" He grabbed his
   head in both hands and groaned. "The Earl was impotent. He
wanted another man's child, my
   child, to be born to his countess."
   Carina tilted her head and studied him. "For a business man
reputed to be the most cold

blooded in the city, I'm surprised that you're distressed over the trivial matter of

impregnating another man's wife."

"How dare you joke? The thought of bearing a child to a man who was a complete

stranger must have revolted you."

97

"At first, yes. Then I realized that having your baby would be my only chance."

"Chance for what?"

"Having a child to love, my own family. My stepbrother sold me and sent me away from

my sisters, and both he and the Earl told me I couldn't see my family again."

"You—" He swalowed past the lump in his throat. "You wanted to carry my child?"

"In my entire seventeen years, you were the first man, the only man, who'd ever been

nice to me."

Max wished her husband lived so he could dispatch the man to a fiery end with his own

hands. As for her stepbrother, he'd deal with him as soon as all the evidence was collected.

Carina had spent a night with a stranger when she was seventeen; the bastard who'd claimed

her innocence—him—and that was her kindest encounter. His own torments paled in

insignificance, as he realized how she'd survived, thrived and created a new life for herself.

When he was younger, he'd accepted his future role as the sixth duke without dispute. As

he'd matured, he'd seen his grandfather frozen in time and had vowed that he wouldn't be merely another feudal Meacham, feared rather liked by his tenants and staff. Yet his attempts

to right past wrongs had moved at snail's pace and the sixth Duke, a powerful man across the

breadth of England, now envied a country widow because she'd outpaced him with her drive,

stamina and determination to change her future.

"My actions were despicable and I cannot fathom how you can forgive me, while

seeking revenge on other men who probably did you less harm. Please, help me understand."

He sounded desperate, but he needed to know what qualified him for redemption.

"Despite the influences of a perverted old man, your inherent decency was evident; you

were a gentleman through and through. You touched me with reverence, as if I were special.

Because of those memories, I'l not al ow you to treat me a whore. I beg you, during our

month: prove that not all men are evil and cruel, and take me to your bed for reasons other

than monetary or an exchange of information."

He paced the confines of the small room, wanting her to see his bewilderment at her

request. "I don't know if I'm capable of relaxing my guard in bed." He gave her a hard stare.

"I was taught that strong emotions weaken a man's character in the eyes of others. What do

you expect of me?"

"Very little realy. Perhaps to think of me between our visits here."

"Ha! Once women walk out that door I wipe them from my mind, and you'l be no

different."

"Then at least treat me with the same respect you showed when I was seventeen."

98

IF THIS COURTESY atoned for anything he'd done, he'd bow to her request. She didn't need

to know that his hunger for her lush body would be satisfied and he'd finally be able to wipe

Carina from his mind

"So be it. Though I can only promise to treat you as a friend."

She dipped her head. "That's something anyway. I don't want to feel like your enemy

while we share our bodies."

He ran his fingers down the soft skin of her face and neck, and she turned towards his

hand and nuzzled like a kitten. His hands cupped her face and his mouth brushed her cheeks,

coming closer and closer to her mouth but not touching. Tenderness was new territory, but he

enjoyed hearing the little whimpers of need she made, and prolonged what he was doing until

her noises grew louder and his enjoyment rose, as did his arousal.

His confidence grew and he was determined to create some beautiful memories for

Carina to remember him by, though it seemed contradictory to want her to cling his memory

when soon he would be outing her out of his mind and concentrating on Alice. Stil , he'd

practiced the science of lovemaking since he was fourteen and knew how to pleasure Carina

until she screamed his name and begged for release, over and over.

His nibbled her dainty earlobe and ran his hands up and down her body, relearning her

shape and escalating her need. Even through her layers of clothing, she felt warm and feminine and his own cravings turned deep and desperate. Quali-fying his gnawing ache as

lust was pointless, because he'd barely begun to take her for the first time and he already

wanted to claim her as his, again and again and again.

"Turn around," he ordered, his voice hoarse. He cleared his throat. "I'll unbutton your

dress."

Carina turned but peered back over her shoulder. "Is this what you normally do, unbutton

gowns?"

"For pity's sake, woman, I'm trying to change my normal habits and yet you're

questioning me about other women's clothing."

"But I don't know how to please you? Isn't that why I'm here, to make you happy?"

"Damn it! You're the most contrary woman I've ever encountered. You only need to go

to bed with me and I'l be happy."

He cursed the tiny buttons running down the back of her gown, while she peered back at

him with piercing green eyes that dared him to drop his mask and reveal something more.

"The answer to your question is no. I've no time to waste on undoing tiny buttons that

aren't made for a man's hands." He gritted his teeth and fumbled with the smal fastenings. "I

99

RARELY TAKE a meal here and I'm not present when they undress." His fingers halted. "How the

hel did they manage?"

She laughed. "Typical male who never considers the difficulties of female clothing. I assume they either wore front closing clothing or had a maid secreted somewhere."

He glanced around, half-expecting to see a maid's head pop out.

Carina chuckled. "I assumed you'd organize our assignation down to the last detail.

Though I should have considered buttons, because I can't picture you ripping the clothing

from my body in a ravenous frenzy like the heroes in one of those penny dreadfuls that my

sisters devour each week.

Max frowned, uncertain if he'd been insulted for his lack of passion or praised for his

organizational skills. Ripping off her gown and throwing her to the floor would prove that he

was a flesh and blood male, who was more desperate to plough her warm depths than he was

to see his ship sail into port.

His entire body jerked at the thought of taking her in the ravenous frenzy that had fuelled

his dreams, and his fingers twisted in a lock of her hair curled near one gaping buttonhole.

"Ouch!"

"Sorry." He touched his lips to her hand, which she rubbed over her scalp on the spot

where he'd inadvertently tugged her hair.

"It's not your fault," she whispered. She slid her fingers out and he pressed his mouth

into her soft red hair, moved from side to side and enjoyment the sensation of springy curls

tickling his face. "My curls are... Hmm." She moaned and wiggled her bottom against his

trousers and his prick screamed for release "...unruly. Curls tangle in everything."

"Your curls are as magnificent as a summer sunrise and, like you, they're vibrant and warming."

He closed his eyes and savored the moment, because moments of intimacy were rare and

likely to be scarcer during an arranged and formal marriage. He held his breath at her long

sigh and hoped his maudlin sentiment hadn't embarrassed them both. Letting his guard down

left him exposed and vulnerable, and he waited for her laughter or ridicule.

"That's the most beautiful thing anyone has ever said to me, especially about my unruly

hair. Thank you."

Thank God she hadn't caled him a sentimental idiot. His prick stirred and prodded him

to take action, but a wish to prolong this moment made him dawdle.

He concentrated on disrobing the lady, though his trembling wasn't helping. "I'm rather

ham-fisted because I've never even seen a woman undress before, let alone assisted her."

100

"I LIKE the feel of your fingers on my skin." She shivered. "Nicer than being touched my

sisters or my maid."

He slipped buttons free of their moorings, one by one, until her gown slid off her

shoulders. When her head dropped forward, he responded to her sensuous invitation by

bending to nuzzle her bare neck, inhaling roses—sweetly enticing roses—and dredging up

memories of another woman who smeled of roses. When he was ten, he'd been stranded at

Eton for term break because his grandfather's carriage was

stopped by a flooded stream.

A school acquaintance, Freddie Hepworth, came from a large and loving family, and his

mother, Lady Hepworth, had scooped Max up and taken him home with Freddie to join her

other five children. What Max remembered was that she'd kissed him each morning and

night as if he'd belonged to her, and when she'd kissed him, she'd smelt of roses. Sweet,

sweet roses and pungent lavender. In a lonely boy's mind, those scents meant gentleness and

love.

He nuzzled closer, inhaling the heady scent and lightly brushing up and down her neck

with his mouth, until she turned to him and tilted her mouth for his kiss. He rarely kissed

anyone, though he'd respond in kind if a courtesan instigated it, while making it clear such

intimacies were unnecessary. Carina's lips glistened wet, red, and her breath held the sharp

tang of red wine; he needed his mouth on hers more than he needed to breathe.

"Soft, so soft and wet for me," he murmured into her open mouth.

His lips moved back and forth across hers in an entice-and-retreat pattern, until her

mouth fell open and her breathing became panting. Even white teeth nipped at his bottom lip,

and she sucked it in a dance of seduction he was powerless to resist, and his own ragged

breathing sent his head spinning.

"Christ almighty!" He gripped her arms and puled back a scant few inches to allow them

more air. Her stunned surprise reflected his.

Her tongue licked across her swollen red mouth and, tormenting him, the tip of her tongue stopped at every reddened spot to touch and access, as if testing to see if her lips still

belonged to her. "If my body sings and screams after a simple kiss, how wil I cope with our

lovemaking?"

"How wil I?" The words were out of his mouth before he thought, and her eyes widened

at his honesty.

"You? But you've done this hundreds of times."

"Never."

"Never what?"

101

"YOU'RE the only woman I've ever kissed that way. In Dorchester, and then now."

Her fingers touched her swollen lips, and he removed them gently and used his tongue to

worship her mouth, licking in sweeping motions until they both trembled and shook.

She puled away. "Are you teling me that you've never kissed any other woman?"

"Not like that, no." He shrugged. "I love your mouth and I enjoy kissing you. Come, let

us go upstairs." He waved towards the steps and she started up but, on the bottom step, she

hesitated and turned to meet his eyes. Her next step was back- wards, so she stood slightly

above him. Letting go of her gown, she shimmied her arms out of the tiny flounced sleeves

and let the bodice slide towards her hips, her eyes fixing him in place the way a cobra

mesmerized its prey.

"If they're usual y naked when you go upstairs, I won't be, because our hour together wil be different in every way."

"Oh, God, Carina, if you only knew."

He ran his hands down her arms and watched her skin shiver with gooseflesh and her

arms tremble in the wake of his touch. He moaned.

"Our time together was destined to be different from the moment you stood in my

drawing room and chalenged me." He shook his head and looked at her with sadness. "Don't

you see, I'm helpless to resist you? You hold me in thral with every word and deed."

"And is that such a bad thing?"

"Ha!" He threw back his head and gave a harsh bark of laughter. "You've no idea what it

does to me, do you? How everything comes tumbling down around my ears when you

challenge me or laugh at me. I erected a wall, brick by brick, to block away the horrors of my

past, so I could face a future that my grandfather arranged, and that I never wanted."

She gave a broken sob and reached for him, but he stepped back. "I'm so sorry."

"No, I don't want your pity. That's not why I said that."

He turned a circle at the bottom of the steps and stayed out of her reach. God knew, if

she touched him and looked at with compassion in her eyes and tenderness in her voice, he'd

break. "Compared to you, Countess, I'm the scum on the bottom of the pond!"

She snorted. "Have you forgotten that you accused me of slaugh-tering the Earl?"

He shook his head. "Stupid taunts and far wide of the mark, because I know you're not

capable of murder."

"I don't know," she said in a wry tone. "I may not have dispensed with my husband, but

when I find the fourth man, meet with him, and if I have my suspicions confirmed-"

"Suspicions? You didn't tel me you might know who he is. What's his name?"

102

She waved a dismissive hand in a gesture he recognized as her way of cutting off a

discussion. "I don't know."

He frowned. "But you suspect someone and I want to know his name."

"Why? So you can charge off on your black stallion and run the vilain through with

your sword. What would Alice say about her intended making a spectacle of himself

defending another woman's honor?"

Guilt stabbed in the same as when she spoke of his forthcoming wedding.

"Thank you for the concern, but I wil do this by myself. Besides which, I don't want to

put anyone else in danger."

"If it's dangerous, I shal take care of it and you won't bc involved."

She shook her head. "The Earl left me in this situation and though he wasn't the best of

husbands, I can't understand why he did it and what he had to gain. When I find out who it is

and why, I can then decide how to solve the problem and make us safe, once and for al."

"You're talking in riddles. Keeping things from me."

"No more. The next hour is about us. We undress here and not upstairs."

He glanced around. They stood out of sight of the street; the curtains were drawn and the

doors were locked. A frisson of excitement shot through him; his blood heated and rushed to

his groin. His erection, not sighted for many months, swelled and shouted for attention.

Imagining Carina's naked body, not hidden under linen sheets, gave him the incentive to

forget old habits and start anew as she wanted.

"Yes." He struggled out of his tight-fitting coat and, with one strong tug, unraveled the

intricate knot his valet had spent fifteen minutes perfecting. Now it seemed ridiculous, but

he'd been nervous earlier and had fretted and fidgeted in front of his mirror. If his valet had

guessed the reason, his training stopped him from mentioning it, though he'd rolled his eyes

and huffed in a put-upon fashion when Max had rejected item after item.

After taking over an hour to dress, he stripped himself of all but his trousers and boots in

minutes. His linen shirt landed on the fast-growing pile of garments, before the sight of

Carina stepping free of her second petticoat stopped his progress. His chest tightened with

that now familiar ache which happened when he was with her.

She loosened the laces of her short corset and pulled the boning away from her body,

letting it catch on her hips before she shimmied it down to the floor, leaving her covered only

by a transparent shift. They stared with matching hungry looks, as if they were starved and

the sight of the other's body would nourish them for the next year.

"Alow..." He cleared his throat. "Alow me to help. Sit and I'l remove your boots."

103

HER EYES WIDENED IN SURPRISE.

"What?" He smiled. "Do you think that being a duke makes me incapable of removing

boots?"

She returned his smile and nodded. "I assumed you could pul off your own boots when

necessary, but I cannot picture you removing anyone else's."

"My valet believes me incapable of doing anything for myself, but I've undressed and

dressed in this cottage for many years with the aid of whoever is present."

Carina's smile upended and become a grimace. Damn! Another reminder that she was

one of many women who'd visited this cottage. "Sorry. I only meant—"

"Please!" She covered his mouth with her hand. "I'm under no il usions about why I'm

here."

"You're wrong. Give me a chance to prove that this means more than the usual." He

guided her to the fourth step from the bottom and sat below her. He lifted her foot and

unwound the fastenings of her half-boots. Removing them and her stockings became a

forerunner to the sexual act and a pleasurable interlude he'd never indulged in. By the time

the second finely-knit stocking slid through his fingers and he lifted her foot to his mouth, her

breathing came as a series of gasps. His breathing wasn't much freer as he nipped each toe, before soothing her hurts with a swirling lathe of his tongue.

"Oooh." Another deep growl rumbled when he lifted her leg and nibbled upwards to the

tender skin of her thigh.

"Sweet Lord in heaven," he whispered, before burying his head between her bent knees.

"I can see al of you. You're beautiful."

"I didn't bother with layers ..."

After he eased her knees wider apart, then slid both hands up and over her thighs to raise

her shift higher, her head went back and her eyes drooped shut. His gaze fixed on the clefts

and curves of her body that he'd exposed.

"...As I couldn't see the point if..." Pushing up the folds of her shift, he let it puddle

around her waist before he reached out to touch her apex. "... when you were going to remove

everything."

The first pleasure he allowed himself was threading his fingers through her thick nest of

curls and resting his palm over her mound.

"Red," he announced with a low growl, as his fingers wove in and out in and tested the

spring in the curls. "I didn't know. I dreamed and, believe me, I hoped."

He shifted sideways on his stair, and so his body rested closer to where she sprawled

104

DOWN THE LENGTH of four steps. Using his free hand, he reached up to stroke the matching locks

on her head and twirled a stray ringlet around his finger.

"Crazy crimson up here," he brought the loop to his mouth and slid it across his lips in a reverent caress, "and down here, sly scarlet." Tickling scratches, a long sweep of a finger

through her moist crevice, and she wriggled and writhed. "Both are so sexy, but I need to see

al of it, al of you. Let your hair down, please."

When she reached up to release her hair, pin by pin, he watched in fascinated silence.

One ringlet after another hit her shoulders and bounced to land in disarray around the pale

skin of her neck; the startling contrast between the brilliant red hair against the stark white of

her neck stirred the first crack in his armor. Never in all his years had he wanted to unleash

his dominating character more than now, to forget finesse and abandon refinement and

plunge deep inside her hot passage. To claim every inch of her as if she belonged to him.

He looked up to find her watching his face and judging his expression, and he jerked

back, uncertain of his welcome. She was no common slut, no practiced prostitute, nor an

overpaid courtesan. This was Lady Dorchester, a countess, and a woman he'd normally not

dally with. He withdrew his two questing fingers and waited.

"It's al right, and in fact, it's perfect. You're perfect, and exactly how I remembered. So

many nights, I waited for the Earl to stop his useless rutting and I'd think instead of your

fingers inside me, probing so gently. When he thrust and nothing happened, he'd curse and

swear at me as though I caused his unmanliness." She gave a dry laugh. "As he sweated on

me, his stomach rubbing against me like an overfed pig—"

"Enough. I cannot bear hearing every sordid detail, or knowing that the Earl paid for your body and yet never appreciated that priceless gift. To hear you speak so calmly of his

impotence and how he blamed you—" His voice hitched.

She reached down and touched his arm where it rested under the lawn of her shift.

"Memories of us, together, alowed me cope with those nights without losing my sanity. But

now I want new memories. Please touch me. Make love to me."

10

Max shuddered. At Carina's passion-hazed command to make love to her, self-doubts
rose like a thunder cloud. "Love-making between us is impossible." As soon as he'd spat out
105

THE HARSH WORDS, he regretted them. She puled back, "Forgive me, but we cannot forget who

we are and where we are. Let's not delude ourselves, or lie to each other."

She stared with unblinking, moisture- filled eyes, and that blasted pain shot straight

through to his gut and caused a raw burn. She stopped his absent-minded rubs at his midriff.

"Are you suffering some sort of aliment in your abdomen?"

He bristled. "Of course not. I enjoy perfect health."

She lifted a brow. "Your veins may run with the bluest blood, but your human form suffers from the same frailties as the rest of us lower mortals. I've noticed that you rub your

stomach quite often. Perhaps you should consult a physician."

"Ridiculous charlatans. I'l not listen to another swindler promising to cure a simple

digestive disorder by bleeding me dry with leeches."

She gasped and put her hand to her mouth. "Oh, Max. You've already visited

physicians."

"It's nothing."

"You said no lies. I know an excelent physician, a good friend, who is presently in

London and would consult with you."

He started to shake his head, but she squeezed his arm and leaned forward until her nose

almost touched his. Ringlets brushed his naked chest and his senses filled with her essence.

He took her face between his hands and feasted on her sight and smell.

"God, you're beautiful," he murmured, before covering her soft lips with his. He growled

before unleashing his pent-up hunger and ravaging her mouth. Something drove him to brand

this woman, mark her as his, and feed from her goodness until the hollow gnawing in his gut

subsided; until he'd nourished his empty soul but blanked his tormented mind.

His busy hands couldn't get enough of the shape and curves of her body and, in a rush of

movements, he broke the kiss, lifted her shift up and over her head and threw it away.

Burying his face in the exposed skin between her breasts, he whimpered. "Christ, I want you

so much I can't think."

"Don't..." Her words broke off on a ragged sob, as he shifted an inch to the right and

swirled his tongue around the point of her nipple. "Oh, please, don't stop. I can't bear it."

With his left hand, he tormented that nipple, tugging and rolling while his teeth nibbled

at the other. From between her clenched teeth, she made a long and low keening sound that

echoed off the low ceiling, while her eyes squeezed shut and she bucked. He clung to her

nipples and prolonged her wild orgasm until her jerking movements subsided and she

slumped back across the stair treads. She whimpered several times when he rasped his teeth

106

BACK FROM HER NIPPLE, and he leaned on one elbow and watched as she drifted back to

consciousness.

His fingers trailed over her flat abdomen. "I've never seen a woman do that before."

Her eyes popped open. "Never?"

He shook his head. "Despite what you think, I'm not an unfeeling bastard. I ensure that

any woman I'm with enjoys our coupling, though I've never seen any woman respond so

explosively. You're so incredibly passionate."

"Ha! I'm not sure that's a good thing, because my nature often gets me into trouble."

"It also makes you fascinating. Your passion is the thing I love best—" Dammit, he was

treading in quicksand again, but if she sensed his dilemma, she ignored it.

"It's your turn, she said. "Do you want me to help with your boots?"

He imagined her sucking his toes between those sweet pink lips, and his erection jerked

so hard he almost doubled over where he sat.

Her touch on his arm was comforting. "Is it your stomach again?"

He gave a dry laugh. "Lower than that." He put her hand over the hard length inside his

breeches and she moved it in a small exploratory circle. He threw back his head and groaned.

"Yes, rub it like that."

He fumbled with his placket buttons and yanked back the flaps, but when her small hand

ran with tentative strokes from the tip to the base of his penis, he couldn't wait another

moment. He'd waited for years already and if he didn't put his cock inside her in the next few

minutes, he'd break down and beg her for release. Her hand slid away when he bent forward

to pull off his breeches and boots and toss them across the hallway.

She laughed and pointed. "No undergarments."

"Like you," he grinned, "I couldn't see any point, because I knew I'd be desperate to

have you as soon as I arrived. Mind you, I had to wait until my inquisitive valet left the room

so I could whip them off and dress again. If he knew I was going about in public without

drawers, he'd be so scandalized he'd quit."

She gave a gurgle of sympathetic laughter, and any earlier strain dissipated and sexual

tension filled the air. It felt good, even relaxed, but only for scant seconds until her inquiring

hand wrapped around his dick and she bent forward until he was certain her nose would rub against the twitching head. Then all hell would break loose.

"Carina." He tried to draw her back, but her warm breath brushed his mushroomed head

and his shaft quivered like an over-strung bow.

Her giggle started his and she did it again. Blew hot air up and down until his rod stood

107

PROUD AND HIGH and as hard as stone. Playful sex was another thing he'd never lingered to

enjoy, but he suddenly wanted to dally here for days and indulge all their fantasies.

"Lord have mercy," he moaned.

When she bent nearer his thicket of black hair, he couldn't see the focus of her

enthrallment, but her concealed mouth and tongue worshipped his ballocks, which had earlier

constricted to cannon balls, and he bucked off the wooden stair and almost sent her flying. He

took her arms and lifted her to face level and, driven by that same compulsion, laid her back

and began kissing the breath from her body.

Ions later, Carina pushed on his chest. "I need to breathe," she gasped, "and your kisses

rob me of air."

"I can't get enough of your mouth." His open-mouthed, wet kisses moved down. "Or the

softness of your skin."

He licked past her curvaceous belly and down to her groin, once more separating her legs

and reveling in the brilliance of her curly nest and wanting to beat his chest with pride at the

tell-tale wetness trickling down her thigh. He swiped two fingers through her cream and waited til he'd captured her gaze. A slow swipe of his tongue up his fingers and around the

tips had him moaning.

He held his fingers to her mouth. "Taste yourself. Like the sweetest cream."

After a moment of shocked silence, she sucked his fingers into her mouth in a rhythm

that had him groaning again. "Enough enough, minx, or I'l spil before I'm inside your sweet

body." He positioned the tip of his cock at her entrance and pushed inside an inch. Warm wet

woman enclosed him and urged him forward. "Tight. So frigging tight."

"It'l be al right. I remember from last time, a little pain at first." While she spoke, he

advanced, his twitching prick demanding that she open and let him claim her fully. Nothing

mattered except burying himself to the hilt inside her wet and welcoming body. The

opposition he encountered to each advance puzzled him, but his concentration was on the

awe-inspiring feeling of finally being inside the woman he'd dreamt of for years, and his

fuzzy mind couldn't grasp what she was teling him, either vocaly or with her body's slight

resistance.

"Do it. The pain won't last."

Her meaning penetrated his thick skul with the shock of a black-smith's hammer

pummeling his head. He stilled, sucked in a deep breath, and tried to lever himself off her

body, though pulling out of her would have taken a will a lot stronger than his.

"Christ almighty! You're tight and you expect pain."

108

. . .

THE REALIZATION SHOCKED him into retreat, but she wrapped her legs around his and clasped

her hands around his neck.

Inches from his face, she said, "Don't dare leave me. I know what your dammed honor is

screaming at you to do and, yes, I feel tight, and, yes, I expect pain. For exactly the reason

you assume."

"No, no, no."

"I've had no man inside my body apart from you."

While he shook his head and tried to rattle some sense into his addled brain, he held his

lower body motionless. His prick twitched and jerked and urged him to race to the finish line,

and he had to draw on every facet of his fabled control.

"But why? You let me think...There were two others, discounting your husband as he

was impotent." He hissed out a breath when she wiggled beneath him. "For Christ's sake,

don't move."

"I'm sorry I misled you. You believed they'd bedded me, the same as you."

"Of course I did, and you did nothing to correct that lie." With a sigh, he touched his

forehead to hers. "Though I thank heaven they didn't touch you. I've tormented myself with

visions of your nights with them and what they may have demanded in exchange for their

money."

"You thought they'd believed the Earl's claims about my virginity?" At his nod, she

continued, "If I'd told you the truth, you might have refused to help me find them." She put a finger to his lips. "Please, later. Not now."

Between her plea and his body's screaming need, his questions would have to wait,

though he couldn't forget that this lady and her innate sexuality belonged solely to him. She

lifted her hips and pushed towards him, and he responded the only way he could, by giving

them what they wanted. Longer thrusts pushed him higher into her tight passage and he

worried that, despite her soft, wet, wil ingness, he'd cause her pain.

Her frantic cries became louder each time he rammed his length home, time after time,

until nothing existed except two sweat-dampened torsos slapping and sliding as two fraught

people fought for release. His balls pulled tighter and he released with an unstoppable spurt

high in her body.

Carina screamed, a loud, uncontrolled, fish-wife's screech, that rolled on and on,

vibrating against his heaving chest and overriding his own more strangled noises. Her entire

body stiffened and bucked one last time, her back arching up to claim him as her mate and

her inner muscles squeezing him dry of every last drop of seed. Her hot tight clamping

109

PROLONGED his own shuddering climax and he spurted in an endless stream before sobbing

with exhaustion.

He slumped, bewildered and spent, over her quaking form. She nuzzled his face without opening her eyes and, guided by instinct, he met her lips with the softest of kisses. Slow,

tender touches and gentle, open-mouthed kisses made time stand still, and it was some time

before he thought about the fusion of their lower bodies. His deflated member slipped out and

pressed between their entwined legs. They lay in a sweaty jumble that he was loathe to

untangle, though cool air sent shivers rippling across her damp skin.

He made a half-hearted attempt at relieving her of his weight. "Carina." She shook her

head against his shoulder and muttered, "No, no, no." Her reluctance to move pleased him,

but the dim light filtering down the hall indicated a lot of time had passed.

"Sweetheart," he tried again, "this floor is cold and we need to stand."

Despite his disinclination to disturb the peace of their small paradise, he pulled away and

began gathering clothes. In a drowsy move, she flopped one arm above her head in a

nonchalant pose that sent blood rushing south to his groin and, in seconds, his mouth went

dry and his heart raced. He dropped to his knees and stared with a puzzled frown.

He soothed the frown lines with his fingers. "You'll think me insane, but when you

stretch like that you resemble the sun rising in summer."

She shifted and peered at her bared flesh, before giving him another puzzled look. The

flickering lamp-light couldn't hide the pink flush around her navel or the rosy glow spreading

upwards to her cheeks. She snatched the shirt out of his hand and covered herself.

"No, let me show you."

He tossed the shirt away and touched her hair. "The red arc of the morning sun starts

here." His fingers trailed a path down her neck, over her shoulder, and circled her breast until

her nipples stood to attention. Her breath hitched and her back lifted to chase his finger.

"There," he said, circling her nipple but never quite touching. "A crimson line goes from

top to bottom, like the sun moving across the day." He walked his fingers over the hollow of

her hip. "Ends here." Two fingers slid over her mound, pushed through sodden curls, slipped

inside and hooked back.

Her eyes went wide and her mouth opened to a silent scream. Partly for her enjoyment

but mostly for his, he manipulated that overly-sensitive spot until she writhed under his

fingers, as if he was a puppet master tugging at her strings in command. When he started to

withdraw, she clenched her knees and held his hand there while she panted for breath. Both

hands held his arm in place.

110

"I WAS GOING to show you the other colors." His free hand moved over her stomach. "A

line of purest white leads from your toes to your plump thighs."

"Plump!" The first word she'd spoken ended with a glare. He gentled her until she lay

back and he could continue his explorations. "Next time, I'l worship your adorable thighs.

But now, a white blaze rests beneath your outer fiery and goes up and over the mountains to disappear."

Her breaths were shallow pants and her eyes fixed on his hands. He felt as powerful as a

king, and the sight of her spread at his mercy, like a virginal sacrifice before a demi-god,

shortened his breathing and tightened his chest. He shuddered and fought the compulsion to

spread himself across her smaller feminine form and take her again, and again, an obsession

with a cost much higher than paying an escort to relieve his physical urges.

Wishing he could possess this lady and keep her for al time was nonsensical. "No, no,

no."

"What's wrong?"

He stared at the ceiling and its ornate plasterwork rather than meet her gaze, and even

debated if he could live with himself if he prolonged their relationship and hoped his bride to

be didn't learn his secrets. "Wanting things that are impossible."

Carina sat up, scrunching herself into the step and glancing around for something to

cover her nakedness. "Your change in behavior is scaring me."

He sighed. "I was caught up in a romantic fantasy. One that can never happen."

Her shoulders slumped. "I know." She gave him an impish grin. "But I didn't bank you

being so poetic and romantic. Light-hearted."

"Unfortunately, bubbles of happiness drift out of reach, or burst."

"If you've such a pessimist, why marry at al and subject Alice to your misery?"

He shrugged. "I can't imagine how you remain so optimistic."

"I have to believe that I can give my sisters a rosier future."

He puled her close and wrapped his arms around her smal body. "And when I'm with you, I'm optimistic enough to perceive a better future for both of us."

Putting his arms beneath her knees, he lifted her and strode down the hall. With a fire

burning, the drawing room was a cozier option, and nothing to do with sparing her the

embarrassment of becoming another in the line of women who'd used the bed upstairs. He

laid her on the plush carpet before the fire and waggled his brows mischievously.

"Where was I with my sunrise painting?" Using both hands, he sketched the arcs from

top to toe and dalied in every crease and hollow. "Ah, yes, stunning white hiding beneath

III

BEAUTIFUL RED. Scarlet flashes are scandalous and white streaks are virginal, while pink

indicates an underlying modesty. You've never given your naked body to any man except

your past and current lover—me—who gives you so much pleasure that you'l beg to

continue our affair."

They stared at each other in tense silence. "I'm sorry, Carina. I was carried away with

my own fantasies and something that we both know can't happen."

"Any longer and rumors wil fly, and people we care about wil be hurt."

"Yes, thank you for being sensible when I keep forgetting myself." He lowered his head

to her nipple and nibbled it, drawing it out through his teeth until she giggled.

"And my nipple, kind artiste, what does it represent in the

sunrise?"

"These two delightful buds represent your body's strong desire for sex. They protrude in

lustful anticipation while waiting for the perfect lover, again me, who will tease and taunt

them towards fulfillment."

He lifted her breasts higher and gave a light flick with his tongue over each bud, so she

could see the effect of his words on her nipples. "Uh, uh," he said, when she demandingly

arched up off the carpet. "I've something in mind to complete our painting."

"You're torturing me. Our scheduled hour must be wel past, so could you please hurry."

She scowled. "Before I go mad." She puled his head down for a kiss and took his mouth with

hunger and impatience.

He stretched full length between her legs and wriggled forward, so her legs widened and

his mouth blew heat over her curls and folds. Red curls lifted and fluttered, and he murmured,

"So pretty, little Carrot-top."

She gave a shocked gasp and tried to close her knees, but he soothed her with soft

murmurs and light touches until they dropped open. Her groans began the moment he pushed

two fingers past her swollen folds and inside her warm passage. Moisture trickled over his

fingers, the flow increasing as he pushed in and out in a steady rhythm that demanded she

give herself over to sensation and release the orgasms that hovered just out of her reach.

"Oh, Carina, I wish you could see yourself. Shiny and red, and wet, and mine." He ran his tongue up each thigh and between his fingers, keeping up a slow insistent pressure on

each side of her throbbing centre.

"Max!" She sounded shocked when his tongue replaced his fingers, and burrowed inside

and lapped at her wetness. "Surely only a true courtesans al ow that."

He laughed but didn't move from his position of worship, instead giving three swift

circular lashes with his tongue. "Perhaps I should tel you then that, though I've tasted

112

WOMEN BEFORE, I've never wanted to hold up a mirror and share this erotic view with any

mistresses. And I've never lingered and licked the juices flowing down their legs, and then

gone back for more and more."

He swirled his tongue around her clitoris and she jumped. "And there's never been

another woman who gushes like a waterfall after a storm when my tongue is inside her. No

light skirt has ever responded to the things I've done as naturally, or as sexily, as you."

"Oh!" She slammed her knees together and jolted upright.

"Ouch! That hurt." He rubbed at his imaginary wounds, but burst into fits of laughter at

her horrified expression. "If you could see... Stop!"

She swatted wildly at his head with one hand, but he took it and toppled her down to

meet him.

"How dare you! Do you mean you've... done things to me... that...?"

He rolled her to her back, covered her and clasped her hands above her head. He rocked

back and forth a little and groaned. His erection jerked against her stomach, insistent and

urgent, while he struggled to explain himself.

"I've no excuse for my outlandish behavior, other than being with you makes me crazy

and I want to do things to you, and with you, that I've never dreamed of with other women.

Do you understand?"

"Yes." She stroked his hair. "I always understand because it's as if we're—"

"Connected."

She nodded. "A dangerous connection for us both."

"I know."

He kissed her long and hard, pouring all his yearnings into her mouth and, afterwards,

into her body. Words couldn't be spoken, but he wanted her to know that deep down he

wished he could give more and promise more. Their second bout of sex was unhurried and

the incessant ticking of the mantle clock was all but ignored, despite Max unconsciously

timing his thrusts to the ticking of the second hand as they counted off the hours.

Each wet slap sounded joyously and each stolen moment a priceless memory, though the

lingering farewell on the doorstep sliced like a knife blade.

"Thank you," she murmured, as she climbed into the carriage.

He closed the door and said, "We're not finished, Carina. We stil have time."

She shook her head and turned her face away.

He stood outside the cottage and made himself, and the heavens, a promise. "One way or

another, my sweet, you belong to me and I will have you again."

11

Carina let herself into Woods House with her key. She'd instructed the servants to not wait up and, cowardly, she'd left Gertie to explain that she was visiting an old friend.

The Duke's coachman had agreed to put her down at the quietest corner of the square, but sneaking into her house carried risks, grave risks. As she was a rich widow, the gossipmongers would allow more leeway than they would have for an unmarried woman.

However a scandal could ruin her sisters' chances with suitable gentlemen. The sooner Georgie and Lucy were married and under the protection of husbands, the less chance there'd be for their stepbrother to seize control. After enduring so many miserable years, surely they'd earned a little happiness?

She wandered upstairs to her sitting room, reliving each satiating moment of her evening and unable to believe that, for once, she hadn't been dreaming. Their time together had been

amazing and far better than her first night with Max, when she'd been an ignorant adolescent.

But disillusioned widows had no right to believe in fairytales, handsome princes or in love.

An affair was a short term arrangement, and she and Max had different long term objectives.

Max would marry his child-like bride, she'd see her sisters were well-situated and then begin

her travels. Gertie borrowed books from the circulating library and read about the exotic ports

they planned to visit.

She walked to the sideboard to pour herself a tot of brandy and heard a soft knock.

"Come in, Gertie."

Her friend would want to reassure herself that Carina had survived the evening

unscathed. Gertie accepted a small glass of brandy too and they sank into the fireside chairs

to slowly sip their drinks, a habitual ritual enjoyed by two close friends.

"Wel? Don't keep me in suspense. Are you alright?"

Carina nodded. "Max would never hurt me, nor anyone else." Max had reintroduced her

to passion with such exquisite care that she felt empowered, and yet sad. "He has his faults:

smugness and pompousness."

Gertie chuckled. "Self-righteousness about his unbeatable heritage."

"Pig-headedness.

Gertie laughed. "And his blind faith in Augustus's teachings. And yet..."

114

. . .

CARINA NODDED HER AGREEMENT. "Despite his upbringing, ingrained decency won't alow

him to ignore injustice, and he'd defend a woman with his life."

"Ah, I see." Gertie stared into her glass.

Carina narrowed her gaze at her friend. Gertie was a shrewd judge of character and an

astute observer of human nature; little escaped her notice.

"What do you see?" Though Carina could predict the answer.

"Max treated you wel this evening, so you couldn't blame him for anything, or

everything." She arched a brow. "Am I correct?"

Carina snorted. "Blast you, yes. I wish I wasn't so transparent."

"Never fear, your inner thoughts are only decipherable to me and your sisters."

Carina smiled. "After tonight, you could possibly add one more name to that list."

"The Duke of Stirkton?"

She nodded. "He read my thoughts and anticipated my every wish. It was a trifle

disconcerting, though rather pleasing. Which worries me, because I don't know how to resist

a man intent on pleasuring me."

"Pleasuring? What a delicious thought. Now, tel me al, so I may live vicariously

through you and what was obviously a passion-filled evening."

Carina shook her head. "No, no, no. It would be unladylike to reveal any intimate details,

though I wil say this." She sighed. "Max is a very skil ful lover. His experiences with the

prostitutes his grandfather selected—"

"And his recent mistresses."

Carina scowled. She dismissed Max's encounters with earlier prostitutes because he'd

had no choice, but imagining him with talented courtesans in their cottage was painful. No, she must think of it as the Duke's Brent Street house and not *their* cottage, despite her

stomach squirming at the notion of her duke with any other lover.

When she'd tried to rise and dress, he'd enticed her back to the carpet for one last

interlude and she'd taken little persuading to make love with him one more time. No matter

how much she tried to deny it, they hadn't had sex. They'd made love. And that catastrophic

knowledge had stunned them both to silence afterwards. She'd donned her clothing in a

haphazard rush and had scurried out to his waiting carriage.

She stared into the fire and thought of the nameless parade of women who'd walked on

that carpet and felt unclean. She shook her head. "No!"

To survive a month, she needed to harden her heart. At this very moment, Max was

certain to be doing the same thing, while berating himself for letting down his guard.

115

"A penny for them." Gertie had a smal knowing smile on her face.

"Not worth a penny."

"Are they worth an introductions for your sisters? Take care that Stirkton's price doesn't

prove too costly, because I fear he may have to hurt you in order to protect others."

"What is al this doom and gloom? Has something happened?"

Gertie took a long swallow of brandy and then fussed over placing her glass on the side

table. "Your stepbrother came here tonight."

"Peter? Oh, no. What did he want?"

"To speak with you on a matter of urgency. I informed him you were out with friends

and wouldn't return until very late."

"Did he ask to speak to Georgie and Lucy?"

"Yes, but I said they'd retired early after draining social outings. I'm not sure if he

believed me, but he'l most likely be back. He was adamant that he'd speak with you."

"This can't be good. I hoped to avoid him until the girls had been introduced to a wide

circle of gentlemen."

"Hm. And you wanted more time to spend with Stirkton."

"If I don't uphold my part of our bargain, he'l be entitled to break his promise and I'l

never find the hidden documents, nor locate the two men."

Gertie sighed, "I've said this before, but perhaps this is a sign to forget finding those

men. Max was your first lover and you now have more good memories of being with him."

"I have wonderful memories, but I'm also too close to verifying the next man on the list

to abandon my search."

"Your suspicions are shocking." She shuddered. "I can't bring myself to believe it. The

idea sickens me. But you've enough problems right here, without inviting more trouble."

"I've no intention of stirring up trouble or disrupting their lives. It's simply to confirm

what happened and why those two particular men were chosen."

"For the same reason Max was chosen. Money, four times over. The Earl was renowned

for his greed."

"And his perversions."

"Thankfully, his perversions were only known to a few people."

"I stil wonder how Augustus knew of the Earl's plan for an heir while keeping his

impotence secret." She grinned. "Perhaps they collided while peeping like lecherous

schoolboys through the knotholes in the same brothel wal?"

Gertie giggled. "That's a dreadful thought to take to bed. We'l have nightmares."

116

CARINA LINKED arms with her friend and, still giggling, they walked to their bedchambers.

The best way to cope with memories of what her husband did was to trivialize it and laugh.

Gertie constantly reprimanded her for dwelling on the past, but until she'd spoken with

the two men who'd paid an enormous amount to spend a night with her, the past would

continue to haunt her. Once she'd confronted them and decided they didn't threaten her

safety she'd move on, though curiosity would drive her to ask questions.

Were they bullied into spending a night with her the way Max had been pressured? And

if so, by whom? Augustus was an evil man, who would have threatened retribution on either

her, the Earl or the hapless inn keeper. Though blaming Augustus didn't mean she'd

completely absolved Max.

Gertie labeled it her morbid obsession, but she couldn't rest until she knew if paying for

her virginity had been nothing more than a lark for two men of good breeding, or if there had

been more sinister reasons? The first gentleman—the youngest—had family, who'd thought to browbeat him into foregoing a vow of chastity until he married. After climbing into the

inn's bed, the two young innocents had clung together and whispered their dreams and fears.

Joseph had planned to be a country minister who tended his flock, took a sweet wife and

produced a brood of children. If he'd stuck to his plan, he'd have been easy to forgive, and no

doubt his church would have appreciated a gift of a new roof or more bedrooms added to the

vicarage to house his numerous offspring. A cloud of doubt hovered over the other one, as

she was unsure how she'd feel or react.

An hour later, Carina tossed and turned in her bed as her mind and body recal ed Max's

whispered words and the feel of his hands caressing, teasing and arousing. She longed for his

muscled heat to be pressed against her, skin to skin, and to feel his warm breath hovering

around her neck and ears. Her nipples tightened at the thought of his tongue wetly lashing

them, over and over. She groaned.

If one night in his arms disturbed her sleep and made her yearn for the forbidden, she'd

be a wreck after weeks with a man who'd promised to teach her lovemaking skils from Asia,

where men and women routinely reached the highest peaks of pleasure. A young girl's

adoration for a virile lover instead of a fumbling old man was one thing, but tumbling time

after time into Max's waiting arms was another. Part of her wanted to explore the desire that

rose between them every time they were together, and to understand the joy Gertie had

experienced with her husband for many years.

After restless sleep, she went downstairs to join the others for breakfast. Lucy, as usual,

was chattering a mile a minute about their planned activities and guessing which gentlemen

117

THEY MIGHT ENCOUNTER on their morning excursions. As a rule, Georgie was more subdued. But

today she smiled as she had when a child, openly and sunnily, as if she'd shrugged off her

previous melancholy and happily welcomed the new day.

Carina bent to kiss her sister's cheek and Georgie surprised her by reaching back to pat

her cheek. The returned touch by her sister, who had avoided all physical contact for so long,

gave Carina heart. Perhaps launching Georgie in London had been the right thing to do, and

she thanked God that she and Gertie had made the right decision. And with Georgie staying

at Woods House, she was out of Peter's reach for the time being.

Carina slid into her seat and forked up her breakfast with a suddenly increased appetite.

More than half her plate of eggs and sausages had disappeared before she realized that she

was being watched. "What is it?" She frowned when Gertie smirked, Lucy giggled and

Georgie smiled.

"You've not eaten such a hearty breakfast for some time," Lucy said with wide-eyed

innocence. "Your evening with your friend must have been very energetic."

Carina choked and Gertie laughed behind her napkin. Lucy and Georgie exchanged

puzzled glances, until Gertie finally came to her rescue.

"Carina must have *danced* for several hours to build up such an appetite." She glanced at

her friend. "We're glad you're feeling more like your old self, because we've been worried

about you."

"About me?" Carina was stunned.

Georgie spoke first, an unusual occurrence. "You've been so busy fretting over us, that

you've worn yourself to a frazzle. And with the preparations for the bals Max has arranged,

you've barely eaten enough to keep a sparrow alive."

"You're thinner." Lucy gave Carina's figure an assessing look.

Before Carina could voice her protest, the butler announced a caller. She picked up the

embossed card from the salver and felt an acute premonition of danger.

"Georgie, Lucy," she said, trying to sound calm, "our stepbrother is here."

Georgie gasped and paled, and Lucy fidgeted. Carina walked to Georgie's chair and

gently laid her hands on her sister's shoulders. "I'l not alow Peter to take you away."

Lucy's red face was a startling contrast to Georgie's palor. "Peter can't force me to

marry an old man like he did you, can he?" Her agitated gaze swung back and forth between

Carina and Gertie. "No, no, I won't do it."

Gertie put her arms around Lucy. "There, there, pet. Nothing bad is going to happen,

because we won't alow it."

118

THE FOUR WOMEN linked arms and walked into the drawing room with their heads held high. Peter stopped his pacing and scrutinized each of them in turn. By the displeased

expression on his face, they'd once again failed to meet his lofty expectations.

"Gertrude," he snapped. "You're stil in residence. Haven't you outstayed your

welcome?"

Carina bristled, but Peter had never been able to intimidate Gertie.

Her friend bobbed a quick curtsy. "Lord Lindsay, always a pleasure to see you."

Carina stepped towards Peter and scowled. "Hold your tongue, Peter. Mrs. Carlyle is my

guest and the length of time she resides with me is none of your concern."

"Everything you do is my concern. I am the head of this family."

Carina clenched her fists into the sides of her skirt. "May I remind you, sir, that I'm a

widow with my own income and therefore not dependent upon you."

He glared at her. "Unfortunately, Georgiana isn't as rich as you and Lucille is unmarried.

I'm taking them home. Girls, go and pack your belongings."

"No." Carina stood, hands on hips, and looked Peter in the eye, knowing that cowards

like their stepbrother couldn't deal with people who stood up to him. Georgie moved behind

her and Carina could feel her tremble when she pressed against her back.

Brave Lucy faced her stepbrother. "I shal remain with Carina. The Duke is coming

here."

"Huh!" Peter ignored Carina and addressed the girls, who he saw as easier targets. "I imagine you're referring to the Duke of Stirkton. That haughty brute seen associating with

you for the last two weeks."

Georgie's eyes were round with terror, but she stepped out from behind Carina. "The

Duke is not a brute. He is a gentle and considerate man."

"You're trailing after him because he's rich. Acting like sycophants and embarrassing

our family, and after al I've done for you."

"You've done nothing for us," Lucy said, pointing her finger at Peter. "Apart from

treating us like servants and...stealing our dowries."

Carina moved to shield the girls. The look in Peter's eyes was threatening and she'd seen

it before. "They're not going with you, Peter. They're under my protection."

"Your protection? Rubbish! They belong to me."

"No," Lucy pushed forward again. "Georgie and I are staying here at Woods House. If

you try to make us leave, we'l —"

"What can you do?" Peter sneered. "Lock yourselves in your bedchamber? Report me to

119

A MAGISTRATE?" He picked up a statuette of a shepherdess from the mantle and tipped it over to

read the maker's name. "Nothing but the best for the Countess of Dorchester. This little

trinket wil make a nice gift to quiet my nagging spouse. Something to satisfy her until I..."

Carina snatched the porcelain out of his hands. "Until you what, Peter? Sel Georgie for a

second time? Promise Lucy to a rich old letch?"

Lucy shook her head. "No, you'll not decide whom I marry.

Carina, tel him." Lucy

wrapped her hands around Carina's arm. "We'l tel the Duke and he'l stop Peter."

"Wel , Lucille," Peter said as he ran his hands over another porcelain figurine.

"Unfortunately for you and your sister, the Duke has no say in the matter. I'l decide who you

marry, and when."

"To the contrary," a deep voice said from the doorway. "The Countess requested my

assistance in presenting her sisters in society, and I take those responsibilities seriously."

"Max," Georgie cried in relief. To their astonishment and most of al, Max's, Georgie

ran around the table and threw herself into his arms.

His arms closed around her and held her tucked under his chin for a few moments. He

gently unwound her arms before speaking. "Georgie, my betrothed is looking forward to your

shopping outing, so perhaps you should go upstairs and prepare. You wouldn't wish to be

late."

Georgie smiled at Max. "I'm so looking forward to our morning together." With a little

wave, she flitted out the door, leaving Carina and Gertie staring at her retreating back.

Lucy looked awed by her sister's calm composure. She turned to Max. "Please, I need to

stay here with Carina. I want to see you and Alice every day."

"Of course, Lucy. Until your sister releases me from my promise, I hold myself

personally accountable for your well-being."

Peter's face contorted with anger, and Carina knew he wouldn't let the presence of a powerful duke stop him from unleashing his temper. She moved to stand one step in front of

the stepbrother she loathed and placed her palm squarely on his chest.

"The Duke of Stirkton kindly offered to assist me in introducing our sisters to society.

We owe him our gratitude."

Peter pushed her hand aside and sneered. "You're naïve if you believe a man like

Stirkton offered to help without expecting something in return." He moved to face Max. "I

know your reputation, Stirkton, and you're not known for helping women. Quite the opposite,

in fact."

Carina and Gertie both gasped. "Peter," Carina said. His recent behavior had shown a

120

DISREGARD FOR SOCIAL NICETIES, but to deliberately insult a duke was beyond appalling. She tried

to move between the two men. "His Grace is a friend and my guest, so please remember your

manners."

Max laid a hand on her arm and gave her a smal smile before edging her aside. "Lady

Dorchester, please do not take offence on my account. I, in return, am aware of the reputation

of Lord Lindsay." He held her arm so she couldn't move in front of him. "So I expect nothing

more of him."

"No, please stop," Carina said. "This isn't necessary. Max, perhaps I speak to Peter

alone."

Peter nodded. "I prefer speaking to my sister in private."

"Ah, but I prefer that the Countess has a friend supporting her." Max's cool tone was at

variance with his warrior-like stare. "Though I've no wish to interfere in family matters."

"Then go away," Peter said. He pointed at Gertie. "And you can leave, too. This is a

family matter."

Carina puled away from Max and nodded to Gertie. "I'm fine. Gertie, could you see if

the girls are ready so His Grace's horse aren't kept standing."

Gertie shot Peter a look of pure hatred and left the room.

Max ignored Peter. "Countess, I'd like to hear what Lindsay plans for your sisters, as I

feel responsible for al of you while you're in town."

Peter sneered. "Everyone can see what you feel towards my elder sister."

"My arrangements with the Countess are between the lady and me, and no one else."

Carina knew Max's temper had risen to match Peter's. "But, Lindsay, we were discussing the

younger ladies, Georgiana and Lucille."

"Peter, tel me what you want. I've no secrets from Max."

"Huh! You mean he's curried favor with you and ingratiated himself into the household.

But I hope to hel you've not succumbed to Stirkton, because he's a known womanizer. He

buys courtesans and whores the way he buys cravats." He looked Carina up and down. "He's

only after you for one thing. The only thing women are useful for."

Max stood less than an arm's length from Peter. "Not one more word, Lindsey. I'm an

excellent shot and if you malign Lady Dorchester, or me, one more time, my seconds will be

paying you a visit."

Peter looked momentarily taken aback, as he was unused to facing an opponent of the

same gender, one who seriously outweighed him in power and strength, but conceit wouldn't

let him back down. "I've made plans for my sisters."

121

"Stepsisters!"

Peter ignored her. "It's of no consequence to me whether you stay or leave."

Max walked to the closest armchair and sprawled across it in a pose of elegant

indifference, yet he was fully alert and his presence boosted her confidence. In years past,

she'd not been able to stand up to Peter's bullying, but her title and wealth had elevated her

above him and his grasping wife.

"Georgiana and Lucille are happy to stay with me and nothing would be achieved by

disrupting them. They can live here until they marry, or until I return to the country."

"No, they're coming back with me. I've gone to a lot of trouble to find them husbands.

And those men are anxious to become acquainted with their brides."

"You'll not do that to them." Carina rushed towards him. You forced me into marriage

when I was far too young. You did the same to Georgie, and look what happened. We both

suffered in those miserable marriages."

"Suffered? You were married to titled gentlemen. And you, my dear, inherited a lot of

money. How is that suffering?"

"You know how badly Georgie was treated by Lumley's family." She growled. "And

you, more than anyone, know the type of man I married. You sold a sixteen-year-old girl to a

man with known perversions. I won't alow you to do it to Lucy."

Peter laughed. "How wil you stop me? I'm Lucy's legal guardian. Georgiana's husband

is dead, a pattern for the Griffith sisters, and as she has no money, it falls to me as head of the

family to arrange her second marriage."

He picked up the figurine again, and stared at her calculatingly. Max watched, fingers

pressed together, and his silent presence comforted her and stiffened her backbone.

"Unless," Peter said smugly, "you wish to spare one of your sisters."

"How?"

"You could stand in for one of you sisters and marry the man I've chosen."

Max leapt to his feet, but she put out her hand to stop him. "I'l never marry again."

"So you've said, but I know how devoted you are to your sisters. You'd do anything to

save them from more unhappiness. So tell me, will you be able to cling to your vow when

one of your sisters is standing at the altar beside a man you dislike?" He snickered. "Or wil

you overcome your own squeamishness about men and stand up in their place."

"There's no rush for either of them to marry. They're being introduced to the ton slowly

and they're already making friends."

"Huh! I don't want them making friends. I need them to marry wel so I can recoup the

122

MONEY I'VE WASTED SUPPORTING you three ungrateful girls al your lives."

"That's ridiculous. We were no longer girls when our mother married your father.

Georgie and I spent very few years in your house before you arranged our disastrous

marriages. It wasn't our fault that you spent our dowries before we debuted."

"Then Lucille should be grateful that I've alowed her longer before selecting her

husband and arranging contracts."

"Who with?" Max's barked question made Carina and Peter jump.

She should have insisted Max left before they aired their dirty linen, but she'd been

relieved to have someone other than Gertie stand by her during Peter's barrage.

"Max, perhaps Peter and I should discuss this by ourselves."

Max smiled at her before, once again, standing face to face with Peter. "I ask again, who

is the man?" His tone was cold enough to freeze a pond.

"None of your business, Stirkton. This is between me and my sisters."

"Step-sisters," Carina said, though neither man looked at her.

Max kept his frosty stare fixed on Peter. "Either you tel me his name, Lindsay, or I'l

find out by other means." Carina shivered, but Peter was blind to the danger. "Though I'm

warning you, Lindsay. You don't want me as your enemy. I can, and I wil, make life very

unpleasant for you and your wife, financially and socialy."

Peter frowned. His arrogant belief that no one could stop him using the women in his family as pawns whenever he needed to pay gambling debts wouldn't alow him to back

down. Though Peter knew Max had the power to carry out his threats.

He shrugged. "Very wel. Lucille wil marry Baron Mitchell."

"Mitchell."

Max sounded appalled, and Carina's anxiety ratcheted up several more notches. "Who

...who is he, Max?"

"A man three times Lucy's age and rumored to be riddled with the pox."

Carina whacked Peter's chest. "Not even you could do something so vile. Not to your

own sister." Peter grabbed her arm before she could hit him again and she stiffened.

Though she didn't suffer Georgie's fear of being touched by a man, she loathed her

stepbrother, and having her arm held by him made her feel as helpless as when he'd sold her

to the Earl. She pulled out of Peter's grip before Max swung at him with the fist he'd pul ed

back in readiness. She took Max's hand and held it at her side, earning them both another of

Peter's sneers.

"As you've so often reminded me, Carina, we're only linked because of our unthinking

123

PARENTS. We've no blood relationship, and therefore I don't feel guilty about handing over

three troublesome women to whichever men can best compensate me. The Baron wants to

sight Lucille and then the papers wil be signed."

"What does he want? To check her teeth and hooves?"

Peter shrugged. "Or that she'l warm his bed nicely and that her hips are wide enough to

carry his children."

"You're teling lies," Max said. "The pox means that the Baron cannot bed a woman, nor

can he sire a child. He's outlived three wives, yet has no offspring."

"Peter, no." Carina wrapped her arms around her stomach and shook her head. "I won't

let you do the same thing to Lucy as you did to me." She took Max's arm and turned him

towards the door. "Please wait outside. I need a few minutes alone with Peter."

Carina tugged Max forward, but he'd dug in his heels and wouldn't budge.

"I'm not leaving you alone with him, Carina. Not for a minute."

Fortunately for Carina—though unfortunately for Max—Georgie and Lucy tripped

down the stairs and straight towards Max. They were dressed ready for their outing and Max

had no choice but to escort the girls to his coach.

He whispered so the girls wouldn't overhear. "Carina, Lindsay's plans are despicable.

Let me deal with him."

"His plans are always despicable, Max, but this time I'l fight him tooth and nail. I know

what to do and it'l be easier to convince him without anyone else around."

"Very wel, but I'l be back as soon as I've delivered the girls into safe hands." He

looked back and glared at Peter. "I want them out of Lindsay's conniving grasp first."

"Trust me. Lucy wil never go to the Baron."

"What can you do to stop it?"

Carina stayed silent and Max tilted her face up to meet his eyes, trying to read her thoughts. He shook his head. "No. Don't even think of taking Lucille's place. I'l marry you

myself before I'd let the Baron touch you."

Carina straightened. "You forget yourself, Your Grace. You're already betrothed."

Max sucked in a harsh breath, and she knew he'd indeed forgotten his own situation for a

moment. She didn't want him involved any further, because Peter's disgusting schemes

dirtied everything and everyone and Max had his future planned.

"I'l be back." He sketched a quick nod and went to the carriage.

Gertie hovered near the door. "I won't leave you alone with that man, Carina." She

waved her hand towards where Peter waited. "We stil don't know how involved he was in

124

THE PAST. Nor his intentions towards you in the future. "

Carina put her hand on her friend's arm. "He isn't going to harm any of us again. I'l

make sure of that."

She held her head high and walked back to Peter. He was lounging on the settee and

flicking the pages of a book with his usual insolence and disregard for her belongings. If

she'd left him in her study, he'd have rifled through her account books and letters as if he had

the right.

"We must reach an understanding. Several eligible gentlemen have shown interest in the

girls. Young and respectable men who'd treat them with care. Wouldn't you rather they were

happy than sharing a bed with an old or diseased man?"

"That's where you and I have always differed." He shrugged. "I don't give a damn about

happiness. Only money. But to prove that I'm not an unfeeling monster, like Stirkton, I'l

wait two weeks. If the girls don't bring two men up to scratch, men who can be trusted to pay

off my debts without squabble, all three of you will wed whomsoever I dictate. And if you

resist, I'l tel the world that you gave yourself to four different men while you were married

to the Earl."

"You bastard! That's not true, and you know it."

He shrugged. "You and I may know the truth, but the stories I tel wil be far juicier and

the gossips will enjoy spreading them across every part of England. Even your country

neighbors wil shun you when you return there."

"I had no part in the Earl's arrangements and you can't prove otherwise."

"Ah, but I do have proof. One of those men at the inn told me what happened. Even how

much he paid the man who arranged the transaction. Your husband, I presume."

Peter might be guessing in the hope that she'd share more information, but she couldn't

be certain how much he knew and one small slip could land her in prison.

"The Earl told me nothing of his business affairs."

His laugh was that mad sound again and shivers ran down her spine. "That's the irony,

isn't it? Your husband wasn't incapable of having affairs. The man was impotent."

She didn't flinch and held herself rigidly, so not even the flicker of an eyelash would

give her away. Peter thrived on weakness, but he'd not find any in her these days.

"Was he? I was unaware of any problems."

Peter frowned. Good, play the ignorant wife and leave him scrambling.

"Are you saying that he wasn't impotent with you, when he couldn't raise a cockstand at

al with other women?"

125

HER TURN TO SHRUG. "You had the Earl investigated. What did your spies tel you?"

"They said he couldn't sire children. That's why he paid so much money for you. Why I

arranged––"

"Arranged what?"

The ghastly suspicion lurking in her mind for several months solidified. No, please, not

even Peter could be so depraved. But she knew better. Gambling held him in its grip, and no

deed was too sordid if it put money back in his pockets and allowed him to return to the hells

and lose even more money.

He tugged at his coat cuffs and refused to meet her eyes. "Arrangements such as those

are between men. Women have no say in what we decide."

Nausea roiled in her stomach and bile rose to her throat. "Men such as the Earl?"

He looked her over from head to toe, more ogling than appreciating, and her skin

crawled. She desperately wanted to question him further, but she dared not give Peter a hint

of her own increasing conviction that he'd taken part in, or organized, the dealings at the inn.

By remaining close-lipped, he'd assume she was another fearful female who'd obeyed her

husband without question. Though her growing horror at being near him would soon disrupt

her composure, and she'd leap up, grab his neck and squeeze until there was no breath left in

him. The urge to do him harm was becoming so insistent that she sat on her hands. If she

surrendered to violence now, she'd never get the last piece of the puzzle.

Slowly and carefully, she reminded herself. Don't reveal your hand and frighten away

the main players in this drama. Soon the curtain would fall on this chapter and, if luck was on

her side, she and her sisters would be free to start new lives. She rose to her feet, hoping Peter

would leave. But the bastard stayed seated and ignored Gertie's knock.

"Carina, we're expected at midday for luncheon and it's now a quarter of the hour."

She nodded, thanking Gertie silently for rescuing her before she murdered Peter and

ruined their chances of uncovering everything he'd done. Her investigators were shadowing

Peter, learning how much he owed and who he expected to save him from debt. Until this

morning, however, no one had realized that he'd go so far as to toss Lucy to a pox-ridden

baron, like feeding fresh meat to a crippled lion.

"Thank you, Gertie. Lord Lindsay is leaving."

Peter scowled but only said, "Two weeks. No more."

While Gertie ensured that Peter left, Carina slumped onto the settee and gave in to the

trembling she'd hidden from Peter. Gertie poured wine, and Carina clasped the glass tightly

and took three large gulps.

126

"Is he doing what we predicted?" Gertie asked.

"Yes, everything. My informants believe he's picked his next guls and is desperate to

get hold of their money. Despite being prepared, I was shocked that he'd attempt it again."

Gertie hugged her. "This time we'l stop him."

"Deep down, part of me hoped I was wrong. That he wouldn't destroy his family."

"When we hand over the proof for the magistrates, Peter wil have to leave England.

You'l be free of his sick machinations."

Carina gave her a weak smile. "I'm not convinced I can pul it off. So until he's on a ship

I'l not rest easy."

"You could ask Max for help. He'd be happy to dispatch Peter to the other side of the

world, so you could sleep through an entire night."

"Nothing sends me to sleep anymore."

Gertie grinned. "You slept wel after your recent bout of exercise with Max." She

chuckled. "I prescribe a large dose of wil ing and able male before bed every night."

Carina choked on her drink. "You're incorrigible. Though Max does meet the

requirements: male, large, and judging by last night's perfor- mance, extremely wil ing, though

he's only available at bedtime for a month."

"Wait and see," Gertie said sagely. "Not that I've heard al the deli- cious details yet."

Carina laughed. "And you're not going to hear."

"Too cruel. I miss having a man in my bed, so I need to live libidi- nously through your adventures."

Carina hugged her friend. She prayed for a miracle because they'd need one to catch a

viper like Peter. And she must hold her cards close to her chest, trusting no one, and pray she

could stay one step ahead of him, until they could all wave a far from fond farewell.

12

M ax lay slumped back on the bed, totally spent. Carina had joined him at the cottage every afternoon, or evening, for ten days. Yet he stil couldn't reconcile himself to these

feelings. After each time he enjoyed her lush body, he immediately craved her again.

He forced himself to stand and not glance back. He plucked up her chemise, fine white

linen embroidered with dozens of lavender flowers, meaning to toss it back to where she

SPRAWLED across the tangled mess of sheets. Unable to help himself, he pressed it to his face.

He closed his eyes and moaned. Lavender-scented today, and his favorite. He flicked the

garment over his shoulder, and then watched it flutter and float until it settled on her bare

legs.

There were more than sixty tiny purple flowers, lovingly embroidered by Georgie,

around the hem. While she'd dozed, he counted them. He also knew her perfume was

sometimes rose and that her underwear on those days was decorated with sweet pink buds,

once again sewed with care by Georgie. Others times she wore jasmine, or gardenia, or some

other fragrance designed to send his senses spinning and his mind reeling.

Hours after he left Brent Street each day, he'd be swamped by floral aromas and pass

anxious minutes trying to work which garments the scent clung to, and if anyone else noticed

that his normal pungent pine cologne had been replaced with something more sweet and

cloying. He scolded himself that he was Stirkton and not a besotted swain who couldn't take

his eyes, or his hands, off a woman.

Today, he'd decided to leave as soon as he'd withdrawn from that snug feminine

passage, so he could avoid the temptation to linger, to gaze, to sniff.

"You should get dressed." He sounded harsh.

"No."

"What do you mean, no?" He swung to face her.

Propped on one elbow and with the sheet at her waist, her breasts were bared to him and

he watched, fascinated, when she wiggled and set the twin globes swinging gently. To add to

his torment, she pushed back her swathe of tumbling red curls and moved her magnificent

bosom until his mouth dried and his breath was ragged.

Her deliberate teasing drove him insane and he was helpless to resist. As a man of power, he controlled situations and people. They didn't control him. But every time she

teased him with her body, or perused his body with her tongue caught between her teeth, his

heart beat faster and his blood heated.

Nothing had any significance beyond the wet welcome of her body when he thrust into it

long and deep. Nothing mattered beyond the sight and smell of this temptress. The Countess

had bewitched him. The witch gave him an amused smile.

"Has no one ever denied you, Your Grace? Though I know you're desperate to keep to

your usual schedule, I've decided that I'm ..."

She languidly stretched and spread her limbs across the four poster bed, and then lifted

her breasts. Beneath the curls at her apex, he could see her center glistening, begging him to

128

PUT his tongue there and lick and taste until she screamed his name and flooded his tongue

with her essence. She was pink and perfect and he yearned for one more taste, and then

perhaps another.

"...not yet satisfied."

He couldn't think, couldn't speak. She'd cast a spel and enthralled him.

"Not... not satisfied," he stuttered. "I don't... know... what you mean."

"Don't play the fool. You know exactly what I mean. For two weeks, we've followed

your ingrained timetable. And I imagine, the same guidelines you've used every month and

with every nameless, faceless woman. Am I correct?"

"I said from the start that nothing would be different between us."

"Rubbish. I'm more than your next whore."

"Not once have I caled you a whore."

"Whore, prostitute, courtesan, wife. There's no difference."

"Of course there is. Though I don't understand what you want."

"You, Max. I want you."

"You've had more of me than any woman. Ever."

"You've given me more time, but no more of yourself. Because you're scared."

"Of what?"

"Scared of repeating your mistakes from our first night together. Afraid of not measuring

up to your heritage standards. Did your grandfather find out?"

"Not about that first night. He and the Earl hadn't thought to cut the holes in the wals.

That came later."

"So we're the only ones who know what we shared. Tenderness, acceptance and even

fun. And that's what you can't admit. No matter what you were taught, you treat women with

care. And at least one woman—me—relishes every moment we spend together. I've never

known such happiness, such pleasure."

He shook his head, despite knowing that she was correct and he'd ignored the rules.

"Having sex is a man's way of easing his body's urges, and nothing more."

"Poppycock! Women also enjoy sex. And you've given me much more than physical

pleasure. "

"What about our first time? Virgins usual y feel pain rather than pleasure."

"You took care of me that night too. Made sure I was ready. I had little pain the first

time, and none the second or third times. Do you remember?"

Of course he remembered. Hel, he'd never been able to get her out of his mind. After

129

THAT NIGHT, he'd been watched and every performance with a virgin had been evaluated, then

humiliated by having to account for every action the next day.

"My grandfather was furious about that night, with me and with the Earl. From then on, I

wasn't alowed stay with a girl for longer than an hour in case I formed an emotional

connection with one of them."

Carina stroked a hand down his bare back and though he remembered little about his

mother, he knew she'd touched him with those same feminine comforting gestures.

"Are you worried about getting emotionally attached?"

Max puled away from her roving hand. "We're drawn to each other, yes, but trust me

when I say that what you're feeling is lust, and lust fades and desire shrivels. Sex is good but

after that men and women have little in common."

Carina surprised him by laughing. Her full-throated merriment stirred his sense of the

ridiculous and, despite being the brunt of her joke, he wanted to join in.

"Stop being such a prude. Us, together, isn't to satisfy an urge. We're sharing much,

much more."

He sighed. "Fine. I admit that when I'm inside you I feel things, and I wonder if it might

last. If it's possible to enjoy being with one person long-term." He stretched out beside her on

the bed. "Which is why I want to keep meeting here for longer."

"What? No, no. We might pass each other in the street or meet at a bal, but by

Christmas, you and Alice wil be man and wife."

"My intention has always been to keep a mistress. Girls like Alice can't be expected to

welcome their husband more nights than necessary, so a true gentleman takes his lust

elsewhere."

"Rubbish! Why would any lady want to share her husband with another woman?"

Max felt his face heat. "You're twisting my words. Ladies are entitled to be left alone

after they become *enceinte*, as I've no doubt Alice's mother wil explain. I shal do my best to

ensure that Alice enjoys my visits to her bed. But with an experienced courtesan I can relax

my guard."

"Your plan for bedding Alice sounds like animals being mated. Personally, I enjoy your

baser urges. A lot. Isn't that why women, especial y widows, have affairs? Because they miss

having a virile man between their legs."

"If you enjoy what I do, keep coming here until our liaison runs its natural course and we

tire of each other."

"I couldn't do that to Alice. Guilt would eat me alive. But out of curiosity, why do you

130

THINK we'l grow tired of each other?"

"Because nothing lasts forever, especial y not anything good."

"Oh, Max." She stroked his bare arm and he shivered. "But there are both good and bad

marriages. My mother and father were very happy."

"But her second union wasn't good, was it?"

"She wanted security for us, but she'd turn in her grave if she knew how dearly her

mistake has cost us."

"You dealt with a stepfather whom I gather you disliked and a stepbrother you loathe,

yet you stay optimistic and you shower others with warmth and goodness"

"Believe me, I'm no saint. I committed adultery with you, and supposedly with other

men. I've grappled with that guilt for years. In the eyes of God, I'm a sinner."

He touched her cheek. Warm, alive and wonderful, and he wanted more. He kissed her

and lingered at her mouth, unwilling to leave her sweet and tempting lips.

"Sweetheart, your heart's too pure for you to be a sinner. God would never condemn you

for something you couldn't control and berating yourself is senseless. Remember your

achievements and don't dwel on your imagined failings."

Carina smiled. "That's the nicest thing you've ever said to me. That anyone has said in a

long time."

"The ladies adore you and appreciate the sacrifices you make for them."

"It's not a sacrifice when it's people I love." She ran her hand down his bare chest. "It's

a privilege."

Max groaned, before kissing her with hunger, need and desperation. Her inner goodness

warmed him like a fire and he yearned to keep her close. "I need you. Stay with me. If we're

discreet, no one wil know."

"I've barely been able to keep our secret from my sisters." She frowned. "And when we

dined with Alice's family, Lord Johnston watched me like a hawk. As if he knew what we

were doing and was condemning my black soul to hel."

"Nonsense. Besides which, Johnston is a man of the world and wil assume I'l keep a

mistress. He'l probably applaud my good sense for not bothering Alice."

"I think you're wrong. His wife wants their daughter to be the most revered woman in

England and, mark my words, she'l not tolerate her son-in-law dallying with courtesans. And

he obeys his wife, so you'l not be let out of their sight."

Max glared at her. He did as he pleased and nothing would change because of a few

church vows. "I'l speak to Johnston. Neither he or his wife wil dictate to me."

131

CARINA LAUGHED. "If you think to cower Lady Johnston through her husband, you sadly

underestimate the power females wield in households."

Her assumption that his wife and her parents would have any say in what he did was

irritating. "I swear I'l take care of everything."

"Your past liaisons were common gossip and your future affairs will also be discussed

in every house and at every bal. I can't be involved with you, because of the damage it

would do to my sisters' reputations. Perhaps Johnston wil turn a blind eye to your normal

habit of setting up a courtesan, but anything more will bring Lady Johnston's wrath down on your head. I can't risk that, not when my sisters' welbeing is at stake."

"For God's sake! Why can't you trust me?"

"Because I learned long ago to make my own decisions and not depend on a man. Not

you, and not my stepbrother."

"How dare you lump me with that vilain! My investigators are following Peter's trail of

debt through a string of clubs and I'l soon hold proof of his perfidy. I want to see him

prosecuted for gambling away money that rightfully belongs to you and your sisters."

He pressed a kiss into the palm of her hand. "Trust me on that at least. He'l never harm

any of you again."

Carina sighed. "You're the only man I'l trust. But when so much is at stake, I must be

careful." She linked her hands behind his neck and pulled him down for a kiss, and he forgot

the problems she spoke of and thought of the warmth and the pleasure.

Lust, he reminded himself, and nothing more. But then he looked into her clear green

eyes and fel under her witch's spel. Somehow, he'd convince her to extend their time

together, at least for the few weeks needed to satiate himself with her lush body. Or, until he

convinced himself that he could give up her passion and zest for life and accept Alice's cool

reserve as the correct path. After al , he'd accepted Alice's nervousness before, so why was

he now filled with doubts?

"Getting back to what I said before," she said with a cheeky grin, "I need another reminder of how *not* to feel pleasure." Her tongue flicked along the seam of his pursed lips,

but he resisted her unspoken request the way she'd refused to agree to a longer liaison. No

woman with a strength of will to match his own had ever been at this cottage until now, and it

was hard to know if she was the best decision he'd ever made, or the most catastrophic.

While he waged a fierce internal debate, she took the decision out of his hands by lifting

and spreading herself full length on top of him, skin to skin, and with her soft curves filling

his hollow spaces. She entwined their fingers and lifted their hands high, so they strained

132

TOGETHER FROM HEAD to toe with each hot place pressed against its opposite. Her tongue speared

his ear, before she licked a path down his cheek to his open mouth and dived inside, swirling

wet circles over his teeth and tangling with his tongue.

He rarely kissed women, yet he wanted to wrap her in his arms so she couldn't lift her

mouth from his. "You make me yearn for things that can never happen."

She rested her forehead on his and her warm breath fanned his face. He shut his eyes and

blocked out everything outside their cozy cocoon.

Lifting her head she faced him, her eyes inches from his and met his stare with a depth of

emotion that shook him to his toes. He was awed, amazed and yet tormented. "You believe

the same, don't you?"

Her face creased with pain before she dropped her gaze and

shook her head, unwittingly

teasing him by flicking her hair back and forth across his bare chest. Lifting her chin, he

watched her expression.

"It's in your eyes. Tel me, because for once in my life I'd like to hear someone express

their true feelings and not tel me what they think a duke needs to hear." He captured her

tongue between his teeth and bothered it with his tongue and mouth until she panted. "Not

false praises from paid companions on my excellence, nor buttered compliments from

debutantes hoping to become my duchess."

She caressed his face and pressed her lips to his. He liked the games they played with

lips, tongues and mouths. Advance and retreat, until they quickly outgrew foreplay and he

pulled her thighs apart with rough desperation and slid deep inside her, making them both

moan and groan and demand more and more from each other.

From their first time together, she'd ignored his rule about kissing and had opened her

mouth over his with no finesse but a bucket-load of love, until he craved the feel of her lips

moving over his; craved the volcano of feelings she effortlessly stirred.

"Poor, Max," she murmured. "Hasn't anyone praised your bedding skils before? I lose

myself and become a wanton woman with you, so I can't under-stand why your other consorts

didn't applaud your obvious talents, especially when you arouse a woman with such finesse

and then ensure she reaches her pinnacle long before you let go yourself."

He sucked in a ragged breath. "I never alowed it before."

Her eyes closed and she nodded. When she opened them again, she inspected him as if

deciding to lay bare each of his dark and hideous secrets, like serving meat on a dinner

platter. She silently encouraged him to share some his burdens with her in a way he'd never

done before, completely and freely.

133

"I HAVEN'T BEEN PAID to toss out accolades and further inflate your enormous ego, and

I've been married off to a title and have no interest in bowing and scraping to a peer again."

She laughed. "I'm certainly not looking to marry again anytime soon, so I say this in all

honesty. When you make love to me, with me—"

"No!" He replied by rote. "We share a bed."

She shook her head and smiled. "You and I, Max, make love. Beautiful love. The reason

I let you blackmail me into these meetings..." He raised his eyebrows. "Fine, I amend that

statement." She waved a hand between their bodies. "This was why I agreed. Passion, desire

and lust. I wanted to enjoy myself, rather than be the novelty act. The chance for an unknown

man to add another notch to his bedpost by deflowering a virgin."

Max winced. "I'm sorry."

She placed a finger over his lips. "Shush."

He removed her finger and kissed the tip. "You may not want to speak of it, but the guilt

stil keeps me awake at night. I've been unraveling some of the mysteries from my teens, and

there are things that concern you and questions I need to ask."

"I know." She sighed against his lips and he had to taste her again. Breathe in her scent

and absorb her moans and sighs with his mouth. Feasting on her lips, tasting her body, had

fast become an obsession.

"This," she said, looking around, "is our sanctuary. Let's enjoy what little time we have,"

she begged, "because there's certain to be a reckoning soon."

She dipped her head to hide her tears but drops trickled through the hairs around his

nipple and ran down his torso. Each drop cut like a knife blade. She shifted and leaned on his

chest. "This respite wil give me strength for later."

He frowned. "What are you planning?"

"No, my darling. I can't tel you, so please don't ask."

He finally nodded. Delaying their parting would allow more time to solve their problems

with Lindsay. Legally, the bastard was in the right. Morally, he was lower than a slave trader.

"Only for a short time, but then I expect answers. Promise?"

She gave a sketchy nod and he mentally loosened the reins, but he couldn't, and

wouldn't, let her run free for too long. Not when the danger was a man as unpredictable and

unstable as Lindsay.

"I do like the idea of us being equal."

She rose on one hand and studied his sprawled nakedness, as if standing in a lolly shop

and deciding which sweet to bite into first. His shaft bobbed and she licked her lips. "Oooh,

134

PERHAPS I'L START THERE."

Christ! No matter which part of his anatomy she touched, he wouldn't survive, because

they were both approaching foreign territory. Her cheeky grin showed the unfettered girl

she'd once been.

"I want to do something." He swalowed hard. "Do you trust me?" Unable to speak, he

nodded. "Put your hands above your head and hold onto the bar. Don't let go."

His cock leaped to attention, quivering above his nest of dark hair. His cock's antics

made her smirk and all he could think about was tossing her on her back and fucking her until

they both passed out from pleasure. He gritted his teeth.

"You want me."

He threw his arm across his face and snorted his self-disgust. "Carrot-top, I always want

you, no matter how strongly I resist." He looped an arm around her neck and puled her

mouth closer. "I lust for you day and night." He devoured her mouth. "And I don't know

what to do about it."

He slumped across the bed, arms open wide in supplication. After gnawing her lower lip,

she wiggled down until her face was level with his unruly dick. Her pink tongue flicked out

to moisten her lips, making clear her intention.

"Christ," he spluttered. "You can't do that."

She frowned. "Don't you like it?"

He swalowed hard. "It's ... it's not for ladies."

Her face lifted. "Do mistresses do it?"

He threw back his head and groaned. "I'm not discussing that."

"Ah, so they do. Though I'm surprised you'd alow that."

Despite longing to change the subject, curiosity won. "Why?"

"In drawings, in books, it seems that to..."

She waved her hand at his groin and flushed. He grinned at his intrepid lover's struggle

with earthy sex words.

"Ejaculate?"

She ignored his offered word. "You don't like handing over the reins."

"Huh! Am I so easy to read?"

"Only to people who know you wel."

"Few people know me." He stared hard. "It's not easy for me to surrender."

"I know." She pushed him flat and bent towards his groin.

Despite his alarm, he held his breath and waited. Many experienced whores refused to

135

SUCK A MAN'S PENIS, so when her tongue touched his purple bulb of his cock he jumped so

high he almost landed them both on the floor. She laid her hand on his stomach and eagerly

applied herself, her mouth sliding wetly around and over his swollen head until his eyes

rolled, and he flopped back and encouraged her to do more and more with his painfully

engorged shaft.

Tentative licks had soothed, but now her long tugs stretched his size and made him

wonder how much he could tolerate before he exploded. Teeth grazed the sides when she

plunged and pulled back in a slow experimental torment that had him squirming and panting.

His hands dropped from the wooden rung and she stopped.

"Ah, ah." She shook her head and he felt like a boy being chastised by the school

mistress. "Stay stil or I'l stop."

"Oh, God, don't stop. Don't ever stop."

His ballocks tightened and his prick stiffened, ready to release. With what remained of

his strength, he tugged her away. Sucking him off, swalowing his salty seed, wasn't

something he'd ever contemplate asking from Alice, and nor should he ask it of a countess.

She reluctantly allowed him to pull her upwards to meet his mouth. He poured his

feelings and yearnings into the kiss and tried to roll her beneath him, but she refused. Seizing

control once more, she straddled his hips and rubbed her dripping cleft up and down his shaft.

He obliged her unspoken wants by thrusting upwards and impaling her on his length.

He'd never been so engorged before and every inch screamed at him to plunge deeper, until

his shaft touched her womb and he claimed her completely. She gasped and he plunged inside

again, setting up a slow and constant rhythm of advance and retreat until sweat ran from his

brow and her teeth bit down on her bottom lip.

She leant forward and offered her breasts. The position offered more control than tossing

her to her back, as she'd been afraid would happen each time at the inn. Nor would she feel

trapped as when the Earl had uselessly grunted and rutted on top of her. He nuzzled at her

rose-scented neck while adoring her breasts with his hands, rolling and tweaking her tight

nipples until she threw back her head and climaxed with a long and loud scream.

Damn, but she was magnificent when she did gave herself over to her own enjoyment

and forgot everything else. He loved watching her lose herself, knowing that he'd done that

for her. Push her to such an exquisite peak that her screams echoed around the old plastered

walls and rattled the used tea cups on their tray.

He pushed up hard to increase pressure on their joining and reached between them to tug

on her swollen nub the way he pulled and tweaked her nipples. She spasmed again. Her walls

136

TIGHTENED and squeezed his cock as tightly as when he used his fist for several months

recently. He wouldn't be able to hold back much longer. Every male part of him clamored for

release. Begged him to let go. Urged him to claim this woman with his seed.

Circling her clitoris with his fingers, he varied the speed. Fast then faster, her sweet little

bud twitched and shivered and orgasm sent her into another drawn-out scream. Her protracted

climax pushed him quickly to the top and over. Thrusting hard and urgently, once, twice, and

then on the third he exploded.

Endlessly, he filled her with streams of hot sperm and chanted her name over and over,

uncaring if she saw his raw need for her and read more into it than he could ever say aloud.

Release had been too swift and earthshattering to withdraw ful y, and he'd be damned if he'd

worry about that right now. Not when she'd collapsed on his chest, panting and gasping, and

her smal continuing contractions milked him of every drop. Dammit! He'd barely

withdrawn and certainly not enough to be safe. Other times he'd tried to pay more attention

until the last so he could protect her better, because she wasn't a prostitute who knew a

multitude of ways to prevent pregnancy. Or knew which East End alley to visit to rid herself

of an unwanted babe.

She lazily stroked his chest and murmured, "Each time is better." Her breathing evened

out as she fell asleep, draped across his chest and breaking another rule about post coital

behavior. He should quietly extricate himself, let her sleep, and leave, yet he couldn't bring

himself to abandon her in this place, their shared haven. The tiny house had felt different,

more comforting, since she'd joined him here and he was loathe to break their intimate spel .

An hour later, he stared at the ceiling with Carina's head tucked under one arm and the

other draped possessively across her tiny waist. Her ful woman's breasts rose and her nipples

beaded in the rapidly cooling air. He was half aroused already. Inwardly, he groaned. Would

his hunger for her never be sated? He could almost laugh at his stupidity in thinking that he

could use her body as unemotionally as normal, and that having her again after years of

searching and not knowing would instantly cure his obsession.

Repetition normal y left him grateful that a month's end was in sight and he could pay

his light skirt and send her away with good grace. To his bewilderme nt, nothing in his life

was predictable any more. Exchanging banter with Carina was invigorating, rather than

boring, and taking her to bed was playful and exciting, rather than calculated.

He shook her gently. "You need to return home before you're missed."

She sighed. "And you must dress for your evening with Alice."

"We both have responsibilities."

137

"REALITY CALS."

'I stil don't believe that our times together must end so soon. Why not wait until closer

to my wedding."

"Listen to yourself. You're talking about keeping me as your mistress and marrying

Alice in one sentence. If we're found out, I'll be shamed and shunned more than in the past.

A soiled dove, or the other woman. I can't do it."

He held her in his arms and kissed her one last time, showing his desperation and need,

yet his confusion was crystal clear to them both. Carina might be set on the righteous path,

but he wasn't so noble and, for the first time, he had no clue how to proceed.

13

Max considered the reasons Carina refused to commit to him and, as any good strategist does, envisaged the best way to change her mind. No woman had ever refused him, because,

for better or for worse, he was Stirkton, blue-blooded and wealthy.

Widows and bored wives had strewn themselves in his path for years, until he'd become

an expert at dodging entrapments and avoiding women who would disrupt his carefully

ordered life. Men of less breeding jumped out of bedroom windows to evade enraged

husbands, but he'd been taught how to sate himself with women without getting caught with

his pants down. So he understood why a woman of Carina's status refused to be the mistress

of a married man, especial y when he'd be expected to be dance attendance upon Alice for at

least the first few months.

If he was a ruthless and despicable Meacham, he'd remind Carina that a woman sold

several times had no right preaching to him about proper behavior, but in truth, he admired

her ethics and felt guilty that his own conduct was blemished. Ironically, while Carina taught

him kindness and compassion, she used his name and titles to elevate her sisters and didn't

care a fig if he was uncomfortable with this whirlwind of socializing, something he generally

avoided.

He sprawled in a chair before the fire and pondered the unexpected twists and turns

disrupting his heretofore straight pathway, uncertain if he was satisfied or exasperated. He

138

POURED A FOURTH GLASS OF BRANDY, another oddity considering that he rarely over-imbibed.

Alcohol muddled a man's brain and he held a deep-seated fear of being pitied or looking

foolish before his peers or servants.

Benson knocked and entered, carrying a silver salver holding a white embossed calling

card. "Your Grace, Lord Johnston requests an audience."

The last thing he wanted was his future father-in- law seeing him coddling brandy and

reeking of spirits. Settlements had been discussed long ago, lawyers had had papers drawn

up, and only final signatures were needed. Whatever Johnston's concerns, they wouldn't be

pleasant because, apart from financial decisions, the man obeyed his wife unquestioningly.

And he'd sensed that Lady Johnston wasn't happy with him. He rose and adjusted his cravat,

sighing inwardly at this unwanted interruption.

When Benson announced his lordship, Max forced himself to appear unperturbed and

welcomed his unexpected visitor with a casual air, while silently preparing to defend his

interactions with Carina and her sisters, if that was Johnston's reason for caling.

He extended his hand. "Lord Johnston, a pleasure to see you."

"I'l come straight to the point. My good wife and I are worried about your relationship

with Lady Dorchester, though we know you are old friends."

"Yes, we've known each other for several years."

"While it's commendable to assist old acquaintances, it's not acceptable for a man about

to be married to devote so much time to other women. We realize you're busy with

investments and estate matters, but we insist you spend more time with Alice."

"Does my fiancée have any specific complaints?"

"Alice doesn't know I'm here. Best to discuss this man to man before she learns about

your frequent meetings with the countess."

"Frequent meetings?"

"Yes. Before I alowed you to court my daughter, I naturally made enquiries."

"But my grandfather had already arranged our match."

"A father cannot be too careful with his daughter's welbeing. Circumstances change,

and we want the best for our daughter. I'm a wealthy man, so money was never the deciding

factor in our agreeing to give you Alice."

"Of course not," he said with a sneer. "Titles are far more appealing to matchmaking mothers than money."

Johnston either chose to ignore the sarcasm or was impervious to it, and considering he

dealt with Lady Johnston every day, perhaps the latter was true. The lady had a sharp tongue

139

THAT MAX TOOK pains to avoid, but her husband would have no escape.

"Even your titles won't protect you if there is a public scandal breaks concerning you

and Lady Dorchester. I need your promise that you'l finish whatever the two of you share."

"Are you threatening me, My Lord?"

"I'm displeased at having to make this cal to your house as I'd already made my

thoughts clear to you, but if you ignore my warning I wil retaliate. I realize that it's accepted,

and possible expected, for gentlemen such as yourself to take a mistress, and I've no

objection to your liaisons at your cottage—"

"My cottage? Who told you anything of my private life?"

"I've kept a close eye on your finances and your personal habits."

"You had me followed?"

"Only for a short time before your betrothal. Until I was satisfied that you'd not harm my

daughter. However, watching you fawn over Lady Dorchester over the last few weeks has left

me feeling uneasy. Very uneasy indeed. Fucking a courtesan is permissible. Ploughing Lady

Dorchester at your cottage like any other courtesan is not to be tolerated."

"How dare you speak of Lady Dorchester that way. She's a lady of good breeding."

"In my experience, good breeding doesn't stop women being money grabbers or from

exploiting men with their sexual charms. Quite the contrary."

Max no longer cared if the man saw his fury. How dare the man threaten him? More and

more, he saw Carina's predictions coming true. He mightn't be hen-pecked by his wife, but

his in-laws could make life a living hel , for himself and for Alice, who wasn't strong enough

to stand up to them. For Alice's sake, he needed to find neutral ground with these people as

they'd be required to deal with them on a regular basis.

"How exactly do you see the Countess exploiting me?"

"Huh! She seduced you because she wishes to usurp Alice's position and become your

duchess instead."

Max let out a guffaw of laughter. "I assure you that's far from the truth. Lady Dorchester

didn't seduce me, nor does she wish for another marriage, to me or any other man. Though

none of this is your concern, especial y not who I choose to bed."

"Damn you, Maximus. I'm making it my business. I'l have your promise to stop

consorting with the Countess, or I may withdraw from our arrangements. If my daughter cries

off, she'l be free of scandal and you'l be blamed."

"The difference is that I'm a wealthy and influential man. If your daughter withdraws, I

can guarantee that before Christmas I'l have chosen another chit from the endless line of

140

DEBUTANTES EAGER TO MARRY ME. Can you say the same for Alice? Will she have gentlemen lining up to beg for her hand after she refuses a duke?"

"You're despicable. You'd see Alice ruined?"

"Only if you leave me no choice. Now, I suggest you leave before I reconsider and break

the betrothal myself. I wouldn't like to be in your shoes when you inform your good lady that

your daughter is back in the marriage mart. Humiliation will be hard to swal ow, I'l wager,

for a woman as ambitious as your wife."

Max pulled the bell pull and Benson instantly appeared, obvi- ously having listened at the

door. "His lordship is leaving." After a moment's thought he said, "And please have my

horse brought around. I shal cal on Lady Dorchester."

Lord Johnston pointed his finger at Max. "You've not heard the last of this, not by a long

way."

Lord Johnston's departure was hurried along by Benson, and Max poured himself

another large glass of brandy. For a man of moderate habits, he'd begun drinking a lot

recently. His preferred method of relaxation, taking Carina a dozen different ways at the

cottage, was becoming harder and harder to arrange. He put his glass down, considered it for

a moment, and then lifted it and defiantly drained the contents in one large gulp, despite there

being no one present to witness his moment of rebellion.

He hiccoughed, shocking the footman holding open the front door, and then mounted up

and set out for Woods House. At least, he hoped he was headed that way, but his head was a

little woozy and he couldn't concentrate. Probably the worst thing he could do was visit

Carina, considering his conversation with Johnston, but none of his recent actions could be

labelled wise.

When he reached Woods House, he slid from his horse, righted himself, and took a few

minutes to reconsider his rash and brash actions. Throwing away his planned future with

Alice for the sake of two weeks of snatched hours with Carina made no sense, despite being

able to imagine how they'd spend those enjoyable hours. As usual, his body was hot and

aching and his mind dwelt on their next meeting, when he'd impatiently strip the clothing

from off her lush body and embed his shaft in her welcoming channel.

Blocking Johnston from his mind, he took the front steps two at a time and rapped loudly

on the door. The moment the butler admitted him, he demanded that the Countess was called

immediately. Carina heard the commotion in her hallway and popped her head out of the

sitting room door, followed by her sisters and Gertie.

"Max, whatever is the matter?" Max lurched a little and she hurried forward to take his

141

ARM. "Are you il? Come sit down."

He leaned towards her and muttered, "I won't tolerate it."

14

Carina looked up at Max and breathed in alcoholic fumes. She pulled up short and he stumbled. "You've been drinking! Brandy, by the smell."

The lofty Duke of Stirkton grinned at his audience with the mischievous air of an

unapologetic schoolboy. Gertie, Georgie and Lucy gasped and then, in unison, smiled back at

him. Carina stared at Max. He stood, grinning like an idiot, and listing from side to side like a

ship in a storm, he couldn't help herself. He looked so ridiculous, so unlike himself, and so

damned adorable that she laughed.

Georgiana helped her steer him through the door, staring up at Max in adoration. Her

sister's severe case of puppy love would make their situation more complicated.

Sharper than she intended, Carina said, "Leave him, Georgie. I'l attend to the Duke,

who is clearly in his cups."

Much to Carina's surprise, Georgie didn't budge. "I'm quite used to dealing with men

who are under the weather." Georgie smiled at Max. "And even half-shot, the Duke would

never raise his fist at a woman."

Georgie put her shoulder under Max's arm and steered him to the settee, with Carina

helping her in awe-struck silence. Lucy and Gertie watched with open-mouthed amazement

and jumped when Georgie issued orders in a tone that brooked no arguments. "Ring for tea,

Lucy, strong tea. Carina, stop fussing over the poor man and allow him breathing room."

Carina stepped back. She had indeed been hovering, checking Max's color and

breathing. She flushed. Hovering indicated a deep caring, and though she didn't love Max,

she really didn't, this implacable man would only have drunk to excess after a major

catastrophe. And that calamity must concern them or he wouldn't be here, staggering drunk

and acting so strangely.

Lucy returned and stood side by side with Georgie, both watching his eyes close and

flutter open several times, as if losing the battle against unseen weights pressing his lids

down. Long dark lashes stood out against his skin, especially now he his face was a grayish

142

GREEN.

"He looks like an angel," Lucy said, giving a long sigh.

Carina rolled her eyes. "Not you too? What's wrong with al of you?" She glared at

Gertie who was also smiling down at the sleeping duke. "Perhaps a falen angel, considering

how devilishly he acts."

Gertie glance from Carina to Max. "Ah, but he's your devil, Carina, because it's you he

sped to in his hour of need."

"Rubbish. The Duke needs no one bar himself."

Georgie shook her head. "He suffers greatly, the same as me. Maximus needs someone

who can soothe his troubled soul and apparently that's you, Carina, whether you like it or

not."

"Wel, I don't like it. We have an agreement, a business arrangement."

"Not merely business," Lucy said, "or you wouldn't be so secretive." She looked at

Georgie and Gertie. "We've discussed you and Max."

"You've discussed us?" She looked at Gertie. "Why?"

Gertie answered for them. "Because your feelings go deeper than you're admitting, and

your connection is stronger than you expected."

Georgie nodded. "Your arrangement with Max has something to do with us, we know

that, and something to do with Peter. And while we appreciate your sacrifice—"

"It's not a sacrifice," Carina said. "I want you to marry men who treat women honorably,

and who'l recognize that you're both very special women." She looked down at Max snoring

softly on the settee. "I've been very happy with our arrangement. And when I know you're

both safe and settled, Gertie and I wil begin our travels."

All four women looked at man sprawled on their couch, as if he had every right to take

over their room. Carina smiled because he did look angelic.

Gertie took Carina's hand. "Wil you be happy leaving behind those you love?" She

motioned at the oblivious Duke. "Not just the girls."

Georgie spoke. "Maximus has treated Lucy and me kindly and honorably. But his

behavior towards you, Carina, is not quite so gentlemanly, is it?"

Gertie surreptitiously shook her head, so Carina knew she'd said nothing about the

arrangement between herself and Max. Only Gertie knew the truth about Carina's marriage

and the three sales of her virginity, and her sisters didn't need to know that plans for the

fourth sale were only aborted due to the Earl's demise.

"I...I'm not sure what you mean, "Carina stuttered.

143

LUCY GROANED. "We're not naïve, Carina. We recognize a man who desires a woman and,

on that score, Max is easily read. He wants you so badly that perhaps he'l break his

engagement and marry you instead. That would solve our problems."

"What problems?" Carina felt a trifle nonplussed at her sisters' observations and couldn't

help but wonder if others had also noticed. Because, if so, they were in deep trouble.

Georgie stared at her as if she was slow-witted. "If you married Max, Lucy and I can live

with you permanently, or at least until Lucy finds a suitable husband. We can't let Peter

marry her off at too young an age, as he did to us. Like you, Carina, I've no wish to marry

again, but Peter wil insist upon it, and very soon."

Carina was touched and yet saddened. "Georgie, not al men are evil."

Georgie looked at Max and smiled. "He'd be kind to you."

Carina rubbed a hand across her aching head. "What you're suggesting is impossible.

Have you forgotten that he's already betrothed, and to a lady who is our friend?" She looked

at their smiling faces. "The Duke harbors deep feelings for Alice."

"No, I don't!" They jumped at the loud masculine voice. They'd almost forgotten that

the man under discussion was right in front of them.

He pulled himself into a sitting position and grabbed his head with both hands.

"Damnation," he said with a growl. "My head feels as if it's going to explode. What on

earth happened?"

Carina glared at the other, until Gertie took the hint and shooed her sisters out of the

room. Alone with Max, Carina walked to the tray of china and spoons, and took her time

pouring a cup of strong tea. His hands shook as he accepted the cup and saucer from her, so

she kept her hands in place over his until he had a tighter grip.

"Drink your tea. Cook added some of her special brew to stop your headache. What in

heaven's name were you thinking? You rode here drunk. It's a miracle you didn't fal off in

the street and get run over by a wagon or a carriage."

Max sipped his tea and grimaced, but she didn't care that it tasted foul. Swal owing it

would be his penance for acting so rashly and endangering his life.

"My apologies to al of you." Max glanced at the door, which had correctly been left

slightly ajar by Gertie.

Carina groaned, before marching to the door and pulling it wide so that the three

women, pressed to the other side, almost tumbled to the floor. "Could you please give us a

little privacy?" Three heads nodded before Carina shut the door and turned the key.

"I apologize, Carina. I rarely have more than a glass or two and I've never been foxed

144

IN THE MIDDLE of the day. Nevertheless, you're wrong."

"About what?"

"About Lady Johnston. Alice. There are no deep feelings of any sort of romantic

nonsense between us, and you know that. We've al grown up with arranged marriages and

we know they're not conceived in the heat of passion, but by intelligent men who have the

best interests of both parties at heart."

"Huh! Your grandfather had no heart and he didn't care about Alice's best interests. Or

yours, for that matter."

"Aside from al that, I took umbrage at Johnston's audacity. He dared lecture me, in my

own home, about when, where and with whom I may spend my time."

Carina gasped. "Johnston was talking about me? Us?"

"He knows nothing specific, though he's had me followed to the cottage." He snorted.

"He'l alow me to keep a mistress later on, but for now I must dance attendance upon Alice."

"Oh, good Lord. I knew no good would come of our arrangement. If word spreads that

you and I are..." She waved a hand.

"Carrying on a liaison? Don't fret because I set him straight. I told Johnston to stay out

of my affairs. I'l see whomever I please, and neither he nor his demanding wife has any say

in my life."

"What have you done? I'l be ruined again, and when I was making progress with my

sisters. You must pacify Johnston and tel him whatever he needs to hear."

"You're not listening. I'l treat my fiancée as I have been, with care and respect. But I've

made it clear to Alice what I want in a wife. Someone to organize my households and to raise

our children."

"What of love?"

"I'm surprised that you, of al people, believe in love. I heard you tel your sisters—"

"You were awake?"

"I heard you deny there's anything between us, but you're wrong."

Max stood quickly, ignoring the shooting pain in his head and took Carina by the arms,

upsetting her balance so she tumbled against him. His lips came down on hers, hard and

possessive. He took and took until she linked her hands behind his head.

She groaned against his lips, "Why is this happening? Why do I lose control with you?"

"I don't know why, only that I feel the same when I'm with you." He kissed her again

and again, until she sagged at the knees, but even then he didn't let her go. "You're mine

until I say we're finished and I don't care what Johnston says."

145

. . .

CARINA PULED AWAY. "But he wil be your father- in-law. It's too dangerous to meet

anymore, except in public."

"Forget Johnston, and Alice. Come to Brent Street tonight."

"I can't. Alice wil be humiliated if she learns about your cottage, especial y if she

discovers that I'm going there with you."

"Alice wil be glad of my arrangements after she has born my child. For a titled lady, sex

is messy and unwelcome."

Her hand connected with his face— *whack*—and he rubbed at the spot.

"So what does that make me, Max? I've enjoyed having sex with you for two weeks.

Does that make me il bred?" He frowned, searching for the right response. "Deep down," she

said, "you consider me no better than your other whores."

He flinched. "I told Johnston never to cal you that again, or I'd cal him out, and I won't

let you refer to yourself that way either."

"Why not? I became your whore at seventeen, and I'l end that way. Isn't that what you

wanted; that you'd be my first and last lover."

"That changed."

"Nothing has changed. I'm a woman bought and sold to men, by men. But you're wrong

about one thing. You'l not be my last lover. I've acquired a taste for sex and I'l not give it

up. So when you're on top of Alice, I'l be under another man and putting into practice al

you've taught me."

"What do you want me to say? Yes, I loathe the thought of another man touching you. So

much so that when you meet me tonight I'l prove it to you."

"No. I'm canceling our agreement regarding my sisters and, in turn, I'm free from my

obligations to you."

"You need me to find those men."

"I'll find them by myself. Good day, Your Grace."

"I'm not giving up so easily. Alice and I wil cal for you this evening for the Longstaff

bal as arranged, and for Alice's sake, we'l treat each other pleasantly."

"I've no desire to upset Alice, but be warned. Even my sisters have noticed our

attraction, so we must be careful. No touching, not even my hand."

Max wasn't happy but he finally agreed. However, as they walked towards the door he

made her a vow that both thrilled and terrified her.

"I wil have you again, Carina. Do not doubt that you wil be mine."

146

15

Dancers whirled past Carina where she'd hidden in the shadows of the potted palms in yet another ballroom. Georgie looked serene in the arms of a distinguished looking

gentleman, a compatriot of the Duke's that he'd introduced to them the previous evening.

Their week had been crammed with so many social occasions, Carina's head was

spinning. She was exhausted from keeping track of her sisters and their suitors, being nice to

Alice, and yet avoiding Max. She rubbed at her head to ease the constant nag of a headache

but, as she had reassured Gertie, the season was winding down and soon they could retire to

the country, or accept invitations to house parties.

Max had kept his vow and not touched her, even for a waltz. Yet his gaze followed her

everywhere, and far too often, to go unremarked. Each time she danced, waves of anger were directed at her and her partner, and if she ventured outside onto a terrace, he'd appear within

minutes. Though he kept his distance, he watched her like a hawk until her nerves frayed, she

couldn't sleep and acquaintances commented on her pallor and lack of focus. She yearned for

the privacy of her bed where she could shed another bout of lonely tears.

She was so engrossed in her thoughts that she jumped when she heard her name.

"I didn't mean to startle you," Alice whispered. "But I don't know what to do. Please, I

need your help."

"Alice, your family and your fiancée wil be looking for you. Perhaps you should return

to your mother."

"I don't want to be near my mother. She smothers me."

Carina sympathized, because few people would be strong enough to defy Alice's mother.

She sighed. "How can I be of help?" Though they weren't far apart in ages, Carina felt old

compared to Alice's virtuousness.

"I need some advice from someone who knows the Duke and understands."

"What do I understand?"

"You know, how large and frightening he can be."

Carina looked at Alice's fraught expression. The girl's demeanor changed from

subservient to quivering in Max's presence, but Carina had been too preoccupied with her

own problems to pay much attention. Which was inexcusable, considering that Alice had

been a good friend to her sisters. For that reason alone, the unfortunate girl deserved her full attention. Though, in truth, having a torrid affair with Alice's betrothed meant Carina owed

147

HER MORE, much more.

She frowned at Alice's hands twisting the strings to her reticule around and around, until

they resembled a sailor's knotted ropes. "Are you frightened of Max?"

"The Duke is a very serious man and I'm worried that when we're wed..." A tear trickled

down her face. "You've been married. I need to know what happens, in the bedroom," she

whispered. "The Duke is very experienced and I'm going to disappoint him, because I don't

understand what happens and I don't know what to do to please him."

Carina held Alice's hands so she stopped twisting the strings. Alice's hands were as cold

as the Thames in winter. "Are you wel? You're trembling."

"I don't know what to do. Freddie, Lord Bromley, said I must be strong. He said the

Duke abhors weak women. Freddie says—"

Carina raised a brow. "You seem to have discussed this a lot with Lord Bromley."

Alice's lips turned up at the ends, a smal sad smile. She sighed. "Freddie takes me

driving in the park. The Duke is always busy, and Freddie doesn't mind driving me. He lets

me talk as much I want and he's wonderful to me."

Alice's face lit with excitement when she spoke of Freddie. Yet when she spoke of Max,

her voice quivered.

"Perhaps you should speak to the Duke and explain your concerns?"

"But he's so much older than me."

Carina couldn't help but laugh. "He's only twenty-nine."

"Twelve years my senior." Another sigh. "Mama thinks twelve years is a perfect age

difference because he'l know how I should act, and I'l become a famous hostess, though it's

a huge responsibility being a duchess, and an honor of course. Stil, I'd much prefer to marry

a younger man. One not quite so... large."

"Someone like your Freddie?"

Alice's expression turned dreamy. "Yes, my Freddie."

Carina forced herself to remain calm. Somehow she must convince Alice that Max was a

kind man, even if he occasionally appeared aloof. Actually, he often projected a restrained

and impassive character in public, so Alice's fears were understandable.

"Your family would be devastated if you broke your betrothal."

"Please, please understand. I cannot marry him."

Alice burst into tears, shuddering and noisy sobs which wracked her slender frame, and

which would alert everyone within ten feet that the drama being enacted would make

wonderful breakfast gossip. Carina drew the girl into the shadows and edged her along the

148

WALL TOWARDS THE HALLWAY.

"Shal I fetch your mother?"

"No, no, not Mama." Alice clutched Carina's arm. "She'll be angry that I'm ungrateful for the chance to marry a duke, and she won't forgive me for speaking about my fears with

anyone." She gave Carina an apologetic look. "Especially with you."

"She's your mother and she wants what's best for her daughter. Tel her how you feel.

Ask her what happens on a couple's wedding night."

"She's told me to expect pain, but I don't like being hurt. I'm supposed to be brave and

pretend I'm happy, or the Duke wil be angry." She clutched Carina so tightly that she

winced.

"I'm not an expert, but I believe that after their first time many women enjoy having

their husbands join them in bed. I'm sure the Duke wil make it pleasant for you."

"Did you enjoy the Earl's attentions?"

Carina was flummoxed. Alice would swoon if she heard the truth about the Earl. "My

family arranged my marriage to a much older man," she said, without thinking.

"The same as me." Alice clung to Carina tighter than a passenger on a sinking ship

clutched at the last life vest.

Carina gently disengaged her arm and shook her head. "My husband was unable to

perform his marital duties and frustration warped his thinking, whereas your knowledgeable

duke wil be a gentle teacher. You'l enjoy being with him and have a beautiful brood of

children."

"No, only his heir. My father said the contract states one son, no others, and Mama

swore I mightn't have to suffer many nights with the Duke because I'm only seventeen and everyone knows young girls catch a babe quickly." Tears flowed and her sobs increased. "But

I'm sure I won't be able to endure one night." She leaned closer. "The Duke tried to kiss me

when we were first betrothed."

"It's natural for your fiancée to want to kiss you."

"But his mouth was hard and ... wet. Not soft and sweet like when Freddie..."

"Freddie? Freddie Featherstone kissed you?"

"Yes, but Freddie's kiss was gentle and romantic." She pleaded. "Won't you please save

me and ask my parents to let me cry off the marriage?"

She patted Alice's hand. "Let me speak to the Duke and explain your concerns." The

irony had her mentally rolling her eyes. "He's the one you should discuss this with, not me."

"No, not the Duke. If you won't help me, I'l ask Freddie."

149

DESPITE CARINA'S CONTINUED PLEAS, Alice wouldn't listen and, soon after, pleaded a

headache and was taken home by her parents without speaking to Max. Before she'd met the

Johnston family, Carina had fretted about her sisters, worried about Gertie and been

frightened for herself. Closure, not vengeance, had been her plan.

Now, she'd inadvertently landed them al in a worse predicament and wished she'd

whisked the girls off to the country without delving into past problems, or seeking out the

virile man of her dreams in the hope of easing her loneliness. Memories of Max had driven

her to long nights of writhing under her bed linen until her hand crept between her thighs. She and Max had shared only one full night, nevertheless their connection had formed faster and

deeper than many life time affiliations. They shared an illicit sin that shaped their entire lives.

A younger and almost reticent Max had demonstrated the mechanics of swiving as

learned from prostitutes. She'd learned that being bedded by a man involved far more than

physical release, or a need to procreate, and though he'd denied it, Max also remembered. His

eyes revealed his bewilderment as he grappled with the concept of spiraling intimacy. Max's

reticence came across as coldness, which Alice interpreted as indifference.

She waited until another dance was in full swing and then slipped out a side door.

Waiting at the shadowed end of the verandah, she thought about Max's habit of following her

and knew they'd been foolish to think no one knew of their affair.

"Why are you alone?" he murmured near her ear and, despite expecting him, she was

startled. "A beautiful moon is meant to be shared with a lover."

"I was waiting for you."

He shifted to face her. "Surprising." He raised an eyebrow. "After forbidding me from

approaching you in public."

"And stil our relationship causes upsets."

"What's happened?"

"Your affianced bride went home."

He glanced around as if expecting to sight Alice, and Carina realized that she'd been

used as a shield against Max too many times.

"I don't understand why Alice left without speaking to me first."

"You left her alone and went to the card room."

"Hardly alone. Five hundred people are crammed into that ballroom."

She wanted to stomp her foot at his obtuseness. "Alice wants me to speak to you because

she's terrified of you, and if you don't try harder, she'l do something rash."

"You're not suggesting she'l run away?"

150

"THAT'S EXACTLY what I'm suggesting. Fred... another man kissed her and she enjoyed it.

But your passion frightens her."

"Passion? Good Lord. I kissed her, a very chaste kiss, when we became engaged. How

wil she cope with anything more? You, however, welcome my earthier appetites."

To her dismay, Carina blushed like a schoolgirl. "I despise married men who pursue

other women, but perhaps you should keep mistresses because you're a lusty and virile man

and Alice won't survive your demands. But talk to her. Reassure her that you won't push

your way into her bed. She might reconsider."

"Reconsider what?"

"Marrying you."

Max frowned, but for the first time took her seriously. "Breaking our betrothal is

impossible, no matter how much either of us wants to cal off the wedding."

"Then pacify Alice and hire another courtesan, before it's too late."

"I don't want any woman but you in my bed."

Her face felt hot and she couldn't breathe. "Shush." She took a surreptitious glance around. "Don't say those things, especial y not here."

"Tomorrow, then, at the cottage. We have to talk about our future."

She moaned. "We have no future. Why must I keep repeating that?"

"If I install another woman at our cottage and make love to her..." A rock settled in the

middle of her chest and left no room for air.

"And show her how to please me like you do, by stroking my cock and sucking me into

your —"

"Stop!" She held up her hand. "I can't listen to any more."

"See, you do care about us."

"Fine, I care. About you, us, al of it." She sniffled. "But how I feel or what I want makes

no difference to what must happen. We can't be together."

"I'l find a way to keep us together."

She stepped away from him. "What you need to do is convince Alice that you truly want

to marry her. She's our good friend and I won't ruin her life. And I've worked too hard to

make things better for my family and I won't let anything destroy their happiness."

"Ah, yes. Your years of plots and plans."

"Scoff if you must, but I survived the dreadful years by planning for a better future. I lay

on my back on cold beds in strange inns three different times and prayed that Fate would

intervene and save me, but no one helped me so I learned to save myself."

151

SHE IGNORED MAX'S WINCE, because after years of her pent-up anger and frustration she was close to uncovering the truth about those nights and the men who'd bought her, and

nothing would stand in her way now, not even six-foot-two of seething male vigor.

"I've apologized for my part, but you can't forgive any of us."

"I've explained about the two men who did nothing." She focused on two people

walking through the balroom doors. "But I want the fourth man."

Carina tried to turn away, but Max was too quick. He led her down the steps to the

garden and hid them behind a brick wal. "No more evasive answers about that man. Or I'l

drag the truth out of you and every guest here tonight will hear you scream, though not in

pain but in ecstasy."

She walked to a secluded bench seat and waited for Max to sit beside her.

"Before I tel you, you must promise to never reveal any of it or act on any of it."

He ran his fingers through his hair and she saw his internal struggle. For a potent man

like Max, relinquishing control wasn't easy, especial y when he was accustomed to taking

revenge on anyone who wronged him. But revealing the truth might make him despise her

and allow her to severe the bonds that tied them together so strongly.

"After the first experiment when Augustus was charged a fortune to have me –"

"Augustus didn't have you. I did."

"He paid for my body to be delivered. Who used me isn't important."

"It's important, because picturing him anywhere near you makes me sick."

"Anyway, the Earl picked a decent man for his second victim and I want to reassure him

that I bear no grudge." She sighed. "We connected, a brotherly sort of bond. I pretended to

drink the drugged wine."

"As you did with me."

"Yes, and I made sure we weren't watched by setting fire to the bedclothes and forcing

them to move us to another room." She braced herself. "Neither the Earl nor Augustus could

see anything."

He stiffened. "Why was my grandfather there?"

"Because he and the Earl had formed an unholy alliance through their common interest

in secretly observing others."

Max groaned. "I thought he only watched me, as he explained it, so I could be tutored on

my performances the next day."

"From what the Earl let slip, the pair paid a lot of money to watch anything and anyone

who caught their fancy." Max looked horrified. "My husband was often drunk and he liked to

152

BOAST about their brilliance in joining forces and partaking of their illegal activities while also

saving money. He drank to forget his impotence. Yet the more brothels they frequented, the

more obsessed they became with their viewings and then, of course, the Earl liked to

describe, in great detail, what they'd witnessed."

"Jeezus! You tried to tel me and I couldn't accept it. Despite discovering more and more of Augustus's sickening habits, I wouldn't believe that someone of my own flesh and blood

acted so shamefully. More fool me for not asking questions a lot sooner. But please, tell me

everything. Then I'll know how to help."

Carina frantically shook her head. "I've revealed this so you'l stay away from me,

before and after your marriage. Apart from my sisters, everything linked to me is perverted

and evil."

He nodded, though the militant look in his eyes made her wary. "Pray continue."

"I knew immediately that he was a gentleman. And I recognized his fear." She gave a

smal laugh. "He shook more than me."

"I can sympathize, because you were so different to other women. You were a highborn

lady, a virgin, and I was petrified."

"You? But why?"

She shrugged. "Failing to live up to Meacham expectations." Vulnerability clouded his

eyes for a moment before he dropped his shield. Max was an expert at hiding his feelings.

"The poor man worried that he couldn't perform. His elder brother had defied their father

by joining the military, but he died on the Peninsular. So the father bought me for his second

son."

"Like a consolation gift?"

"No, because he was only eighteen and hadn't been groomed to take over the titles and

responsibilities." Seeing Max's blank look, she said, "Never sowed his oats in London."

"Ah, so he was the true virgin that night. What happened?"

"We talked, and talked some more, and reached an agreement."

Max smiled. "You know, I'm thrilled that he didn't bed you."

She huffed. "Yet I'm supposed to discount the countless women you've bedded."

"Men are alowed far more leeway than women when it comes to carnal knowledge and

sexual behavior."

"Yes, women, both unmarried and married, are scorned for the slightest violation of our

suffocating moral codes. Though thankfully, widows can have any number of affairs, as long

as the couple is discreet, and the ton wil turn a blind eye."

153

HE SCOWLED. "Some widows may have daliances, but not you."

Carina bristled. "You can't stop me from having liaisons after we've parted."

"Yes, I can." He sounded like a peevish two-year-old. She started to stand, but he

stopped her. "Please, explain about the third man."

She steeled herself to unburden more of her past, when someone called from the terrace.

"Georgie, I'm here." She stepped out of the shadows and hurried towards the terrace,

sensing Max close behind her. She forgot about her past when she saw the worry on her

sister's face and saw her trembles. "What's wrong?"

"It's Lord Featherstone. Freddie. He's searching for Max and he's very angry."

Max looked at Georgie with confusion. "Featherstone follows Alice like a puppy, but

what does he want with me?"

Carina spoke quietly, hoping Max wouldn't explode. "When I spoke with Alice earlier, she mentioned that she and Lord Featherstone…"

"I remember." He took Georgie's hand. "There's nothing to be upset about."

"But he looked very cross."

"Did he frighten you?"

Georgie nodded and looked towards the ballroom doors. Featherstone called out and

Georgie jumped. Max stepped in front and shielded her from Featherstone, who was

marching towards them.

"Stirkton, a word please." He glanced at the women. "In private."

"I'm busy, Featherstone. You may cal tomorrow if the matter's urgent."

"Tomorrow wil be too late." He tried to pul Max aside, but Carina hovered beside

them. "You've upset Alice, Stirkton, and goaded her into doing something rash."

'And what does this have to do with you."

"I'm Alice's friend."

"Apparently, though I'd rather you left near my fiancée alone. And if you ever dare kiss

her again, you'l be dealing with my seconds."

Carina gasped and Max shot her a sharp look, but thankfully Featherstone showed sense

and walked away.

Lucy rushed onto the terrace. "Carina, Georgie, I danced with the most wonderful man

and he's quite acceptable because Lady Malory introduced us."

"What's his name?" Max asked in a severe tone.

Carina smiled. "You sound like a concerned papa."

He shook his head. "Lucille, I'm sure if Lady Malory introduced you, he's a suitable

154

. . .

ESCORT, BUT TEL ME HIS NAME."

"Lord Vaughn." Lucy sighed dreamily.

Max gave a fleeting smile. "Ah, yes. Ladies liken Vaughn to a Greek god."

Lucy blushed. "I...I wouldn't know. Though he is certainly very handsome."

Carina hugged her sister. "Lucy, Max is teasing."

The corners of Max's mouth turned up slightly. "Lucille, I'l make a few discreet

enquiries, but from what I know of Vaughn and his family, he is a decent young man. You

could do a lot worse for a husband."

Lucy grinned impishly. "I'm not looking to marry quite yet." Her happiness died for a

moment as she glanced at Carina. "Unless I am forced to."

Carina shook her head. "You'l marry whoever you wish and whenever you wish. Peter

won't force you into anything. Now, shal we return to the bal?" As she linked arms with her

sisters and walked to the door, Max murmured, "We shal finish our conversation later."

They rejoined the crush and danced for several more hours. Lucy and Georgie chattered

on the drive home, prattling on and on about the wonderful gentlemen they'd met and those

they'd danced with. They were happy and looking forward to a better future, and Carina

would do everything in her power to see that it happened.

Since Max had entered their lives, her sisters had blossomed and were more content.

Even Gertie trusted Max and extolled his virtues. *She* also trusted him, despite their

relationship having begun with lies, trickery, and shame. And she'd witnessed his softening attitudes. Though with Alice, he remained unbending and formal.

If he couldn't treat Alice as compassionately as he looked after her sisters, she'd leave

and let him concentrate on calming and caring for Alice. If he didn't resolve the situation

quickly, she'd solve it in her own fashion by disappearing.

16

The door knocker banged loudly enough to disturb the family seated around the breakfast table at Woods House the next morning. The butler showed in their visitor and announced formally, "His Grace, the Duke of Stirkton."

His Grace, however, hadn't waited for the announcement but stormed into the room, his

155

FACE LIKE THUNDER. He stood, feet braced, hands on the end of the dining table, and stared down its length at Carina.

"What happened last night?"

She dropped her toast and watched jam spread across the white linen tablecloth. "Damn, you frightened me." Glancing at Georgie, she expected the worst. But Gertie took Georgie's hand and rather than cowering, she smiled sweetly.

"Good morning, Max."

The others looked at Georgie in shock while Max, belatedly remembering his manners,

dipped his head towards her. His gaze swung back to Carina and he stretched forward,

looking menacing and furious.

"What did you say to Alice?"

His jaw clenched so tightly as he awaited her answer, she worried he'd break a tooth.

"Why? Has something happened?"

With a loud hiss, he strode around the table to Carina's chair and jerked it backwards,

nearly tipping her to the floor. She grabbed the edge of the table and glared at him. "What is

wrong with you?"

"I need answers." He stabbed a finger towards her chest. "About what's been going on

behind my back." Lucy looked stunned, though unafraid, but Georgie shrank into her seat and

twisted her napkin around her fingers.

Max followed her quick sideways glances at her sisters and he saw Georgie's stricken

expression. "Damnation!" He let go of Carina's chair, walked around to Georgie, and took

the empty chair next to her. He her hand and stilled her compulsive slaying of the hapless

napkin. "I promise I'l never hurt Carina, or any of you. Do you understand?"

Georgie nodded. "You rage made me remember."

"Remember your marriage?" Georgie nodded. "Your husband had a temper. Did he beat

you?"

Georgie first looked to Carina for guidance, before facing Max and nodding. "He was

very cruel to me. He broke my wrist, and another time he pushed me down the stairs and I broke my ankle."

"Dear God," Max said. "If the bastard was alive, I'd kil him myself."

Carina, Gertie, and Lucy watched Georgie nervously. But to every-one's surprise,

Georgie gave Max a small and tentative smile.

"If my husband had lived this long and continued with his torments, I'd have kiled him

myself." She turned to Carina, whose shoulders had slumped with relief. "You understand,

156

DON'T YOU? Disposing of your husband is the only way to be free. I couldn't have survived

much longer."

Carina drew a deep breath. "Yes, I understand perfectly."

Max wondered for the hundredth time if Carina had murdered her husband. Not that he'd

blame her if she'd sent the evil bastard to a fiery hell. Nonetheless society would condemn

her. Men, especially men with titles, held a stronger position than women and if anyone

suspected that Carina had hastened her husband's demise, she'd be in grave danger. The law

seldom judged his male peers harshly; yet any woman, countess or not, could be prosecuted,

tossed on a ship and sent to the Colonies, and outraged men would stand in court and cheer

her sentence.

He averted his eyes, because she read him wel and she'd know his suspicions regarding

the Earl's death. "Ladies, I don't care about the past, only the present. An hour ago, Lord

Johnston came to my house and informed me that his daughter is missing. He believes she

eloped."

Out of the four ladies, Carina was the only one looking unsur-prised. "If she confided in

you, Carina, you must tell me. Has she eloped? Run away with Featherstone? If so, I might

stil catch them before they reach Gretna Green, or wherever the foolish pair are headed."

"I'm sorry, but I've no idea." Georgie made a strangled noise and Carina turned to her

with a frown. "Do you know where Alice has gone?"

"No, not that...only Alice said—"

"What?" Max knew he shouldn't have snapped at Georgie, because she almost jumped

out of her seat. He toned down his frustration and reassured her. "I'm not angry at you, or

Alice, or even Featherstone. But her parents are frantic."

"Alice didn't want to marry—" Georgie covered her mouth.

"Me! Alice didn't want to marry me."

Georgie nodded.

Max accepted the devastating news with as much outward calm as he could muster,

despite his inner pain. Being rejected was nothing new, but it reinforced his belief that his

mother had left because he hadn't been worthy.

After a glance at Carina's face, stark with horror and embarrass-ment, Gertie motioned

Lucy out of her seat and helped Georgie to her feet. "Lucy, we'l take Georgie upstairs to rest

and let Carina and Max discuss this in private."

Max could barely contain himself until the three ladies were well out of earshot. He

didn't want them to witness what was coming.

157

. . .

"Wᴇʟ," he said. "Go ahead and tel me I'm thick-headed and unseeing and uncaring, and

I should have listened to you, to al of you. Alice's parents blame me and they've every right

to do so, because I stupidly expected a seventeen-year-old girl to suddenly mature beyond her

years and accept me for who I am."

"Max, I explained. Alice needs time to grow accustomed to your..."

"Oh, good God. You're going to say my arrogant attitude, my ill-mannered boorishness."

She gave his arms a little shake. "You were brought up to believe that Meachams are one

step below gods, so it's hard to relax your guard. Except at Brent Street of course."

"I'm only comfortable with you." He ran a finger down her cheek. Even when dealing

with rejection by another woman, he wanted Carina's opinion.

"You should treat Alice the way you treat me, with respect and understanding and..."

"And what? Love?"

"Tenderness! You're in lust with me, not love, and that wil fade as quickly as it has with

the others. But you and Alice wil learn about each other and she'l bear your children..."

"You dislike the idea."

"Max, concentrate on finding Alice before she and Freddie–"

"Featherstone. She's with that poetry-spouting whelp?"

"I'm not sure, but yes, she might be with Freddie. He's very nice and he reads her his

poetry, and does al the romantic things that an impressionable young girl appreciates."

"I'm not going to write about my beloved's pink cheeks."

Carina choked on a spurt of laughter, making Max even crosser.

Max scowled. "Go ahead and laugh. I imagine Alice considers me an antique."

"Mmm." Her lips twitched. "She did mention graying hair."

Max's touched his hair and frowned. "I have gray hairs?"

"I didn't know you were so vain." Carina chuckled. "A lady of my age might see a man

nearing thirty as in his prime, but to a young girl like Alice…"

He snorted. "I'm the monster who'l wed and bed a child to get an heir."

"Something like that, yes."

"So why didn't you run from me too?"

"We made a bargain and I always honor my word."

"Is that the only reason you're with me? For honor and our pact."

"What other reason could there be?"

She wouldn't meet his gaze so he tipped her chin up so he could read her eyes. "I thought

you might care for me, even a little."

158

"I CARE MORE than I should, but caring brings unhappiness."

He frowned, trying to grasp her underlying meaning and wondering if she could ever

bring herself to love a man she'd been sold to like a common street walker. "My grandfather

believed that women only love titles and wealth."

"He was a bitter and unloved old man, who wanted you feel as unlovable as him. But

you're not like him and Alice wil come to love you."

"I've ruined my chances." He rubbed a hand over his throbbing head. "I must go and

speak to Johnston and discover if Alice has miraculously returned."

"If it's any consolation, I don't think Alice wil disappointment her parents by doing

something scandalous. I'm guessing that she'l be home today, apologetic and unscathed."

"Then come with me. She'l listen to you."

"You can't imagine that I'm the best person to plead your case with Alice."

"Yes … no. I honestly don't know. My life was charted down to the last detail, and now

everything is in chaos and I don't know what to do for the best."

"Before you see Alice, be prepared to promise her everything she thinks she's missed

until now. Promise her that you'l treat your marriage like a partnership whenever possible,

and that you value her input and presence in your life."

Without thinking, he said, "That'd be easy if you were my wife." Neither spoke for a

minute. "Perhaps I should break our betrothal, free Alice from my unwanted embraces and

marry you instead."

"You're not thinking rationally. If you cry off, you'll loathe being the subject of gossip

and scandal, and tossing aside nearly thirty years of plans wil tear you apart."

"And if Alice rescinds? I'l be condemned as the evil villain who petrifies chits until

either they faint or run."

"The woman is normally blamed, not the man, and that's why you must protect Alice."

She cupped his cheek and he turned into her warm touch.

"Whether or not I marry Alice, I'l stil want you. Body and soul."

Her hand fel away from his cheek as if burned and he felt chilled. "Please, don't.

Declarations like that are unfair when our being together would cause heartache for others."

He latched onto the only words that mattered. "But do you wish it could be different? Be

honest. Does the thought of me living with another woman, making love to her, make your

stomach churn as mine does?"

Her eyes were damp when she turned to escape, but he caught hold and ran a finger

through the tears flowing down her cheek. "Go, Max, please go. You must be stronger than

159

ME AND WALK AWAY before I weaken."

He kissed her, gently pressing his lips to her pouted mouth, miserable that her lips were

sealed and she wouldn't alow him entrance to her soft mouth. As usual, she perceived the

deeper consequences of their alliance far better than him and understood that declarations,

even private pledges, were futile. Alice and the protection of her good name was his priority

and after that, he knew from his cousin's recent letters that he was close to finishing his

mission to improve the lives of the women from his past.

His mother had been driven away; his father and uncle doomed to misery; and if it

weren't for the few good memories he clung to instead of cowering to Augustus's whims, he

too might have turned to drink, gambling and women. Real courage was standing strong

through adversity and forging a better path, the way Carina had survived, and hopefully

Georgie would so soon.

Carina's quest to grant her second man forgiveness and to perform a cleansing ritual by locating the third was noble and courageous. Yet she'd fixated on number four and seemed

obsessed with exposing the man so he could be punished for an ordeal that never eventuated.

He needed to unravel that particular puzzle before Carina lost patience with their slow and

tedious probing into Augustus's hidden secrets and decided to publicly humiliate the man.

Retaliation was her right, but if the man was disgraced his reputation might be tarnished in

the short term, while Carina's would suffer irreparable damage. Unfair, but in their realm,

men ruled and women were always the losers.

A SHORT TIME LATER, Lord Johnston's butler ushered Max into his Lordship's study, where

JOHNSTON PACED and grunted and looked to be at his wits' end.

"I spoke with Lady Dorchester and her sisters and, yes, they were with Alice shortly

before she left."

"It's her fault!" Lady Johnston barreled through the doorway and screeched her

accusation. She caught her hip on a side table and a vase rocked, but obviously well used to

such catastrophes, Johnston grabbed the porcelain before it crashed to the floor.

"Now, Gloria, some blame must lie with Alice for disappearing without a word."

"How dare you blame our sweet daughter? She's been wronged by a devil in disguise."

She sneered at Max. "Had I known the true character of her

intended, I'd have protected my

angel from your cruel and calous treatment."

"Madam," Max warned, "take care. No man, or woman, besmirches my name. I accept

that in this instance, a portion of the blame lies with me."

160

"IF YOU'D DEVOTED a trifle of your precious time to Alice, she'd have learned to accept

your severe mannerisms. But no. You've been preoccupied with that woman, the conniving

Countess, and ignored Alice's distress."

Max flinched at yet another taunt about his affair with Carina. He'd taken pains to keep

his liaisons secret and could have sworn no one knew the identity of any woman he visited.

Yet he'd not remained vigilant when he began his affair with Carina, arrogantly assuming

that she'd welcome a month as a duke's lover and, if anyone discovered her identity, would

shrug off any smear to her name.

"I owed Carina a debt from our younger days, and I was glad of a chance to repay her by

presenting her sisters social y. Alice knew, and understood."

"Carina! You cal your lady love by her Christian name, yet in al these weeks you've

not addressed my angel by her beautiful name."

"Gloria," Johnston said, leading his wife to a chair. "You're over-taxing yourself. I set

runners on the roads out of London and I'm confident we'l soon hear good news."

"We'l al be ruined," she moaned. "The jealous harpies would like nothing better than to

bring down my angel, as she's a diamond in a sea of plain stones."

She pressed her

handkerchief to her red eyes, while tears continued to flow down her pudgy cheeks.

Max was about to console the lady when the door flew open and in rushed his would-be–

bride, closely followed by Featherstone. Seeing her distraught mother, Alice threw herself at

her mater's feet and sobbed as loudly as her parent. Johnston glared at Freddie, obviously

wishing he could throttle the hapless young man, but Max stepped between them.

"Featherstone, please explain where you've been and why you're Alice's escort."

To give Featherstone his due, he faced his elders with a straight back and his head held

high. "Alice is unharmed. Her maid is seated outside and wil verify that she's been with her

mistress every moment."

"But where in hel have you been?" Johnston barked the question at Freddie, obviously

recognizing the futility of asking his sobbing daughter.

"Your daughter, Alice—"

"I know her name, you blackguard. Answer my questions."

"Papa!" Alice jumped up and rushed to Freddie's side, and Max was impressed that she

was, at last, showing some backbone. "Don't speak to Freddie that way. You should be

thanking him and praising his efforts to keep me safe. After rescuing me, he took me to his

family and he's returned me here, unharmed, and he stopped me making a huge mistake."

She glanced sideways as Max, who bowed slightly in return. "Freddie showed me that

161

. . .

MARRYING the Duke is my duty and that by running away, I nearly destroyed everything Mama

worked so hard for." She stiffened. "I'm ready to marry you, Your Grace, if you can bring

yourself to forgive me." She stared at him for a moment before turning to Freddie and

reaching for his hand.

Freddie addressed Max, while keeping a firm clasp on Alice's hand. "You're a lucky

man, Stirkton, and I hope that you'l show a little more appreciation for the paragon you'l

have as your duchess. If Alice was mine..." Freddie huffed.

"You'd treat her better than I have, is that it?"

"Yes, by God, that's exactly it. Alice is a jewel, a rare beauty, who deserves to be

worshipped and treated like a princess. Not neglected, as you've done."

Alice listened to Featherstone's prosing in rapt adoration. "Thank you for helping me,

Freddie, and for being my friend." They gazed at each other like a pair of lovebirds.

The excess of publicly expressed sentiment was slightly nauseating, but who was he to

gainsay young love? Even a jaded man recognized the symptoms and these two were

blatantly in love. Only a few weeks ago, Max would have utter some caustic remark about the

stupidity of any gentleman who found himself tangled in love's web, but then he'd been

conscious of his promises to Alice and the rules for arranged marriages, all of which ran

contrary to him finding eternal happiness. Or whatever drivel the poets wrote about endlessly.

Max puled on his haughty ducal mask. "Might I be alowed a few moments to speak privately with Alice?"

"No!" Freddie yeled. "I'l not alow you to browbeat her again."

"Browbeat?" Max raised an eyebrow at Alice, though inwardly amused that she'd seen

his attempt at flirtation as browbeating.

Alice had the grace to blush. "Perhaps browbeat was too harsh, Your Grace, because I'm

certain you meant well, Your Grace, with you instructions on how I should behave, Your

Grace." She dropped a curtsy.

"Three Your Graces in one sentence make me feel like a bishop, an old one at that, rather

than your betrothed. And we agreed that you could address me by my given name."

"Oh, yes, Your Grace. I mean, Maximus."

Max inwardly groaned. Recently, he'd come to resent being addressed so formally by

those closest to him and especially when his baptism name was spoken with such deferential

reverence. The cheeky informality Carina applied by shortening his name to Max, as his

mother had called him long ago, fitted his new persona far better.

Lord Johnston helped his wife from her chair and escorted her to the door. "A few

162

MOMENTS ALONE IS ACCEPTABLE." He ignored Freddie's disgust. "Perhaps you can ease any

worries Alice harbors over your wedding. Though I'm positive it's merely pre-marriage

jitters."

Freddie glared at Max. "Alice is a sensitive woman, so please don't upset her."

Max dipped his head.

"I'll wait in the corridor, Alice," Freddie murmured. "Cal if you need me."

Max rolled his eyes. "I'm not going to beat her, Featherstone. She's perfectly safe."

When he and Alice were alone, Max paced around the room, taking care to stay a good

distance away so he didn't frighten her. "We should discuss our forthcoming marriage."

"Yes, Your Grace."

"Max!" Alice jumped. Despite her thinking him an ogre, he rarely raised his voice with

anyone, and especial y not with a lady, so it baffled him why she'd reverted to her habit of

twisting her handkerchief into knots. Thankfully, she undid the soggy of mass of linen and

dabbed at her tear-streaked face. He took a chance and dropped to the settee beside her,

offering her his pristine white linen and pleased when she accepted the monogrammed square

to dry herself.

"I'd like a truthful answer, Alice." She nodded. "Do you wish to marry me?"

"Mama said it was my duty because Papa and your grandfather had signed the contracts

many years ago and it would be wrong to change it now, and I don't want my parents to be

upset. I know it was pointless to see Freddie last night, but I wanted to ask ..."

"Ask Freddie what?" Max used his kindest voice and even patted Alice's hand, though

he recognized the irony as the gesture placed him firmly as a father figure and not a husband,

and definitely not her lover.

"What I should do to please you."

He choked on his own laughter. "You asked Featherstone for

advice on us?"

She nodded. "He's the wisest man I've ever known."

This time, he couldn't contain his mirth. Good Lord, he was treating their problem as

irreverently as Carina treated their so-cal ed friendship. "I'm certain Featherstone, Freddie, is

a fount of information. What did he advise?"

"He suggested that you might postpone joining me in bed until I became more

accustomed to your ways and felt more at ease."

Max couldn't believe his ears. The interfering pup was suggesting to a duke that he not

bed his duchess, though, in truth, he understood Featherstone's rationale. Given time, and a

great deal of patience from said duke, Alice might accept him into her bed, at least for the

163

REQUISITE NUMBER of visits to beget her with his child, without screaming the roof down.

Perhaps, then, Alice could be coaxed into conceiving a second child. Though swiving his

duchess had suddenly become responsibility rather than pleasure and, for Alice, the

fulfillment of a horrifying duty. His future looked bleak and unpleasant. Ploughing his wife

without any satisfaction, while using an endless line of inter-changeable ladybirds to relieve

his lust had become an insufferable burden.

Christ Almighty, he wasn't even thirty years old, and he had no desire to couple with a

woman who thought it her duty to lie beneath him in a duchess's luxurious bed and ensure that a lineage of dubious merit continued for a few more centuries. "No!"

Alice startled and stared at him blankly. "So you'l insist upon consummating our

marriage on our wedding night?"

"No, no, I didn't mean that." He shook his head. "I'm no more eager to take your

innocence than you are to surrender it to me."

Her were as wide as saucers and she twisted his kerchief around her fingers this time.

"Please, Your Grace, give me another chance. I'l try to be a good wife and learn what you

want and what you like and..."

Max's laugh was full-bellied and so out of character that Alice stared at him as if he

turned into someone else, a man who laughed and smiled. When his mirth had settled to

chuckles and he'd regained his composure, he said, "I imagine Featherstone wil be eager to

teach you how to please a man between the sheets. How to engage a duke."

At that he doubled over with laughter and clutched his aching stomach. After he'd wiped

the irreverent tears from his eyes, he patted her hand. His decision was made so easily that he

was stunned that he'd taken so long to think rationally. He mentally tossed the last of his

grandfather's dictates into the flames and began his new strategies.

'Are you quite wel? You're laughing and I've never seen you do so before."

"We're free, Alice. Both of us, because I'l not marry you."

Color drained from her face. "You're rejecting me over my foolish behavior."

"No, we're rejecting each other. Thanks to your cleverness, we've realized in time that

we don't suit and staying together would make us both unhappy."

"But my parents...They'll be angry that I was unable to hold onto a duke, especial y

after al their arrangements."

"Believe me, my dear, that scandals are soon forgotten, even those involving dukes. The

important thing is that we can follow our heart's desires. You and your beloved Freddie are

free to be married."

164

"OH, HOW WONDERFUL!" She flung her arms around his shoulders and hugged him. "But

our separation wil cause so much talk. Won't you be devastated?"

"I'l survive. People don't question a duke, no matter how bizarre his actions."

"And the best part is that you can now propose to the woman you love."

Max was stunned. "The woman I love?"

Alice patted his hand this time, giving him the impression she was far wiser than he in

matters of the heart, which she was. "Women understand better than men and despite you

trying to hide your feelings, I knew that you loved Carina, and not me."

"Carina and I are close friends."

She shook her head and gave him an understanding smile. "You do love her, though you

mightn't be ready to admit it, and I'd be thrilled if you found the same happiness that I'l find

with a certain gentleman. One I'm eager to marry, if he'l have me."

Max smiled. "Your certain gentlemen wil be delighted. It's best if I explain to your

parents that our decision is mutually acceptable, and that I wish to pay for your wedding with

Featherstone. If I stand at the altar with Freddie, no one will dare object, or mention the

change of groom."

Alice launched herself at him and kissed him full on the lips. "Oh, Max, Max, you're a

truly wonderful man."

He chuckled. "That's the first time you've caled me by my Christian name."

They chattered comfortably, friends at last, until Max summoned the courage to quiz

Alice. "Do you think I might have a chance—" He pushed down the large lump that blocked

his throat. Asking for advice, or assistance, was difficult. "If I were to ask Carina…"

"Yes, Max." Alice's eyes shone with female wisdom. "Take a chance and ask Carina,

because you both deserve to be happy. Don't think of marriage as tradition and heritage, but

as a chance to be with the woman you love."

Together, they faced Alice's parents, and Max was astounded at Alice's calm composure

when she automatically led her mother to a sofa and fetched smelling salts. Featherstone

looked stunned, overcome and grateful all at once that his wish was about to come true and

he could marry Alice. But he rose to the occasion admirably and handled Alice's hysterical

mother with aplomb, admonishing her for upsetting her daughter and earning Alice's undying

gratitude.

Before he said his farewells, Max arranged a meeting with Freddie at his fencing

academy the next morning, where he promised to give Freddie a few pointers. Electing to act

as advisor to a younger man was a novel experience, but one Max envisaged as enjoyable for

165

BOTH TEACHER AND PUPIL. He'd had little time for male bonding, as friendships had been

discouraged because they drained a man's reserves of time and money. Now, he looked

forward to the simple pleasures he'd been denied.

17

_____

"I'm free, Carina." Max said, within minutes of rushing into his house and into the drawing room where she was waiting. Though it was stepping over the line of propriety,

she'd wanted to be here when he returned and hear news of Alice.

"I'm now unattached and begging you to please, please be my wife." He took her hands

and smiled, and she saw his sincerity. "Alice's future is with Freddie, who incidentally adores

her, but you already knew that. Before you came back, my life was sterile and hollow and I

can't, I won't, go back to that miserable existence. People look at me and see titles and

lineage, but I want to be more. To be a good husband and a doting father to our children.

Help me prove that this Stirkton is a man of substance, and a man with a heart and soul."

His words were like a knife's twist to her gut and she was wavered, mind spinning, not knowing which way to jump. Heaven knew, she ached to say yes. Longed to grab hold of

Max's offering with both hands and cling to the idea of a happy future together. But there

were too many questions that needed answering and people who threatened their existence.

"I'l never be your ideal wife, Max. Your grandfather would turn over in his grave

hearing you propose to me, an outspoken widow with a shady past."

"You could already be carrying my babe, perhaps a Meacham heir."

"I'm neither stupid nor naïve, so I understood how risky it was giving in to our passion

with no thought to the consequences." She touched her stomach. I've imagined, many times,

that your seed is growing inside me and giving me a precious babe."

Max grimaced. "I'm entirely to blame for taking those risks, and for that I apologize.

You're not a courtesan, and know little about preventing conception, yet I didn't wear a

sheath and didn't spil outside your body. Deep down, I wanted to impregnate you because

then I could claim you as mine and have legitimate reasons for keeping you close."

"You've always been cautious and calculated, and yet you wanted me to carry your babe

and out of wedlock. Why?"

166

"I DIDN'T EXAMINE my reasons. Only that I was compeled to spil myself inside you, high and often, and provide myself with a legitimate excuse for claiming you as mine."

"Huh! Putting your stamp on me, the way a protector claims an expensive ladybird after

he's paid a considerable amount of money for her. Parading women as trophies so their

friends can see their enhanced status and die from envy."

"You're wrong. Even at first, I didn't think of you as a bought woman. I pictured you

round and ripe with my babe in your belly and saw you as the woman I wanted to shelter and

protect forever."

"While giving no thought to how society would shun me if I bore you a child at the same

time you were bedding another woman, your publicly acclaimed duchess. The ultimate irony

would have been you juggling two pregnant women at the same time."

"Dammit, I thought Alice would make a good duchess, but you're the one who said she

considered me a monster."

She nodded. "Poor Alice. Knowing she wasn't loved and that you only wanted what she

represents: virginity, innocence, and good-breeding. You and her parents traded the girl like a

commodity to be bought and sold, without thought to the contents."

"Thank you for reminding me of my more loathsome traits. But though you've had good

reason to despise my conduct in the past, I've changed."

"But can you open your heart and let someone love you? Because if you can't love, and

be loved, I can't marry you."

"Give me time to prove myself. We've located almost every woman from my past and, between my cousin and me, we're making amends and giving them a new life. A better life

than they came from. So please, let me prove I can be a good husband."

"You're a duke and you should be choosing someone more suitable, another young girl

to replace Alice. Because I'm not young, pure or unjaded. Right now, you're suffering from

wounded pride, but I won't be your second best choice for a wife."

"My love, you're good, kind and generous and you survived where most young girls

would have surrendered. You emerged from a ghastly marriage as a strong and wonderful

lady who I truly admire."

"Yet you've never exonerated me of my husband's murder."

"You didn't kil him. But even if you had it wouldn't matter, because I know more than

anyone how much he deserved to die. If the Earl stil lived, I'd take great pleasure in sending

him to hell with my own hands, squeezing the breath out of him and stopping him from

spying on any other women, or men."

167

SHE SNORTED. "I never knew you were so blood thirsty. But thank you for believing in

me." She frowned. "What about Alice? Are you disappointed to have lost her?"

He shook his head. "I'm relieved that we parted amicably, because I wouldn't have been

able to proceed along that path anyway."

"Why not?"

"You, my sweet, are being deliberately obtuse. After sharing so much with you, I realized what truly mattered between a man and woman and I wouldn't have been able to

settle for less. Not for Alice, and not with any other woman. You have to believe me."

"What you're saying is so contrary to everything you believed. I believe in the sanctity

of marriage, one man and one woman, and it would rip my heart from my chest if I learned

that you were still dallying with other women."

He lightly shook her hands and spoke directly into her eyes. "With you in my life, I'l

never want anyone else."

"I want to say yes to you, I realy do. But there are other considerations and people who

depend upon me, and until that's al sorted, I can't give you an answer."

"Then tel me this: do you love me?"

Carina looked into eyes so very familiar and so very dear, heard the quaver in his voice

and saw the vulnerability behind the question. Max was pleading for her reassurance, which

was laughable considering that her feelings refused to stay hidden, and despite him knowing

that his kisses made her knees give way, and that making love with him made her body mclt

and her heart race. This man, her duke, made her feel more precious than all the jewels in his

family's extensive collection.

Each evening, heedless of other balroom guests, Max's greetings had been enthusiastic,

as if her presence tipped his world back onto its correct axis. Being the focus of a powerful

man was intoxicating, while saving him from noisily squawking debutantes whenever he shot

her beseeching looks, strengthened her sense of purpose. In some respects, Max had already

won their silent war. She craved his touch, yearned for his mouth meeting hers, and longed to

feel him slide into her body and ease her loneliness and pain.

She laid her palm on his cheek. "You know I love you, and with al my heart."

Max sagged with relief. Despite knowing it was best, Alice's rejection had stil stung his

pride, though left his heart untouched. Carina's rejection would have torn his heart into two

pieces and reduced his past, and his future, to a pile of meaningless thoughts and useless

actions. He needed her, desperately, to anchor him and help him achieve his goals.

Carina's eyes were as dark and green as a stormy sea. "But can you let go of the past and

168

LEARN TO LOVE YOURSELF, and to love me?"

No one had dared ask him personal questions and he'd never explained his feelings, but

he couldn't bear to lose her love. So how did he speak of something intangible, like love, or

swear a lifetime's commitment when he'd no experience with any of it? He wouldn't lie, yet

his knowledge of love wouldn't fil a thimble.

"My feelings are self-evident. I want you to be my wife."

"You also asked for Alice's hand in marriage, yet you've said you didn't love her.

This proposal might be exactly the same; a way to tidy up your messy life without

exerting any effort on your part."

Max frowned. "What more do you want from me? Poetic words, me down on one knee and sprouting nonsensical notions of romance?"

She shook her head. "Not poetry, but I want you to say you love me, out loud, and mean

every damn word."

"Our marriage wil be a hel of a lot better than most, because we're friends and lovers.

Isn't that enough?"

Carina shook her head. "I've had a loveless marriage and I won't have another."

"Do not compare that sham with the Earl to the union I'm offering. Tel me it's different.

Tel me you love sharing my bed."

A solitary tear ran down her cheek. She'd told him she didn't cry, yet he'd driven her to

tears for a second time.

"You're a wonderful lover: giving, passionate and considerate, and I love every minute

with you. But don't you see? Without mutual love, I'd resent that you couldn't open yourself

to me and return my love."

"You'd have me and my protection for you and your sisters."

"I love you for that, but if you can't openly admit your love, I'm scared you never wil.

And I want our children to grow up in a warm and loving home and not a cold mausoleum."

"I've been changing things within my household ever since my grandfather died."

"I'm truly happy that you became close to Wil iam during your years of searching and

making amends, but for now it must be goodbye."

"I think you're carrying my child; our child."

Carina ignored his wistful look. "I don't think so." She suspected that she was *enceinte*,

but until she was certain she'd admit nothing because Max would override all her protests and put his ring on her finger. And she refused to marry for the wrong reasons.

"Time wil tel," he said. "I think your bely wil soon swel with my babe. You've not

169

BLED IN SEVERAL WEEKS."

"How do you know that?"

"Huh! I've had plenty of experience with women's cycles and moods. Besides which, I

know your body better than I know my own."

"Ah, yes. The legendary Stirkton and his knowledge of the female anatomy. Developed

over countless years with innumerable women. Nature would have disrupted your schedule

on occasions, I imagine, forcing you to avoid the cottage and messy women."

Max flinched. Despite the truth behind her words, her blunt delivery made him even

more ashamed of his past conduct. "I meant that after being so close these past weeks, I'd

have noticed signs of your menses. Alice's wedding is in a week's time and, by then, you

should know for sure."

"Possibly," she said.

He stepped closer and touched his forehead to hers. "I'll be over-joyed if you are

expecting, though I've no idea how wel I'l do as a father. Stil, I look forward to being a

parent alongside you."

"Stop. Don't make this any harder. Please let me go, for now at least. With al that's

happened, I can't think clearly."

"I'l leave, but if you carry my child, nothing can prevent me from claiming you as my

duchess." He puled her to him and kissed her hard and long until she trembled in his arms.

Her face flushed with desire and she instinctively pressed her curves into his body. "You

want me as much as I yearn to claim you."

"Then say you love me. Say the words and we'l be married today or tomorrow, as soon

as possible. Otherwise, let me go."

His mouth opened and he tried, he really tried, to give her the words she needed.

Pointless to blame his cold upbringing, when the fault lay directly with him and his dread of

open displays of emotion. Carina gathered her cloak and walked out of his door and his

house, and possibly his life.

When his butler spoke several minutes later, he realized he hadn't moved but stil stood

in place, as cold as the marble busts dotted around the walls of his study.

"Your Grace, wil there be anything else?"

He shook himself. "No, Benson, nothing."

His butler walked away, though Max longed to call him back and solicit his advice,

despite keeping the regulation distance between he and his staff and never having confided in

a servant before. Still, Carina spoke to her butler often, as equals and even friends.

170

HE CLEARED his throat loudly and waited until Benson turned and came towards him. "You were employed in my grandfather's household when you were younger."

"Indeed I was, Your Grace." Benson sighed. "I was present when Your Grace returned

home from Eton each Christmas."

"Do you perhaps remember my mo...mother?" He'd been forbidden from ever speaking

of his mother, so it was difficult to cal her by that familial name. "Or how the Hal flowed

when she was alive?"

"Oh, yes, indeed I do." A happy smile creased Benson's face. "Things were very

different then."

"How so?"

"Your mother, the late duchess, was a wonderful lady. She spoiled you every year at

Christmas to make up for not being alowed see you during the rest of the year."

"I spent Christmas with my mother?"

"Yes, Your Grace. When you were younger, your grandfather allowed you to spend

Christmas with your mother in the country."

"So, even then my grandfather made al the decisions about me."

"Before your sire was kiled in that hunting accident, he took control, especial y at the

Hall, though no one was allowed forget that your grandfather controlled the finances. When

your father was killed, your mother was distraught, and not only because of how much she

loved your father."

"What do you mean? I thought my mother and father lived separate lives."

"Your grandfather tried to force them apart after you were born. One heir was sufficient

and he didn't want your mother conceiving a second time."

Max's thoughts spun faster than a child's wooden top. Augustus's version of this story

had been the opposite to Benson's. "My grandfather deliberately kept my father away from

my mother?"

"Your father was dispatched to London on one sham pretext after another, and women,

lower class women, were pushed into your father's path time and time again."

Max rubbed his temples. "He wanted my father to take mistresses so he'd stay away

from my mother?"

"It wasn't the staff's place to judge, or to reason with the late master, but we al

understood his intentions. He wanted your lineage kept pure by having one perfect son in

each generation. Siblings would have divided your attention and distracted you from your

studies. And, they might have expected a share of the family's wealth."

171

MAX SHOOK his head in disgust. He'd been robbed of parents to love and siblings to

relieve his loneliness because one sick, perverted old man had been obsessed with creating

his dynasty. His stomach heaved and he feared shocking Benson by retching. For himself, he

was past caring about the strictures and rules he'd been indoctrinated with, because it seemed

so pointless.

"Benson, what a fool I've been. I believed al the lies. Believed that my mother rejected

me and refused to have other children."

"We always regretted that your childhood was so short-lived. Cook, the housekeeper, all

of us at the Hall, tried to give you a little bit of the love you lost when your mama died, but

the old master threatened us with dismissal if we stepped out of line. No descendant of

Augustus Meacham was to be mollycoddled."

Max was heartsick, especially when he opened his mind to memories of his mother. "Did

my mother grow roses?"

"Oh, yes." Benson smiled again, his face lighting up and replacing his normal, austere

expression with glee. Max felt worse when he realized that Benson was a man with emotions,

expressions and memories and he could have shared things years earlier if Max hadn't been

a...What had Lucille called him? A stuffed shirt.

"...They were her pride and joy." Benson had a faraway look in his faded gray eyes.

"After you, of course. The house was filled with roses and when you were home, you helped

cut blooms for the vases. Your mother distilled oil from her roses to wear as a fragrance on

her person. The Duchess smeled beautiful."

"She smeled of roses."

"Or lavender," Benson said, "or any other flower she could distill."

No wonder those floral scents filled him with joy when Carina wore them, and why

being hugged by his school friend's mother had comforted him. His mother had loved him,

and her young son had adored her.

The Countess was mistaken because this duke was capable of loving and accepting love,

and he'd prove it to Carina, even if it took a lifetime.

"Thank you, Benson. I never knew that Mama, or anyone else, loved me."

"Begging your pardon, Your Grace, but aren't you forgetting someone?"

"Someone?" Max was more than a little bemused. To be having his first personal conversation with Benson at twenty-nine was bizarre, but he suddenly wanted to know other people's opinions on al sorts of things, and make decisions based on facts and not beatings.

Benson shuffled his feet. "I...that is ..."

172

"Spit it out man. I'm not going to bite your head off for speaking frankly."

"We, your staff, have noticed the changes in recent weeks, in Your Grace's mannerisms and behavior."

"For the better or for worse?"

"Oh, definitely for the better. Since you met the Lady Dorchester and her delightful sisters, you've found a purpose for joining society, and that involvement with others has, in return, made you more relaxed. If I may be so bold, more human."

"And is being human good?"

"Most assuredly. You've dealt with those poor ladies in a commendable fashion and your feelings have become obvious to al of us."

"What feelings would that be, Benson."

"The consensus below stairs is that you've falen in love, and those feelings are so intense, so unusual for someone of your upbringing, that you're floundering. Feeling out of your depth and uncertain how to proceed."

"Humph! I never knew my staff were such keen observers of human nature." Odd that

his household knew better than their master about feelings and emotions. "So you've

concluded that abnormal behavior means that I'm having romantic feelings but I'm unable to

progress because I don't know how."

"Exactly. You love Lady Dorchester. You should follow your heart and let nothing

prevent you from securing the Countess as your duchess so that... Wel , so that al our lives

can be meaningful and enjoyable once more."

Max meekly nodded. "I'l consider what you've said."

"We have faith that you'l arrive at the correct conclusion, because you're like your

mother and she was a very wise, considerate and loving lady."

Benson left Max alone with his thoughts. He'd learned more about his parents, and

himself, in a single day than during all the years with his grandfather. He now knew that he

was capable of loving and of being loved. At long last, his heart was light and he felt ready to

conquer the world, or at least the small part that Carina inhabited.

Whatever she needed from him he vowed to give, and he'd revel in every new discovery.

Rules he'd thought written in stone could, and would, be broken. Wherever they resided

would become his home, as long as it was with the woman he loved. And yes, he did love

Carina and he was finally strong enough to admit it.

Now, he needed to tell her and, if necessary, to go down on one knee and beg her to give

him a chance to prove how much, and how deeply, he could love.
173

18

Carina's week had passed as quickly as the previous eight weeks. However, her personal enjoyment of the social flurry had greatly diminished. Max's carriage arrived punctually

every evening and whisked them off to London's most prestigious bals, routs and musicales,

and they often crammed three or four events into an evening.

To her dismay, Max had fallen into the habit of arriving with them, lingering around the

edges of rooms for half an hour, and then disappearing. If he wanted to punish her for not

accepting his offer, he was succeeding because thoughts of where he went, and who he spent

time with, were robbing her of sleep and raising her temper.

Though exhausted, Carina was delighted with the progress they'd made for securing her

sisters' futures. Georgie's quietly reserved, though ardent, admirer had asked for her hand in

marriage, and her quiet sister had stunned them al when she'd declared that she loved Daniel and couldn't wait to become his wife, share his home and his bed. Georgie had blossomed

from a pale and retiring girl who was scared of her own shadow into a confident woman, who

was looking forward to her future with open delight.

Carina couldn't be happier, because Daniel was a steady but strong man, whose wife had

died three years earlier. Though devoted to his two small girls, he had been desolate and

lonely, and not looking for another woman to replace his much loved wife. Then he and

Georgie had bumped into each other, literally, while both hovering on the edges of a

ballroom and seeking an escape route.

Sharing confidences and past hurts, their mutual love had quickly grown and, with

Daniel's children already pleading for Georgie to become their new mother, the pair would

shortly become husband and wife. The announcement had been in the morning paper, banns

had been read in church, and their quiet and stable alliance had thrilled and relieved Carina,

so much so that she, Gertie, and Lucy had already shared several bouts of happy tears.

Gregarious Lucy had, as expected, taken to ton life like a duck to water, though she

missed riding, fetes, afternoon visiting and all the other more relaxed aspects of country life.

To compensate, she'd arranged to spend a few weeks with friends at their smal estate in

Surrey after the season finished.

The family had six siblings, one son and five daughters, and as that son was smitten with

her and openly praised her sunny and caring approach to others, including his sisters, Carina

174

EXPECTED an announcement within the next six months. She couldn't
believe that Fortune had,

for once, smiled on them, or that she and Gertie would soon be
free to start their Continental

adventures. That left one major hurdle to be jumped.

Standing at her bow window, Carina watched one part of her
major problem march down

the street towards her house. Gertie had been so certain that Max
would arrive with first light,

she'd set an extra place at their breakfast table. Carina, however,
understood him better and

knew he'd gather al available information before confronting her.
She'd calculated to the

half hour how long before word of last night's incident would
reach Max's ears, and how

much time he'd need to extricate himself from whatever, or
whoever, occupied his evenings.

She shuddered at the image of Max being summoned from his
cottage—their bed in their

cottage—and reluctantly dragging himself away from the naked
woman sprawled across his

tangled sheets. Those thoughts tortured her, yet she clung to the
belief that Max cared for her,

and about her, and wouldn't hurt her by taking another mistress,
at least not until she'd left

London. He'd have issued orders to the numerous men assigned
to follow and protect her,

and her household, and he'd have sent a pack to hunt down her
assailant from last evening.

Max held himself ramrod straight and his fisted hands swung
wildly as he took the stairs

two at a time. Heaven save her, their confrontation was going to be worse than she'd feared,

because the Duke had clearly unleashed his normally controlled temper and she was about to

receive a blast of that fury.

She sighed. She'd hoped Gertie would be proved wrong and that Max would be occupied

with interrogating inspectors and constables, or anyone else he could squeeze for information.

Because, last night, someone had tried to kill her and she suspected that her overly-protective

lover was not about to be appeased by her reasonable explanation.

She pulled a chair up before the unlit fire, willing her trembling to cease, and forced

herself to appear calm and composed. Not that she feared Max, quite the opposite, but being

attacked had sorely tested her physically and stretched her nerves until, suffering after-

effects, she feared she'd swoon at his feet when Max let fly with his outrage on her behalf.

Crying before him would be akin to setting a match to his fire and her would-be assailant

would find himself in more acute danger than when horses' hooves had thudded down onto

the road mere inches from her head. Not waiting to be announced, Max strode into the room

as if the devil were chasing him. Carina shivered, but she wouldn't back down.

Her enemy would certainly target Max next, and she'd die before she alowed him to be

harmed. She'd divert his attention away from this house, from her, and from them, so she

could retaliate against the person she believed responsible for assaulting her, but without

175

Max's involvement or interference.

"What happened?" When he loomed over her, she barely resisted the urge to shrink back

into the chair. If ever she needed a clear head, it was now. Because she had to damp down his

worry, pretend her whipping had been accidental, and send him away once more.

She waved a hand and shrugged. "An accident, nothing more."

"I'm in no mood for lies. A rider doesn't skirt the pavement of a busy theatre by

accident. Nor does a man carry a cattle whip if he's simply riding home. You were his target

and he deliberately rode close and unfurled his whip. If he'd struck you about the neck, he

could have kiled you."

"There's nothing to prove that he intended me any harm. Several groups were walking

from the theatre towards their carriages, so it's impossible to say whether the whip's stroke

was aimed at anyone." She slid her hands into the folds of her gown, and then held her breath

when his gaze focused on her arms.

He frowned. "Are you cold?" She shook her head and looked down at her lap. One hand

was firmly tugged out from her gown and Max lifted it higher. "Then why are you wearing

gloves inside the house?"

Damn the man and his sharp eyes.

"I dressed for a walk in the park."

Quick as a wink, he undid the tiny buttons at her wrist and, ignoring her protests, pushed

up her sleeve. His breath hissed, harsh and long.

She tugged on her sleeve with her other hand but, once again, he moved too fast and her

sleeve was pushed higher until her forearm was fully exposed. She heard a tortured sound but

couldn't see his face, as his head was bent close to the vivid red streak running wrist to elbow

up her arm. He unbuttoned her glove, pushing aside her arm when she tried to stop him, and

carefully slid the glove off her palm and away from her hand.

She thanked providence that, though her hand was grazed from the road, it wasn't badly

injured. Her gratitude came too soon, because it took him mere seconds to secure her other

hand and strip away its glove. Gertie had covered the largest cut with gauze but it was already

blood-soaked, causing another agonized groan from Max. Her plan to exclude him from a

dangerous situation took another downhill turn.

Max's inherent nature was imperious and unbending, so she accepted that diverting him

for any length of time would be difficult, but he dismantled her defenses within minutes. A

smal part of her remained grateful she'd not been forced to tel lies, while the larger part had

dreaded his reaction to both her wounds and the danger she'd faced. Though his arrogance

176

AND SELF-CONCEIT MADE him difficult to deal with emotionally, she'd never doubted that his

protective instincts were for the benefit of others, not himself. He was a fighter and a warrior

and would gladly give his life to save another.

He frowned over her hands, before placing the right in her lap and unwinding the gauze

from the left. Dried blood clotted the wound where the whip had laid open a gash of around

four inches diagonally across her palm, and the bandage was stuck fast.

He gently puled it away. "Jeezus." His eyes closed, but then he hauled in a deep breath

and lifted his head.

His face was a picture of shock, horror and pity, and his agony was more than she could

stand. She sobbed, breath-seizing sobs that shook her from head to toe and sent tears rolling

down her cheeks. Once her emotions escaped, she couldn't rein them in and her sobs

increased, rolling on and on. Max dropped to his knees and gently pulled her towards his

shoulders, tucking her into him and holding her until her weeping wound down and ended

with a stream of hiccoughs and wheezes.

She pulled away and sat back, trying to brush her wet cheeks with the backs of her

hands. Though what she really wanted was to fling herself into his arms and feel them close

around her and know that she was safe from any more shocks and horrors. If only she could

hand over her problems to someone else, for once.

"Here, let me." He used his handkerchief to blot her face and dry her eyes, before

dropping it onto her lap. He clearly thought she wasn't done with her bout of self-pity, but

she had to collect herself and continue with her plan.

He puled up a footstool and sat before her, wedged between her knees so she couldn't escape. Max wasn't about to let her go again, so her next decision had to be whether to reveal

everything and accept his solid support when she confronted her fourth man, for she was

certain that was who had attacked her at the theatre; or bluff and lie and, for the second time,

give him his marching orders.

"This time, you'l tel me everything. The entire story, and I'm not budging from this

room until I'm certain you've spiled every last secret. You know who attacked you, don't

you? Was it your fourth man?"

She nodded. Despite having spent several years trying to come to terms with the

treachery involved, she shook with a mixture of horror and abhorrence. "He's a monster."

"I was also a monster when two evil men sent me to rob you of your innocence." He

smiled and stroked the skin of her inner arm, a soft and soothing touch. "And yet, when

you're lying under me, naked and open, you don't cal me a monster."

177

"Mmm. I've caled you many things, but never monstrous."

"I know. When you climax, you cal my name loudly and often, and not once have you

caled me a monster."

"Even at sixteen, I saw you as another victim and knew that any monstrous notions had

been beaten into you over many years."

"The others were victims, and yet you've now met and made peace with them. Al but one. You have to tel me why you're shaking in your shoes and can't speak about him?"

"Apart from him wanting me dead?" Her jest fel flat, and Max kept his steely gaze fixed

on her. Inwardly writhing, she held her head high. "Fine. I first discovered his name in the

Earl's account book, but wasn't certain what it meant. Gertie and I have spent every spare

moment sifting through those boxes you've been giving me each week and reading your

grandfather's letters."

"I've read boxes of his letters, over and over, but couldn't connect al those names and

places and the amounts of money mentioned."

"None of it made sense to us either, until the last dozen letters we read yesterday."

"That last box was one I found by accident, and only this week, because it was hidden in

a wardrobe under some gowns and shawls that must have been left by my mother. Her room

was locked and the staff weren't alowed inside." He sighed. "I begged the housekeeper to let

me see my mother's belongings once, but Augustus held the keys and she would have been

dismissed if she'd tried to let me into my mother's room." He shook his head. "So what was

remarkable about those last letters?"

"The same name from the Earl's earlier account books cropped up, alongside my name."

He frowned. "William and I saw your name on one letter, along with your stepbrother's,

plus the mention of seven hundred pounds. But we decided that referred to years ago when

you and I ..." Max shuddered and closed his eyes, and she knew his agile mind had made the connection. "Oh, God, no." He shook his head. "Tel me it's not true."

She and Gertie had made the same mistake as Max originally, but they'd then held a

magnifying glass over the faded date on the letter. The date hadn't been seven years ago, but

much later.

She laid her hand on Max's knee. "I wanted to spare you." She moaned. "Because now,

like Gertie and I, you won't be able to wipe the idea from your mind. They planned it, all

three men, together. Money was exchanged, but, fortunately for me, two of them died before

they could proceed with their fourth auction for a night wit me. Gertie and I think that the last

man alive has spent the last few months trying to dispose of any evidence against him, and

178

FAILING THAT, wil dispose of anyone who could testify against him. I presume he's had us

watched, and heard that you've been delivering boxes of papers here. He panicked and tried

to kil me last night."

Max gasped. "I can't believe he'd go that far. To try to kil you, and perhaps the rest of

us, so he can cover his tracks."

"His wife is a harpy and wil probably kil him herself if she learns what he's done to

cover his gambling debts. The only way to avoid exposure, and prison, is to rid himself of the

family members he loathes."

"How can you speak of him so calmly?"

She shrugged. "You forget that I've known him for a long time.

He's greedy and

manipulative and has never been bothered with ethics or good behavior. The Earl, the old

Duke, and my stepbrother organized the most despicable acts, probably more than we've

uncovered. As the sole survivor, Peter would have arrogantly assumed he could continue by

himself and not have to share the profits. But sadly for him, I returned to London because I

wanted closure, and I wanted to see you again. Now, Peter's only choices are to locate and

destroy any incriminating papers, and do away with anyone he sees as a threat."

"Your own brother."

"Peter isn't our blood relation, though we spent years together as family after our parents

married."

Max had thought that Augustus's death had freed him from people who enjoyed

depravity and cruelty, and had assumed that Carina would name a peer that they only knew

vaguely, and that the saga would end with him being jailed. But the cunning Earl had chosen

his previous marks carefully and picked men known to overindulge in London's

entertainments: gamblers and men obsessed with very young girls.

He steeled himself to ask, despite knowing the answer to his question. "The Earl truly

knew that Peter was the fourth man and that he was buying his stepsister?'

'Oh, yes. The Earl wouldn't have turned down such a lucrative arrangement because

he'd win in three separate ways. He'd punish Peter for selling him a useless wife who, despite being given to three different men, didn't deliver an heir."

"Despite the Earl and his impotency being the problem.'

'By his reasoning, three wives unable to bear children was the fault of women in general:

that we are contrary and unaccommodating. Yet he'd been incapable of sex since contracting

a disease from street whores, the only ones who'd suffer his perversions.'

"Rather than concede that he was impotent from the pox, he punished his wives."

179

"PUNISHED THEM TO DEATH. Wel, except for me of course, because he died first."

"And the other ways in which he'd win?"

"Gaining seven hundred pounds wasn't to be sneezed at." She gave a brittle laugh. "Plus,

he'd settle his score with me by drugging me and handing me over to Peter, who'd relish

swiving his despised half-sister. They knew that shame would drive me to the brink of

despair, and to possibly to take my own life."

"Such a pity you'd didn't get that chance, dear sister." Peter stood in the doorway, a

pistol in his hand. "If you'd disposed of yourself, I wouldn't have to dirty my hands by

shooting you."

Max leapt to his feet, but before he could move Peter raised his hand and leveled his

weapon directly at Max.

"No, not him!" Carina screamed. "Me, it's me you want." She shoved herself in front of

Max, stretching against his arms when he tried to push her behind him.

"Very touching, dear sister. If you'd shown me some of that warmth and concern years

ago, we wouldn't be standing here now." He grinned as he waved the pistol between both of

them.

"You won't get away with this," Max said, easing sideways a step. He needed to distract

the bastard so he aimed at him, and not Carina. "Though if you leave now, you can be

halfway to the coast before we have time to alert the authorities."

Peter sneered. "I'm not going anywhere. You're the ones leaving, though it won't be for

anywhere else in this world." He chortled, a chilling sound that screamed insanity, before

waving someone forward from the doorway with his free hand. "Bring them here, dearest."

Carina gasped when Clara, Peter's wife, ushered Gertie and her sisters into the room and

then stood beside her husband. Clara also carried a weapon and held it high for them to see.

Her pistol was smaller than Peter's and similar to the one Max had seen in Carina's reticule, a

lightweight gun made for women's protection, though only dangerous when fired at close

range.

When Carina took a step towards her mad stepbrother, Max frantically waved her away,

saying, "Stay back. Let me deal with him."

"No, it's me he wants." With her eyes on Peter's, she pointed at herself. "I'll go with you

if you let the others leave unharmed."

"Sorry, but it's much too late for that. While any of you are alive, I'd always be looking

over my shoulder and wondering if one of you had been brave enough to reveal all our sordid secrets to the police." He glanced at Georgie who was closest to him and, to Max's eye,

180

LOOKED REMARKABLY COMPOSED CONSIDERING that her stepbrother spoke of shooting her. "Not

you, Georgie. You're too frightened of your own shadow to walk into a police station with

your complaints."

Max saw Georgie stiffen and hoped she didn't pick this moment to prove her courage.

He edged another few inches towards the side table, where he could see Carina's sewing

scissors and hoping he could pick them up without Peter noticing.

"You're wrong as usual, Peter," Georgie said, stepping away from her sister-in-law and

facing Peter.

Carina and Max yelled at the same time, urging Georgie to move back again, but she

ignored them and stood face to face with her brother and, by doing so, put herself in the firing

line for both pistols. Gertie and Lucy looked frantic, but neither could move without risking

Clara firing straight at their backs.

"Georgie, please move away," Carina implored her sister.

Max could hear the desperation rising in Carina's voice and knew that one of the women

was about to risk their own life by drawing fire. He held up one hand and said, "Wait.

Everyone stand still." He looked between Peter and his bitchy wife, and decided she was the

easier target. "Did you know that your husband has always been obsessed with Carina? So much so that he was wil ing to risk everything to spend just one night with her in his bed.”

Clara gasped, staring at her husband with fury and horror.

Max slid the scissors off the table and into his hand, hiding them behind his back as he

walked forward two steps. “Ah, so Peter didn’t tel you how he paid Carina’s late husband

seven hundred pounds.”

She swung towards Peter, eyes wide and her pistol pointing straight at his podgy

stomach. “Seven hundred! You sold my diamonds because you said we had no money.”

“Be quiet, woman. It’s none of your business how I spend my money.”

“Those diamonds belonged to my mother. You sold my jewelry so you could...”

She waved her hand towards Carina and Max held his breath. He hoped to God Clara

wouldn’t fix her attention on Carina, though her stunned expression showed he might be able

to turn her fury back towards the husband who’d cheated on her.

“Yes,” Max said. “He sold your valuables to satisfy his long-held obsession with his

stepsister. So he could have ilegal sex, incest if you like, with his drugged sister.”

“Stepsister!” Carina unwisely yeled, causing Max to turn towards her and stare her into

submission.

The damn woman would be the death of him yet. He swung back towards Peter and

181

CLARA, thinking their momentary distraction would give him the opportunity to charge at Peter with his impromptu weapon: Carina's scissors. The loud discharge of a pistol stopped him in

his tracks. Stunned, it took a few seconds to comprehend that the smaller pistol had been

fired, though the target hadn't been one of the girls, but Clara's own husband.

Peter stared at Clara in disbelief. He clutched his stomach and, in slow motion, crumpled

to the floor. Max jumped towards Clara and, using the scissors in a wide open position,

jabbed her wrist.

The woman gave an ear shattering screech and dropped her pistol, which Max quickly

snatched up and shoved into a pocket. He swiveled towards Peter, spread at his feet on the

floor, and did a fast search for the second weapon, only to discover that Georgie had already

swooped down and twitched the gun out of her stepbrother's life-less fingers.

Georgie dropped her arm and the gun dangled beside her thigh. She clearly didn't know

how to handle a weapon and her sheet-white face showed she was fast falling victim to

shock. Very carefully, Max stepped towards her, anxious to remove the dangerous piece from

her fingers, but someone else had anticipated the danger and moved beside Georgie. He

gently unwrapped her fingers from the trigger and slid the gun out of her fist.

Max heaved a sigh of relief when Daniel, the man Georgie was to marry, eased the gun

away and efficiently disarmed it, before securing it in his coat pocket. Max's relief was so

profound he could have married the man himself or, at the very least, hugged Daniel. In the end he didn't need to embarrass Daniel, because Gertie and Lucy took his place and gathered

both Georgie and her intended into their arms for a long hug.

Clara had slumped to the floor beside her husband and was using the hem of her gown to

staunch the flow of blood from her wrist wound. She rocked back and forth, moaning and

cursing her unresponsive husband with language Max hadn't expected her Ladyship to use, or

to know. He felt Peter's wrist, looking for a pulse, but when Carina caught his eye, he shook

his head. The man was dead.

As if the room wasn't crowded enough, Carina's ancient butler huffed and puffed his

way to their side, clutching his chest and gasping for breath as if he'd run a mile. Max

understood that the old man had run at least to the corner of the square when he saw three

burly constables charge in.

He raised his hand and silenced the chattering and squawking all around him, before

succinctly describing to the constables what had occurred and asking that the ladies be

allowed to recover in a separate room before they were questioned for their version of events.

He'd presided, as a magistrate, over many dramatic circumstances on his estates and knew

182

HOW LONG IT would be before Peter's body could be removed and his wife taken away to be

questioned at the station.

A footman was dispatched to summons his cousin, William, who was the best person to reveal al they'd discovered in the boxes of letters and papers. Bil could explain what he'd

learned during numerous conversations over the past three years with nearly a hundred

women, or their descendants. The more they'd discovered about Max's so caled sexual

initiations, the deeper the quagmire, and despite his worry over the scandal that might ensue,

Max had prompted William to share his findings with a mutual friend assigned to restructure

the new police force.

He was doubly grateful to his cousin at this moment, because Bill had insisted that

preparations for a rendezvous, possibly involving Carina and made not long before

Augustus's death, had sinister undertones. His cousin was convinced that clandestine

activities started years earlier were still proceeding, but under the control of a mysterious man

who'd remained invisible.

Thanks to Wiliam's warnings, Max had doubled the guard around Carina's house and

had men following Peter and his wife, because Peter seemed the most likely person to want to

harm Carina and her sisters and he held a special loathing for Gertie. Despite Daniel's arms

supporting her, Georgie looked to be wilting and Gertie to have aged another ten years. Max

gave instructions for tea to be brought to the breakfast room and urged all the women, bar the

soon-to-be-prisoner, out of this room and across to the hall to another where they could sit,

talk and recover.

Carina, barely meeting his eyes once, took charge of the staff and sent someone to also fetch Lucy's admirer. He was, like Georgie's new man, a stalwart who the girls could lean

on, and who would stop Lucy's fidgets and soothe her into amenability. And frankly, Carina

needed all the support she could gather, because if her nerves had been strung tight during her

earlier discussion with Max, now they were stretched to breaking.

Four hours later, Max slumped into one of Carina's armchairs and stared blankly at the

low burning fire. Carina had thought to direct a maid to light it when rain had started outside

and the temperature inside turned frigid. Peter's body had been examined where it lay before

being wrapped and carted away in an ambulance wagon. The cause of death was noted as a

gunshot wound at close range above his stomach, which in turn had ruptured an artery, and

bleeding had resulted in almost instantaneous death.

Each person present had given their statement. The official verdict would read death by

misadventure, the consensus being that nothing would be gained by holding a public trial for

183

PETER'S WIDOW, as within minutes of shooting her husband she'd retreated into some private

world and was incapable of speaking. Carina has cleaned and bandaged her sister-in-law's

hand but had said little, either to the catatonic woman or to Max.

He'd been informed that the four women from this household had all retired to their

bedchambers and, after seeing that the constables and others who were milling around writing endless reports had been fed and watered, the majority of the staff had retired below stairs to

recuperate. When Max had recovered enough energy to stand and walk, he discovered that a

lone footman had been posted near the front door with instructions to lock the door after the

last person departed.

Carina had left a simple message to be given to the Duke, himself, and he listened to the

footman with half an ear. He looked upwards to the next floor, and Carina's bedchamber, and

wondered if his weary body could run up the sweeping flight of steps and evade the footman

who most likely had orders to stop him. He sighed. Probably not a good idea considering his

state of mind at the moment.

With Peter dead and his wife locked away, possibly in an asylum, there was no urgency.

He'd best leave Carina and the girls to their grief, if they could find it in their hearts to shed a

tear for the stepbrother who'd betrayed them on so many levels. If not grief, they'd be

suffering shock and would need to rest.

Apart from those considerations, Carina's edict had been succinct and final. She might as

well have had the footman put his boot to Max's rear end and kick him to the pavement than

have the hapless messenger repeat, goodbye and thank you.

19

Saturday had at last arrived and Max stood impatiently on the sidelines, while the church
filled to overflowing with well-wishers for the joining of Alice with her beloved Freddie.

Squeezed alongside the couple's friends was a large number of London's busybodies, eager
to witness, firsthand, the latest installment in the ongoing saga of Lady Dorchester, her sisters
and companion, the Johnston family and, to his dismay, the Duke of Stirkton.

Max ignored the stares of those eager for a new chapter in their drama and scanned the
heads of those already seated, trying to locate Carina. The gossips were going to be sorely
disappointed when the minister called for any man who objected to Alice marrying

184

. . .

FEATHERSTONE to stand to his feet. He had absolutely no objection to their marriage, though he

wished to God he hadn't been directed to the front row and the pew occupied by the Johnston

family.

Half the congregation craned their necks to catch his every movement, or leaned forward

in their pews so they could overhear his muttered words to Lady Johnston when he passed her

a clean handkerchief. He wasn't sure if the lady cried over losing her chance of playing

mother of a duchess, or because the gossips expected waterfalls of joyful tears at seeing her

only daughter standing at the altar.

But Max had paid for this extravaganza for the sole purpose of informing the *haut ton*

that he held no grudge against the two young lovebirds. However, enough was enough, and

an hour and a half of pledges and prayers was more than any sane man could endure. He

caught himself in time before he stood up and ordered the bumbling minister to hurry up and

finish so they could move on to the wedding breakfast.

Coming to his feet would have been construed as an objection, rather than a wish for this

ordeal to finish so he could move on to his main goal. The only reason he wanted to start the

feasting was to capture Carina, alone, and demand an answer to the questions roiling through

his mind on an endless cycle for the past few days. Each time he'd cal ed at her house, her

decrepit butler had lifted his nose in the air and informed him that his mistress wasn't home

to callers.

Now he was desperate to know if Carina would agree to marry him and if she was

pregnant with his child? His plans had been foiled in church when he'd spotted Carina

standing beside Alice at the front of the assembly. Though why Alice needed her support he

couldn't fathom. He'd have been happier to see Lucy or Georgie supporting Alice and

leaving Carina free to sit here, tucked into his side, and putting the world on notice that the

Countess belonged to him.

Finally, when he was at the end of his tether, the pianist played several resounding

chords to signal an end to the interminable service. The bridal party turned glowing faces

towards the cheering crowd and he thanked the Lord that the things could proceed.

Unfortunately, his happiness was short lived.

Lord and Lady Johnston stepped into the aisle immediately after the bride and groom,

and accepted congratulations as they made slow progress down the aisle and towards the

church doors. The Featherstone family, not wanting to be outdone, also clogged the aisle until

the procession moved at less than snail's pace. The slower they moved, the quicker Max's

frustration rose. In a few minutes, Carina would be too far along in the crowd for him to

185

CATCH, which meant he'd have to survive another hour or two before he had an answer.

In a moment of clarity, he understood that if he didn't put his ducal stamp on Carina here and now, she'd elude him. Possibly disappear before he had a chance to maneuver her into a

side room and have their overdue conversation. Upward of two hundred people would cram

into the Johnstons' balroom and he might lose Carina in the crush.

He'd lost her once before and he couldn't, and wouldn't, let her slip through his fingers

again. Decision made, he jumped onto a wooden pew and called across the heads of the

crowd: "Lady Dorchester!"

The procession in the aisle halted so suddenly that people ran into the back of those in

front, creating the toppling effect seen when children played Simon Says and stopped on the

spot. Heads turned back and up, and he was subjected to the stunned and questioning looks of

at least a hundred people in the first rows. But, as far as he was concerned, they were

invisible. His focus was on Carina as he tried to read her expression. Shocked, yes, but also a

little intrigued, an encouraging sign considering he was to make an absolute fool of himself

before the very peers he'd bent over backwards to impress with his hauteur previously.

"Carina, before our family and friends," he waved his hand around, "and this entire

assembly, I'm asking you to do me the great honor of becoming my wife." He sucked in a

huge breath. "You suggested that I become more human and acted more like a man in the

throes of love, so I'm doing exactly that. Only a man in love would to embarrass himself by

asking for her hand in marriage in front of a packed congregation, knowing that she'd refused his previous offers. But I'm handing you my pride, and my heart, on a platter. I'm hoping

you'l take pity on a reformed duke and say yes to me. I love you, and nothing in my life wil

have meaning unless you're standing by my side as my duchess."

There were gasps and cries and chattering all around, but he ignored them and focused

on the woman he loved. Every head swiveled back and forth, eager to catch every word

spoken, and people shifted and pushed forward in their eager-ness to hear his beloved's

answer.

He waved his hand again. "Everyone is waiting for your decision, so I beseech you to

take pity on a poor man who has learned to love and live and enjoy because of you. But I've

so much more to learn and I'm hoping you'l teach me even more, because you're the most

courageous and loving person I know."

There was stil no reply from Carina and Max's heart sank.

From somewhere within the crowd, a chant started. Perhaps it had been Alice or Freddie

who started it, he couldn't tel for sure, but within seconds the mantra was taken up by many

186

OTHERS until the entire reception was signing the same refrain.

"Say yes! Say yes! Say yes!"

Carina's eyes filed with tears, and he was filled with fear. He'd never wanted anything

so badly in his entire life, and no amount of Meacham influence could win what he wanted

most. She smiled up at him from seven rows forward and he, a reputedly heartless man, felt that organ stutter and trip in his chest, while he held his breath and waited for her to speak.

"Shush, shush, shush," he told the crowd, desperate to catch her answer about the din.

She nodded and smiled again. Daniel, Georgie's betrothed, helped her climb onto the

pew nearest her while others, including Lucy's beau, held her steady.

"Yes."

He cupped his ear, unable to believe he'd heard correctly. "Again. Say it again."

"Yes," she yeled, throwing back her head and laughing. "Yes, I'l marry you. Yes, I love

you. And yes, I'l stand at your side as your duchess for the rest of our lives."

Raucous cheers nearly lifted the roof off the church, when Max leaped to the floor and

worked his way to her side. The crowd, suddenly silent, moved aside and left the path clear

so he could reach Carina. Hands slapped his back, touched his sleeve. But everyone waited

for him to take her hands, pause, and then haul her into his arms.

He tipped her head and covered her mouth with his, oblivious to anything but the urge to

tel her, this time through actions rather than words, how happy she'd made him. Each long

kiss was his solemn oath to love and protect her, and she accepted each vow and gave hers in

return.

"I love you," he murmured close to her ear.

"I know, and I love you too."

"Wel, wel, love is definitely in the air." The elderly minister beamed down the aisle

towards Max and his bride-to-be, and then grinned at the assembly. "It appears I'l be conducting another wedding ceremony, and quite soon." He gave Max a forceful look.

"Very soon," Max and Carina said in unison, before bursting into laughter. When the

crowd also laughed and cheered, Max knew what it meant to be not only a powerful duke, but

a man whom people could admire and love. And it felt good; *very* good.

NOTE FROM AUTHOR: Reviews are like gold to authors!

If you've enjoyed this book, please consider leaving a review, and/or rating the book.

187

EXCERPT LOVING LADY KATHARINE

I lived in Vanuatu, previously the New Hebrides, in the South Pacific for nine years and loved the island life and its fascinating history. Kelly's Justice is set in contemporary Vanuatu and Loving Lady Katharine in historic Vanuatu. I hope you enjoy reading both versions of Vanuatu.

1860 New Hebrides, Pacific Ocean.

At first, all Lord Alexander St. John had gleaned was that Lady Katharine Montgomery was the young widow of a British Lord and yet she now ran, efficiently and unobtrusively, her father's extensive businesses in the largest town in the New Hebrides, a large group of islands in the South Pacific. Her father, a cruel Scots man estranged from his family, beat her whenever he was drunk or whenever something reminded him of their forced and hasty departure from London.

But less than twenty four hours ago, Robert McLeish, Katie's father, had been laid to rest in the small burial ground beside the open-sided erection that passed for a church. Father Bryan struggled to speak complementary words of the man as the coffin was lowered into the ground, yet Katie stood dry eyed, her only feelings being those of profound relief. She was finally free.

Robert McLeish, with his usual arrogant disregard for the native's warnings, had pushed his horse through dense undergrowth on his distant plantation and a wild boar had startled his horse into throwing him, where after he had sustained repeated attacks from the monstrous animal.

People had moved around her at the house, offering tea and sympathy, mainly speaking pathetic lies of what a good man her father had been. No one believed them, least of all his only daughter. The European population on the island was small so Katharine's situation with her father had been well understood although never spoken of as in some way they all depended on their trade business to supply goods to the town. MacLeish's temper was legendary and none had dared to interfere.

'Katharine, please let us know if we can help in any way.'

'Lady Katharine, will you now be returning to England?'

She stared at the speaker intently before replying. 'I have nothing to return to.'

'It is impossible for you to remain alone in the house now. Certainly not fitting for a lady.'

Now she almost laughed, her thoughts mixed with a touch of hysteria. If they only knew. This hell hole was fitting for a woman like her.

Katie stifled rising feelings of frustration and anger with their questions to mingle with her guests, finding it easier to fix her face into her normal unemotional mask and agree with their lies about her father rather than acknowledge the unspoken truth.

Finally the house emptied, except for Alexander. She'd been polite, formal and firm at her first attempt to get him to leave, to leave her alone with her thoughts, but he insisted on staying, worried about her state of mind. After plying her with three whiskies from her father's best bottle, a bottle she'd never been allowed lay a finger on before, he drew her unresistingly to the large bamboo settee on the front verandah.

'Sit, Katie! Rest a while. You're exhausted.'

She stared at him with unseeing eyes. He sat close to her, his thigh almost touching hers through the skirts of her black mourning dress. This dress, like everything else he'd seen her wear, was practically threadbare and hopelessly out of fashion but here on her beloved island, Katie wouldn't have given such frivolous things a thought.

'I know you didn't like your father...'

Expressing the first real emotion he'd seen all day she yelled, 'Like? I despised him. My father was a tyrant just like...'

His stroked her arm. 'Like your husband?'

She shot off the settee, gaping at him. Unused to alcohol, she rocked on her feet but when he reached out to steady her, she jumped backwards. 'No, don't touch me. What do you know about my...my husband? No one knows. Only my father and he's dead. He's dead and I'm happy! Do you hear me, happy!' The last came out as as a shout and she looked skyward, as if expecting to be struck down. Though if she wanted her father to hear, she should have shouted at the floor because a man as evil as her father would be looking up, not down.

Watching closely to make sure she didn't hurt herself, he gave her the space she obviously needed to be able to tell her story. And even then, he didn't think she would have unburdened her hidden story of shame and grief if she hadn't been slightly inebriated. Her arms wrapped her waist in a defensive manner and he tried to picture her life. Being under the control of two men who'd alternatively ignored and then abused her must have been a living nightmare.

Keeping his words soft, he'd encouraged her to share with him. 'Katie, I know your father beat you but I never understood 'why.''

Katie clutched the bamboo railing wrapping the verandah. This house had been her father's pride and joy. 'My father loved to stand here and look down on the town and the docks. High enough to spit on the world down below. High enough for him to feel superior to everyone.' Flinging her arms wide, she nearly toppled over the balcony but waved away his aid.

This was where Katie had first met Alex, less than two months earlier, and from that moment her mind had constantly drifted to him, hoping his ship would return soon. Her father's pompous voice had been disgustingly boastful as he announced one morning, 'I am bringing a guest for dinner tonight. Alexander St.John. Soon to be the Duke of St John as I have heard that his father's health is failing quickly. Alexander will inherit the title, the properties and ships that go with it.'

His sneering glance raked Katie's thin figure. 'It's a pity you are so ordinary or I may have entertained the thought of giving you to him as an incentive to trade, but unfortunately he has been betrothed from birth to some chit in England.' Katie had inwardly flinched at the insult from her father, but she schooled herself to not give him the satisfaction of seeing her mortification.

'Be sure to instruct the cook to prepare an excellent dinner. Mr. St. John will one day be a man of great importance. Work in the back room at the warehouse today but return to the house in good time to ensure everything is in place for dinner. We will be at the house at six o'clock. I expect everything to be perfect because if you embarrass me in any way, you know the consequences.'

Katie knew exactly how many lashings her father would deal out for each imaginary sin she committed. Her father enjoyed inflicting pain and even the mildest protest would see him double the lashings. She depended on the healing lotions Tong Lee prepared to prevent further scarring on her back.

The menu had been perfect, her father drooling with greed at the memory of the lucrative business deal he had just concluded with his guest. Conversation had been intelligent and enjoyable and for the first time in many years, Katharine was able to relax in the company of a well bred man. For the first time in her twenty six years, she felt a flutter in her stomach, her body heating as she met his direct, appraising glance. Something flashed between them. Something she had no knowledge of previously and didn't know how to deal with now.

Then the unthinkable had happened. Alex had spoken directly to her. Simply addressed a question towards her across the dinner table, unleashing a chain of events.

'Lady Katharine, your father tells me you attend to his accounts in the warehouse. I am impressed with your talents. Do you enjoy working there?'

Even as she raised her eyes to answer, a fleeting smile on her lips, her father burst in with his malicious evil. 'Of course she doesn't enjoy it. Who would enjoy living in this God forsaken hell hole, but it is because of her...Lady Katharine...that we are both forced to endure here. She had it made in London, a Lady married to a Lord of the realm with a powerful and influential family. All she had to do was lie in the marriage bed and open her legs to produce an heir. But would she do it? No! She was too good for that, too above herself, thinking she was better than any of his family just because she is educated, reads books.'

Katharine gasped, her face burning and her mortification complete as she staggered out of her chair, knocking it over in her haste but bravely facing her father. 'You forget!' Her voice was reaching hysteria, yet she stood her ground firmly. 'It was your greed that forced me into that situation. You gave me to that man knowing what he was. What he expected.'

Her father's swift answer was an open handed slap across her face that knocked her sideways. Without looking their shocked guest in the eye, Katharine covered her reddened face, regained her footing and turned to escape the room. Alexander sprang to his feet, trying to capture her arm before she fled. 'Lady Katharine...' But she lifted her skirts and flew out the door and into the garden.

Alexander was outraged on Katharine's behalf. In his experience women were to be protected. 'Mr. McLeish! I hardly think this is suitable dinner table conversation. She is your daughter.'

'Daughter! Daughter!' He was choking on the words, drunk on wine and whiskey as he flung back his own chair, slamming his fist on the table and spewing his rage. 'She is no daughter of mine. She disgraced me. I now have to live my life here.' He threw his arm wide to indicate the small cluster of houses grouped below the hill where his house stood. 'This nowhere!' A malicious gleam sprang into his bloodshot eyes. 'But soon I will be rich. Rich enough to return to

London. Then my stupid daughter, the Honorable Lady Katharine, can stay here. She can repay me by continuing to run my business interests here.'

Alexander had been even more shocked. 'You can't be serious! The port is full of rough seaman and unscrupulous men. You can't mean to leave your daughter here by herself, with no one to protect her?'

'Protect her? Protect her from what? You've seen her. No man would want her. I could never imagine why Lord Percival married her in the first place until I understood the true situation later. She should have been grateful... despite what he was.'

Alexander's question was deceptively quietly spoken. 'What he was?'

Under the weather with drink, Robert let his tongue run away with him for a few minutes.

'Well who would have guessed what persuasion he was? How could I have known?' His look was sly, almost evil, and Alexander knew without doubt that this man had known exactly the situation he had sent his daughter into. 'Anyway, it should have made no difference to Katharine. She was his wife regardless and should have done her duty. If she had, the truth would have stayed hidden. That...that... other man's wife would never have found out. Never have found them together and taken a gun to them.'

Belatedly recalling who he was talking to, another peer of the realm, Robert pulled himself together. 'Never mind that now. How about another shot of my fine whiskey?'

Nearly choking on rising bile, Alex forced himself to exit politely. 'I thank you sir, but as I sail on the first tide tomorrow, I will bid you goodnight.'

He desperately wanted to race to the gardens and search for Katharine. To assure himself she was all right, but he couldn't afford to be anything but detached with her father. He'd heard the stories of his repeated cruelty. Yet if he remained in the same room as that vile man for another minute, there was no saying that his rage could be contained and the only thing that held him back was worry.

He strode down the flare lit path away from the house until out of sight and then turned into the gardens to search. When a sound-less shadow stepped out of the bushes in front of him, he jumped. Tong Lee put a finger to his lips in a gesture of silence and beckoned Alex to follow. Wordlessly, they descended to the small cove where Tong Lee simply stopped and pointed. Huddled on the beach, Alex could make out a small figure sitting in misery and staring fixedly out to the ocean. Not wanting to scare her, he cleared his throat softly to announce his approach... but still she started in fright and fear.

'It is only I, Alexander. Please do not fear me. I didn't wish to alarm you but I needed to be assured of your well being before I left.'

'If my father knows you have spoken to me, he'll...he'll...'

Shuddering at the stories of the man's harsh treatment of his daughter and miserable at the thought that he had been the hapless cause of yet another beating for her, sickness overwhelmed him. While he had fought often with his own father over the years, one of the main reasons he'd gladly left England behind, his father would never inflict physical pain on either he or his three sisters.

He cleared his throat and struggled to settle his agitation before speaking. 'He'll what? Beat you? I am so sorry. I didn't mean to cause you any more distress. Is there any way I can help?'

The look in her eyes as she now fully stared at him was a picture of helplessness and hopelessness. 'There is nothing anyone can do for me. Please leave now before he finds you here or it will be worse for me tomorrow.'

Without moving, he raised his face heavenwards as he searched urgently for an answer, any answer. 'I sail with the morning tide, but I return in a month. May I have your permission to search you out privately then, away from your father? I wish I could help. I wish I knew how.

Please know that I will think of little else during the next month, but you. Lady Katharine, I deeply regret the suffering I have caused you.'

Receiving no reply, he gave a little bow, turning to walk away.

Finally the moonlight lit her face with the ghost of a smile as she whispered. 'Katie. Call me Katie. My friends do.'

He halted. Turned to her. Gently, he reached out to touch one finger to her swollen cheek. 'Thank you Katie. My friends call me Alex. Keep well until I will see you next. Watch for me at the next full moon. Perhaps we could ride together.'

She didn't reply, yet as he walked mutely along the sand to the harbor he heard the faintest of whispers, 'Farewell Alex.' The finality in it wrenched at him. She never expected to see him again. In her whole life, she had never been able to depend on any man and she fully expected the same from him. Guilt washed over him at the thought that he may have unwittingly caused such torment in any other woman in his past life. Never again would he be casual with the feelings of women he knew. All women were treasures and deserved to be treated as such.

Tong Lee fell in silently beside him to match his stride. He was becoming accustomed to the Chinaman's shadowy presences and spoke quietly to him. 'Will she be safe? Will he beat her?'

'Yes, he will beat her tomorrow when he wakes and his head is sore. But after I will take care of her as I always do.'

Alex reached into his pocket and pulled out ten gold coins. 'Use these to buy what you need to look after her.'

Tong Lee merely averted his eyes from the money and bowed. 'I will care for her as I always have. As if she is my own daughter.'

Alex insistently pressed the money into his hand and closed his fingers around the coins. 'Please! Keep her safe until I return.'

The ship's sailing kept him too busy to reflect on what had happened but eventually they were under sail and he collapsed onto his bunk. He felt like a miserable coward, leaving a woman with that monster of a father. But what could he do? He had a betrothed awaiting him in England. A girl he hadn't seen for five years yet his family had committed him. To her and to the shipping business. If he stepped in to save Lady Katharine and lost the business, he may well cause the down fall of his entire family. Could he risk it. Two sisters in London depended on his money to give them a season to find a suitable match. Could he jeopardize it all. Risk the scandal by rescuing Katie from her father. But once he had rescued her, what then? What could he possibly do for her.

And so it was that around the next full moon, Katie's eyes drifted continually to the horizon, scouring every boat that arrived, hoping to glimpse Alex's arrival. Her back had healed once again from her father's lashing but this time a new hope blossomed inside her. Not that she allowed her expectations to climb very high. The past had taught her caution.

.

ABOUT THE AUTHOR

Tag Line - Making history fun, one year at a time.

I now live in a sunny part of Australia after spending many years in developing countries in the South Pacific. I love traveling, anywhere and everywhere, meeting crazy characters, and visiting the Australian outback.

My sexy heroes and feisty heroines challenge tradition, and though they might live a privileged life, they also understand the seamier parts of life.

I can be found in many Facebook groups talking about books and history and am always busy on Twitter, Instagram, and my personal favorite, Pinterest.

To learn more about Suzi Love and my new releases, join my newsletter at my suzilove.com. I am on Instagram and Goodreads and have lots of Pinterest Boards as suziloveoz. And please join my Face book Group, Suzi Love's Lovelies, to keep up with my news on books and history.

Please visit my WEBSITE

Email me: suzi@suzilove.com

BOOKS BY SUZI LOVE

Fiction By Suzi Love

Embracing Scandal Book 1 Scandalous Siblings Series

Scenting Scandal Book 2 Scandalous Siblings Series

December Scandal Book 3 Scandalous Siblings Series

The Viscount's Pleasure House Book 1 Irresistible Aristocrats

Four Times A Virgin Book 2 Irresistible Aristocrats

Pleasure House Ball Book 3 Irresistible Aristocrats

Petunia and the Pearl Diver Book 4 Irresistible Aristocrats

Loving Lady Katharine Book 5 Irresistible Aristocrats

Love After Waterloo

Kelly's Justice

Outback Arrival

Old Sydney Town

Non-Fiction By Suzi Love

History Of Christmases Past Book 1 History Events

Easter In Images Book 2 History Events

History of Valentine's Day

Regency Overview Book 1 Regency Life Series

Young Gentleman's Day Book 2 Regency Life Series

Older Gentleman's Day Book 3 Regency Life Series

Young Lady's Day Book 4 Regency Life Series

Older Lady's Day Book 5 Regency Life Series

Self Publishing: Absolute Beginners Guide.

HISTORY NOTES SERIES

Here are some of the many titles in this Non-Fiction History Series.

Coming Soon:-
History Notes Underwear
History Notes Grand Tour
History Notes Mail Deliveries
History Notes Peerage
History Notes Food
History Notes Carriages
History Notes Money
History Notes Sewing
History Notes Hats
History Notes Mourning
History Notes Furniture
History Notes Shoes
History Notes Trades
History Notes Clubs
History Notes Fans
History Notes Sports

Historic London

Overview
Bridges
Hospitals
Churches
Famous

REVIEWS

Reviews are like gold to authors. I would appreciate it if you could leave a review, good or bad, for this book at any book retailer.

And don't forget, to get insider news about my book releases, any discounted books or contests that I am a part of, you should sign up for my newsletter. I promise you will only ever hear from me when I have exciting news, about me or my other author friends. www.-suzilove.com

You can send me an email : suzi@suzilove.com.

Or send a letter : Suzi Love, 258/ 52 University Way, Sippy Downs, Queensland, 4556, Australia.

www.ingramcontent.com/pod-product-compliance
Lightning Source LLC
Chambersburg PA
CBHW050031030726
47506CB00001B/214